Cruel Winter

Also Available by Sheila Connolly

The County Cork Mysteries
A Turn for the Bad
An Early Wake
Scandal in Skibbereen
Buried in a Bog

The Museum Mysteries
Dead End Street
Privy to the Dead
Razing the Dead
Monument to the Dead
Fire Engine Dead
Let's Play Dead
Fundraising the Dead

The Orchard Mysteries
Seeds of Deception
A Gala Event
Picked to Die
Golden Malicious
Sour Apples
Bitter Harvest
A Killer Crop
Red Delicious Death
Rotten to the Core
One Bad Apple

Relatively Dead Mysteries
Watch for the Dead
Defending the Dead
Seeing the Dead
Relatively Dead

The Glassblowing Mysteries (as Sarah Atwell)
Snake in the Glass
Pane of Death
Through a Glass, Deadly

Also Available
Reunion with Death
Once She Knew

Cruel Winter

A County Cork Mystery

SHEILA CONNOLLY

CROOKED LANE

NEW YORK

Published in the United States by Crooked Lane Books, an imprint of The Quick Brown Fox & Company LLC.

Crooked Lane Books and its logo are trademarks of The Quick Brown Fox & Company LLC.

Library of Congress Catalog-in-Publication data available upon request.

ISBN (hardcover): 978-1-68331-100-3
ISBN (ePub): 978-1-68331-101-0
ISBN (Kindle): 978-1-68331-102-7
ISBN (ePDF): 978-1-68331-103-4

Cover design by Louis Malcangi.
Cover illustration by Rob Wood.
Book design by Jennifer Canzone.

Printed in the United States.

www.crookedlanebooks.com

Crooked Lane Books
34 West 27th St., 10th Floor
New York, NY 10001

First Edition: March 2017

10 9 8 7 6 5 4 3 2 1

Is maith an scéalaí an aimsir.

The storyteller likes the weather.

One

～

Maura Donovan all but slammed the front door of Sullivan's Pub behind her. "Why is it so bleeping cold in here?"

Mick Nolan looked up from scrubbing the top of the bar. "Yer here early. And it's no colder than it's been, Maura. Where's yer coat?"

"Don't have one," Maura muttered.

Mick set down his cleaning rag. "You've no coat? It's winter now, isn't it? And you from Boston?"

Maura wrapped her arms around herself and stalked over to the fire, which Mick had started, thank goodness. Stoked with peat, it gave off little warmth, but it was better than nothing. "When I got here it was spring, remember? I didn't think I'd stay long, so I figured I'd never need a coat." But he was right: she needed a winter coat *now*.

She decided not to mention that the one she'd left behind in Boston hadn't been worth bringing with her—she wasn't looking for Mick's pity. After her grandmother's death, Maura had taken care of the funeral, settled the bills, left the rented apartment they'd shared for years, and realized there was little she cared to save. She'd cadged some attic space in a friend's house to store the few boxes she had and taken off to Ireland, the last thing her gran had asked of her. She'd brought little more than the clothes she wore and a carry-on because she thought she'd carry her grand-mother's farewells to anyone who remembered her in this corner of West Cork and then return to Boston a week or two later.

That had been in March. Nine months later, she was still in the tiny village of Leap, where she'd inherited a pub as well as a house up in the hills north of Leap, all from a distant relative of her gran's—Old Mick Sullivan, that was, no relation to the younger Mick who had worked for Old Mick and had stayed on when Maura took over the place. Thank goodness he had, because she had been clueless about running anything, much less a pub in foreign country. To be fair, she knew a bit about Ireland, but all of it secondhand from the various Irish workers who had passed through her grandmother's kitchen and who had usually enjoyed a generous meal from her.

But as it turned out, Old Mick and her gran had kept in touch over the years after Gran had come to Boston with her son, Maura's father. And since Old Mick had never married or had children, and Gran had worried about Maura's future, they'd cooked up a plot to take care of her—without bothering to tell Maura. She still wasn't sure why Gran had kept that a secret.

Maura had told herself back then that she'd wait and see how things went, and now she was closing in on the end of a year in Ireland. Grudgingly she admitted she kind of liked what she was doing, which had surprised her. At least it was nice to be her own boss after a few years of working at dead-end jobs in Boston.

"Is the heat working?" she demanded.

"As well as it ever does," Mick replied. "Leave yer jersey on if yer cold."

"I'm already wearing most of the clothes I have." She actually had on three layers, topped with a heavy wool sweater she'd found in a thrift—no, charity shop in Skibbereen.

"Is the heat working out at yer place?"

"Yes. That was some advice I still thank you for. I think of you every time it goes on." Mick had had to explain to her how the heat in her small and elderly cottage worked and had found someone to supply her with oil, back when it had first turned cold. "What's the heat for this place?"

"You've paid the bills, have you not?"

"Well, yeah, I guess. So it's oil too?"

"That and the fire there. You know as well as I do that once this place is filled with folk, it warms up fast."

"I'm cold now," Maura grumbled, feeling like a sulky child. "Who's coming in today?"

"Jimmy'll be in around midday, and Rose will come if we happen to get busy."

Jimmy and his daughter Rose made up the rest of her so-called staff. "Like that'll happen—it's off-season. Tourists don't come over here to see the rain. They're looking for rainbows."

"The two come hand in hand, do they not? Here, I'll make yeh a cup of coffee—that'll warm yeh up a bit. And then I'll send you out to find a coat. Yeh'll be needin' one sooner than later."

"What's the hurry?" Maura asked, perching on a barstool.

"Do yeh not listen to the weather reports?"

"Uh, Mick? I don't have a television at the cottage, and I don't think I've ever had a radio. Is there something I need to know?"

"You might say that. The forecasters are after tellin' us that there'll be a giant storm, the likes of which we haven't seen in this century." Mick looked like he was looking forward to it.

Now Mick's early arrival made sense to Maura. "So that's why you're here so early. You think people will stop in for one last drink before they're stuck at home?"

"I can't say, but it could happen. And I'd rather be stuck here than at my own place."

He made a good point. Maura realized that it had never occurred to her that she should worry about getting up the hill—steep and barely paved—that led to her cottage. Nobody ever seemed to think of Ireland and snow together. Would her elderly car, borrowed from Mick's grandmother, make the climb? "So where am I supposed to look for a coat?" Maura demanded, sounding defensive to her own ears.

"There's places over to Skibbereen—I seem to recall Rose took yeh to visit some a while back. Try the charity shops—there's plenty of those."

"Right." Great, now she'd be rummaging through a pile of secondhand coats. Good thing she wasn't counting on her good looks and fashion sense to keep Sullivan's going. Rose, who was barely seventeen, would be more likely to bring in customers than she was.

The door opened again to let in Billy Sheahan, most often known as Old Billy by the regulars at the pub. Old Billy was first among those regulars, practically owning the lumpy upholstered chair by the fire, where he held court for anyone who would listen to his tales. He lived in a couple of rooms at the other end of the building, under some arrangement he'd made with Old Mick years back, and Maura hadn't had the heart to toss him out. Not that there was any need to, since she had no other use for the rooms. Nor that she wanted to: Billy was like a walking encyclopedia of West Cork, Skibbereen, Leap, and most of the people in this part of the country. While he was past eighty, his mind was sharp and so was his humor, although he was kind to everyone. Maura felt he was kind of like a grandfather she'd never had.

"You're in early, Billy," Maura said, then realized that meant it must be officially opening time. Billy took care not to look for special privileges at the pub, like coming in early or leaving late. "Have you had breakfast?"

"I have done, although I wouldn't say no to a cup of tea. But I figgered you'd have a fire going, and why waste me own turf?"

"Is your place cold too?"

Billy waved a dismissive hand. "No more than ever. Mebbe it's me bones that're feelin' it now."

"Mick, does our heat cover Billy's space?" Maura asked. She'd never given it any thought before.

"It should do, although I'm guessing the ducts haven't been cleared in a long time."

Maura could handle being cold herself, but she didn't want Billy to be uncomfortable or—heaven forbid—to get sick. "We should look into that. After all, we've got a little more money coming in with the music now." Recently, Maura had revived the pub's long-standing tradition of offering live music, something that Old Mick had begun years back but had let lapse as he grew older. The success of the effort had surprised Maura. "Maybe we should check out the building, see what else needs doing."

"Up to you, Maura," Mick said with little enthusiasm. He filled a mug with hot water from the coffee machine behind the bar and dropped a tea bag into it.

"Yeh might be wanting to turn on the telly, Maura," Old Billy said as he settled himself into his chair.

"To check on the weather?" Maura asked. Why was Billy tuned in to things like that when she wasn't? They had the necessary television above the bar, mainly for sports events. Maura still hadn't figured out which team was which or who cared about which rivalry, but people—guys, at least—seemed to expect to be able to watch them.

"There's talk of snow comin'," he told her. "I heard on the radio."

Maura hadn't seen any snow since she'd arrived in Ireland, and here it was January. Back in Boston, snow had been a normal part of daily life, although the massive drifts, frozen rock-hard, lingered long after the pretty blanket of white stuff did. "Is it rare around here?"

"Yes and no," Mick answered her. "It doesn't snow often, particularly in this part of the country, but it can happen, and it's hard to predict. Most of the time it doesn't last, but on the other hand, it's been known to linger on the ground for as much as ten days if it's cold enough. The thing of it is, if any snow builds up, most everything hereabouts stops in its tracks, save for the main roads, like that one there." Mick nodded out the front window at the highway that ran in front of the pub. Highway was too grand a term for a two-lane road, but it was the biggest one around this part of Cork, running along the south coast.

Maura was about to scoff when she remembered the small lanes that led to her cottage a couple of miles away. The ones closer to the village, or to Skibbereen, might be two lanes wide if you had a small car, but by the time she got to her hill, she prayed she wouldn't meet anyone coming the other way, for there was no room to pass. "I'm guessing that nobody plows the lanes?"

"You'd be right about that. School buses can't make it either. And even if the snow melts, if it refreezes after, things get worse, what with the ice."

"So should we be worried?" Maura asked.

"Wouldn't hurt to check the weather news. Just in case."

Maura retrieved the remote control for the television and clicked on the news report. Apparently, the national weather service had just issued a warning of some sort. "Status Orange? What's that?"

Mick came around the bar to look at the screen. "There are three levels of warnin': yellow, orange, and red. Yellow means there's no immediate threat. Orange means yeh should prepare yourself. And red? That's pretty rare, and it means maybe yeh should think about leaving the danger zone if yeh can."

"Seriously?" Maura said, incredulous. "This building must have seen its share of storms over the years—or maybe centuries. What are we supposed to worry about?"

"The electric, for one thing. Having enough fuel on hand fer a coupla days. Food."

"Am I supposed to send everyone home? Assuming they show up at all?"

"Yer customers, yer asking? If they're smart, they'll tend to their own places. But there's always a few who want one last pint.

At least we've just had the latest delivery, so we can all sit in the dark and the cold and drink while we share weather stories."

Maura took one last look to see if he was kidding, but he appeared to be serious. Mick had removed the tea bag from the mug on the bar, so Maura gathered that up, along with a small pitcher of milk and the sugar bowl, added a spoon, and took it over to Billy. She set them all on the table next to his chair, then dropped into the chair next to his.

"Don't fret yerself, Maura," Billy said, adding two heaping spoonfuls of sugar to his tea, following that with a dash of milk. "Yer right—this place has survived this long because it's solid. You've nothing to worry about here."

"Except a few days of lost customers," she replied. She hadn't even seen a full year's results from running the place, and she had no idea what kind of profit margin she might have. She knew there was money in the bank, but not a lot, and she worried that there were taxes and license fees—the kind of stuff that she hadn't planned on because she had no idea how much they were. She still had a lot to learn about running a pub. "We've fixed the leaks we knew about, and I've been told the roof is sound." Slate, which was plentiful in the area, turned out to be pretty dependable, and Maura was guessing that Old Mick had had the roof replaced a couple of decades earlier.

"Have yeh seen much of Gillian lately?" Billy asked, blowing on his tea.

Gillian was a local artist and fast becoming Maura's closest friend, despite a decade's difference in their ages. "Not really. Mostly when she drops in here. You know she stayed with me for a bit, but then she and Harry sorted things out, and she's been living at the manor since then." Maura had wondered how that was working out. Harry Townsend was the last scion of one of the local aristocratic families—or so Maura had been told—and while he lived in Dublin most of the time, he was looking out for his elderly great-aunt Eveline, the only surviving member of the family living in the Big House overlooking the harbor. He and Gillian had been an on-again-off-again item for years, both in Leap and in Dublin, but Gillian had found herself pregnant with his child recently, which had thrown a monkey wrench into their casual arrangement. To his credit, Harry was standing by her, and now she was staying at the manor house with Eveline.

"And how does that sit with Eveline?" Billy asked.

"From what Gillian's told me, Eveline's glad of the company." Though Maura had met her, Eveline seldom left the manor house these days. "And she's accepted that Gillian is pregnant with Harry's baby. I think she was worried that the family would die out altogether."

"I'm glad to know that. I always thought she was a fair-minded woman. Will Harry be settling here in Leap, then?" Billy asked.

"It's not clear yet, or at least Gillian hasn't told me. You know when Eveline . . . passes, the property goes to the National Trust?" Eveline was roughly the same age as Billy, so Maura wanted to tread carefully to avoid hurting Billy's feelings, but surely he knew that Eveline wouldn't live forever.

Billy nodded. "Which puts Harry out on the street, eh?"

"Well, he's got a place in Dublin that he rents, but it's expensive to live there, or so Gillian tells me. He could probably do what he's doing now in Cork city or Skibbereen, maybe, but they'd still need a place to live."

Billy didn't look worried. "These things have a way of working themselves out, yeh know. Look at yerself."

Maura had to smile at his optimism. "What, you think there's some fairy godfather waiting in the wings to fix everything for Gillian and Harry when the time comes?" Well, in fact, that was just what Old Mick had done for her. Surely that sort of thing wasn't a regular event, even in Ireland.

"Don't borrow trouble, Maura me dear. There's time yet."

That was an oddly Irish way of thinking, but it beat worrying about everything all the time. "I hope so, Billy."

Two

It was a slow day at Sullivan's by any standards. A Thursday, off-season, with looming bad weather? Maura wondered if it was worth staying open at all, but she hated the idea of turning away even one customer—and besides, she was already here. She knew that was not a practical decision, because she'd have to keep the lights and the heat on in case some poor soul wandered in looking for a pint or even a cup of tea. The math didn't make much sense. But she didn't like the thought of shutting down and retreating to her cottage, where it wasn't much warmer and was definitely lonelier. And if the weather warnings were true, she might get stuck up there on her hill for who knew how long. Plus she had next to no experience with driving in the snow, since she and her gran could never afford a car in Boston and really hadn't needed one, and she didn't want to end up in a ditch—or worse, upside down at the bottom of the hill. So she was going to stay at Sullivan's, come what may.

In that case, she needed to do something. "If we're suppo to prepare ourselves for a big storm, what do we need to do asked Mick.

He cocked his head at her. "So now yer takin' this seriously?"

"I guess I should," she replied.

"Mebbe. All right, then. If the winds come up, the power's likely to go when the lines blow down, so we should have some torches and spare batteries on hand."

Maura had a fleeting image of wooden torches, like in some medieval castle. "Torches? You mean flashlights?"

"I do. And the batteries'll go fast at the shops, so you should get yerself up to O'Donovan's hardware and stock up if you can."

"Okay, that makes sense. What if they're out?"

"Then the Costcutter will be out as well. I'd guess there'd be some oil lamps in the cellar here, although you'd need to check for fuel."

Oil lamps—really? Which century was this? "What about the heat?"

Mick nodded toward the fireplace. "The oil tank's half-full. Otherwise, that'd be it. We're fairly well fixed for turf and coal, so long as the storm doesn't last long."

"That's out in the shed behind the building, right?"

"The tank and the rest are, yeah."

"And food?"

"You've no kitchen here to speak of."

"There's a kitchen!" Maura protested. "I'm just not sure any of it works, and it hasn't been used in a heck of a long time. But we would need food. What do we do about that?"

"Check with Anne Sheahan across the way, see what she's got in. Or the other restaurants on this side of the road. I'd send the Costcutter down the road, but that's where everyone and his uncle will be headed, and the same goes fer Fields, over at Skibbereen. It'll be mad there."

A lot like Boston, Maura reflected. She remembered news stories about crazed people going out to local supermarkets and buying up bread and milk—even if they never normally ate bread or drank milk. Sometimes fistfights broke out. "How long do we have to get ready?"

"Depends on the storm. Sometimes nothing happens, but sometimes they move fast."

"That's no help, Mick," Maura said impatiently. "What do you think I—we need to do right now, just in case?"

"Like I said, you've got drink and heat. Make sure yeh've got lights, and lay in some food."

"What about people who can't get home because they stayed too long?"

Mick was beginning to look exasperated. "Are yeh looking fer trouble? Sure, and there'll be some fools who think a bit of snow and ice can't stop them. Send them over to Sheahan's. They've got beds."

"They've only eight rooms over there. What if they're booked already?"

"Then go ask the woman. Doubtless she's been through this drill before!" Mick turned away and started polishing the coffee machine, clearly ending the conversation.

Maura fought down her annoyance. Mostly she was just itchy to do something, because sitting and staring at the fire wasn't her thing. She didn't know what to expect from the weather, and it might be no more than some wind and rain. But if it was worse than that, she wanted to be ready. She didn't like feeling out of control of the situation.

She looked around the room. Apart from Old Billy, there were no customers. She might as well cross the road and talk to Anne Sheahan or her husband Brian at the hotel and see how they were fixed and if they could offer her any advice. "Fine," she announced to Mick, "I'll go over now and talk to Anne." Belatedly, another thought hit her. "Will Bridget be all right?" Mick's grandmother Bridget was Maura's nearest neighbor, and she insisted on living in the cottage she'd come to as a bride. Mick made sure she had what she needed and stopped by regularly.

A brief flash of guilt crossed Mick's face. "I'll go up and check on her once Jimmy comes in. And you get back from the inn."

"Should we tell Jimmy and Rose to stay home if things look bad?" Once again, she realized she had no idea how far away any of her staff lived. She knew Jimmy and Rose lived within walking distance, but where Mick's home was was still a mystery to her. That was the downside of paying their wages in cash. She hoped she wasn't going to have troubles with her taxes—one more thing to check, even though she wasn't sure she had enough knowledge to figure out what she might owe.

She opened the door and had to hold it back against the wind so it wouldn't slam into her, and she was immediately reminded about her lack of a coat. Was this the time to drive into Skibbereen and hunt for one? No, one thing at a time. Right now the item at the top of the list was to talk to Anne about storm prep. The wind cut through her multiple layers of sweaters. Wrapping her arms around herself, she hurried across the road and climbed the steps to the hotel bar opposite. Once she shut the door behind her, she noted that the place was a hundred percent more crowded than Sullivan's: there was all of one person at the bar. That made her feel a little better. Anne—co-owner after her marriage to Brian, whose family had owned and managed the place for well over a century—seemed to be working on the accounts on top of the bar but looked up when Maura came in.

"Maura! How's it goin'?" Anne seemed pleased to see another face.

"About as lively as this place."

"Can I get you a coffee? Tea?" Anne volunteered.

"Coffee would be great, thanks."

Anne turned to the machine behind the bar to start a cup. "What brings you over here on this fine day?"

"This fine day, actually. The news is saying we're in for a storm, and I don't know what I have to do to get ready for it. Can you tell me what I need to do?"

Anne slid the coffee across the bar, and Maura settled herself on a stool there. "Sure, and I might have a bit more experience than you. First, rest assured that yer building won't fall down around yer ears."

Maura laughed. "I figured that, since it's survived this long. But what if it gets bad later in the day, and people can't get home? Or the power goes out? What happens?"

Anne waved her hand. "Electric goes out a couple of times a year, storm or no. The winds comin' up the harbor can be fierce. Usually comes back on in a couple of hours, or maybe the next day."

"What if it's a couple of days?" Maura countered.

Anne gave her a look that mixed amusement and exasperation. "I'd say you needn't worry, unless somebody asks you for ice fer a drink. Which they won't. Me, I've got food in the fridge and freezer to worry about if the electric's out, but yer safe on that count."

"That was my next question. Say people get stuck and want to eat. Can I send them over to you? Would that be a problem?"

Anne shrugged. "Don't borrow trouble. If it comes to that, we've got enough laid in that we can manage our folk and yours as well. Sure, and you can send them here. Or over at Ger's on the corner, although they most likely don't have much stored up."

"What about rooms if they can't get home?"

"Ah, now that's a different question. There's a conference on, over at Glandore, and we've got the overflow guests on our hands. Fully booked, we are, and if those guests are smart enough to listen to the reports and don't head off fer their meetings, they'll be stayin' here, sure enough. And I'd warn them that the road along the harbor is tricky on a good day and all but impossible to drive in a storm. Well, if that even mattered. Did yeh hear part of the road washed out in the last big storm we had?"

"Good grief, no! I don't go that way very often. What happened?"

"A chunk of it fell into the harbor, just past the bridge."

"So you can't get to Glandore from here?"

"Yeh can, by a road up toward the Costcutter, but it's steep, so if the snow's bad . . . Well, I wouldn't want to try it, and I'd tell any strangers as much."

"When will it be fixed?" Maura asked.

"When the government decides. It's not in our hands, fer sure."

"Wow. Thanks for telling me, at least. Anyway, I was just checking on what beds were available. You know Sullivan's and what space we have. There are rooms upstairs, but nothing like furniture in them, and nobody's used them for a long time. If people show up with their own sleeping bags, we might be able to cope, but I can't count on that. Which leaves offering them a piece of the floor, and that's kind of hard."

Anne considered. "Most of our linens are in use with the guests we've got, but if things get bad, I might have some old duvets to lend you, to at least cover the floors. Let's hope you won't need them. And did you come out without a coat, then?"

Was it the blue lips that gave her away? "Well, yes. When I came over here in the spring, I didn't think I'd need one because I didn't plan to stay this long. I've done okay with sweaters so far, but it seems that's not going to work much longer."

"I'm guessin' you don't have wellies either?"

"Wellies? Oh, boots. Nope. I was traveling light back then— just one carry-on for the plane. Where should I go looking for what I need?" *That I can afford?*

"Let me check what we've got stashed away here. People leave stuff behind, now and again. Wellies in particular, if they've had a poor run of fishing. Brian might have an old coat or two from his younger days that'd fit yeh."

"Thanks, Anne. I'd really appreciate it." Maura was oddly pleased at Anne's offer, since they weren't exactly friends.

"Ah, we're neighbors—we've got to stick together. Stay a moment, and I'll see what's in back." Anne darted through a door behind the bar and emerged a minute later holding up a quilted dark-blue coat and a pair of battered rubber boots. "These'll do fer yeh!" she said, pushing them across the bar toward Maura.

"Great, thanks." She slipped into the coat, which fit better than she expected and seemed reasonably clean. "This is fine, Anne. I really need this. Let me know if there's anything I can do for you. Any idea how bad the weather's going to get?"

"Hard to say. Much of the time, it depends on exactly where you are. We might get nothing along the coast here, but there'd be ten centimeters a few miles inland or higher up."

Maura did some quick math: an inch was something over two centimeters, right? So ten centimeters would be four or five inches.

"That doesn't seem like much," she said. "We get a lot more than that in Boston—and more than once a year. Maybe more than once a month in winter."

"Ah, but yer people there are ready for it, aren't they? They have plows and salt and sand and the like, or so people tell me. Here it's a rare thing, so we don't waste our money on such items. Mostly we wait until it melts. Was there anything else you were wanting?"

"Not that I know of—yet. I'm sure I'll find more. You know, I don't think I've ever asked you, but would it be a problem for you if I cleaned up those couple of rooms over the bar and fixed them up as bedrooms?"

"Yeh're sayin' for rentals, or like a B and B by the night?" Anne asked.

"Something like that. The space is there, and it seems a shame to waste it, but that would be one more thing I'd have to manage. Look, if you tell me you can handle whatever business comes along here, I won't get in the way of that. Or you could use my rooms as overflow if you needed to."

"Let me think on it. Or mebbe you could do longer lets if people want to stay around fer a bit. No need to decide right now, eh?"

"Of course not. I guess I'm off to try to find batteries."

"Good luck with that."

Maura slid some euros across the counter to pay for her coffee, but Anne pushed them back toward her. "You'll do the same fer me, later."

"Thanks, Anne."

Maura pushed her way out the door again, carrying the boots. The coat Anne had given her was a blessing. It was freezing, and she couldn't afford to get sick. And she'd never even thought about boots. Where had her head been? Did she really think winter didn't happen in Ireland? Had she let herself get sucked into the green/rainbows/happy cows/tourist junk? She hurried up the street to the hardware store a block away. It was called O'Donovan's. So was the furniture store across the road and the flooring store next to it. And a funeral home at the edge of town. Well, Leap had been named after Donovan's Leap, or so many people had told her, so it made a kind of sense. She had only a fuzzy grasp of what the leap was all about—something about one of the important local guys fleeing the British and clearing the small gorge and the stream that had created it to escape, back in seventeen-something. Every time she walked over the modern bridge that spanned it, she tried to visualize a horse that could make it—and failed.

The owner of O'Donovan's (the hardware store, not the furniture store—Maura assumed they were related to each other somehow and maybe even to her) was a tall, rangy man in his forties, Maura guessed. She'd never learned his name, but she was willing to bet it was O'Donovan. Before she even opened her mouth, he said, "All out, if it's batteries yer looking for." He spoke slowly and deliberately. "You'd be Maura Donovan, am I right?"

Crap. "I am, from the pub. I'm sorry to hear that, Mr. . . . O'Donovan." The man nodded without comment. "Any chance for lamp oil?"

The man raised his eyebrows. "Are you sayin' you have the lamps?"

"I think so. Old Mick Sullivan never threw anything away, so there may be some in the cellar—I haven't looked yet. Not that I know how they work, but I know people who know, if you get what I mean."

"Someone who's a bit older than yeh, mebbe?" He smiled at her.

"Exactly. So, do you have any?"

"What yer after is kerosene, not the fancy stuff in expensive small bottles. We've plenty of that fer stoves or heaters. But yeh'd hardly need that much of the stuff. Wait there." The man disappeared through a door at the back of the shop. Maura looked around, wondering what other things she should have that she didn't. Or didn't know whether she had. She knew how to use a screwdriver or a hammer and maybe a wrench for simple plumbing, but mostly she'd let Mick or Jimmy handle mechanical things, and they had their own tools. And, she realized, she'd never really taken a look at the dark corners of her cellar, beyond where the kegs were stored, and who knew what might be lurking there? Something else she could do while waiting for the weather to go to hell.

The man emerged from the back clutching a plastic gas container. "I've filled a smaller jug fer yeh. Here, take it. It should see yeh through the storm." He thrust it toward her.

"That's great, thanks. What do I owe you?" Maura asked.

"Ah, go on, take it. Yer a neighbor, and it's a big storm."

"Well, thank you. I'm sorry—I don't even know your first name."

"It's Charlie."

"Well, thank you, Charlie." It had stopped surprising her that everybody in the village seemed to know who she was, but she'd come to realize that few new people moved in, so she stood out. And she realized how little effort she'd made to get to know her neighbors in the village. She'd used the excuse that she was too busy learning how the pub operated, but she should simply admit she was kind of unsure of her welcome. Old Mick had been a fixture, and she was very new. "Will the pub be busy tonight, do you think?"

"If yeh've got heat and light and drink, yeh might be. How's it been goin'?" he asked her.

"Not bad, at least since we started with the music again."

"Ah, that was a grand thing, ten or more years ago. Great bands Old Mick brought in. It added a lot to the town. I'm glad to see it again."

"Then you should stop by—the least I can do is buy you a pint."

"After the storm, then. Good luck to yeh."

"Thanks, Charlie." Toting her kerosene container, Maura scurried out the door and down the hill, headed for Sullivan's. The wind seemed to have picked up since she left.

Three

~

Maura fought the wind all the way back to Sullivan's. She burst into the pub, which was at least warmer than outside, and held up her container. "No batteries, but they had this at O'Donovan's— it's kerosene. All we need now is the lamps—and someone who knows how they work," she ended dubiously.

"I'll check downstairs in a bit," Mick said. "You've got another customer," he added, nodding toward the fireplace.

Maura was surprised to see Gillian Callanan sitting next to Billy, deep in conversation. Maura went over to join them. "Gillian! I didn't expect to see you here. Where's Harry?"

"I didn't expect to be here. I've been telling Billy that Eveline's taken a bad turn. Harry's been down from Dublin the past few days because he was worried about her, and when she worsened, he thought it might be better if she was in hospital rather than at home, in case . . ." Gillian didn't finish the thought. "So he dropped me off here."

"You didn't want to stay at the house with the O'Briens?" The O'Briens were an older couple who lived at the manor, both to look after Eveline and to keep the building from falling down.

Maura had met them, but they never ventured into town—and certainly not into her pub.

"Eveline seems to have accepted this"—Gillian laid a gentle hand over her rounded belly; she was now six months pregnant with Harry's child—"but the O'Briens think I'm a fallen woman and won't talk to me. If I get stuck somewhere with this weather, I'd rather it were here, where I'm among friends."

"Well, you're welcome here, of course. But how bad could it get?"

Gillian sighed. "I've no idea. I've spent much of the past few years in Dublin, and the city seldom shuts down, as you might guess. I remember some big storms here when I was younger, but I was small then, so my memories probably aren't accurate." Gillian studied Maura's face. "Go on, then—tell us we're eejits to worry about a bit of snow and wind, after all yer years in Boston," Gillian said in an exaggerated country accent.

"Well, Boston's had some pretty major storms in the last few years. I think the record last time a big one hit was ten feet of snow, spread out over a few weeks, and then it wouldn't melt. I'll let you do the math for what that means in centimeters."

"A lot, I've no doubt," Gillian said, laughing. "I don't think we'll see the likes of that here. But Harry might want to stay with his great-aunt at the hospital, whether or not the roads are clear to drive."

Maura remembered again that Eveline Townsend was the same age as Billy. Did her sudden decline trouble him? He seemed ageless, although he wasn't exactly spry—he moved slowly even over the short distance to his rooms at the end of the building. Maura had known him less than a year, but she'd be sad to lose him. As far as she knew, he didn't have any close family anywhere nearby—he'd never married, and she thought he'd once told her he'd outlived his siblings and even their children. Maura caught him watching her, and he smiled. Was he psychic? Or did anyone who lived as long as he had learn to read expressions and even thoughts? Maura was glad she could at least offer him a safe home and a pint when he wanted one.

Now what? She'd done what she could to prepare for the storm, but was it enough? Or was she overworrying? Maura glanced up at the television, which was still turned on but without sound. The weather seemed to be the major story, with occasional comments about somebody shooting at somebody else in a country that was not Ireland—where nobody ever shot at anyone—and the weather maps seemed to show that the storm had grown. And the arrows on the screen were aimed right at West Cork. Not good. She was torn between wishing at least a few patrons would show up—for one last pint before everything shut down—and hoping they'd have the sense to stay home.

Just past eleven, Jimmy and Rose came in. Rain had begun to fall, and the wind had risen even more; the two looked like wet cats. Maura regretted that she hadn't told them not to bother. "Sorry, you two, but there's not much to be done here. Would you rather be at home?"

"Nah, the oil tank's about run dry," Jimmy told her, "so we thought we'd make use of yer heat here."

"That's fine with me, Jimmy," Maura said, wondering if he'd expect her to pay for his hours at the pub today when there was no one to serve. And Rose's. "How you doing, Rose?"

"Fair enough, Maura." She lowered her voice as Jimmy went off talking to Mick. "I think me da just wanted to get out of the house, and I'd didn't want to stay behind in the cold."

"You don't have to apologize, Rose. I don't know what to expect from this weather, but it looks like we'd all feel happier facing it together."

Mick came up to her. "I'll be checking on me gran now if that's all right with yeh."

"Sure, go ahead. I think we can handle the crowd here." Which was nonexistent. "Will she be all right? Or do you want to bring her down here?"

"No worries—she'll be fine. She has all that she needs up at her cottage. Bringing her down here would probably be more upsettin' to her."

Maura knew that Mick drove his grandmother Bridget down to church each weekend, but she couldn't recall if Bridget had ever gone anywhere else. Mick was probably right: Bridget knew her own home and was safe there, so why make a big thing of this storm? It would all be over by tomorrow, wouldn't it? "Say hi for me, will you? And check out how the roads are up that way. I really don't want to have to figure out how to camp here tonight."

"I'll do that. I'll be no more than an hour or two."

Maura checked the clock again—not even noon yet. This was going to be a long, dull day. "Anybody want to think about lunch, while we can still get around?"

Several hands shot up. "Let me go, Maura," Rose volunteered. "I'll go mad if I'm cooped up all day. I'll see what I can find, but I'm pretty sure it won't be fancy."

"Thanks, Rose. Let me give you some cash." Maura rummaged in the cash drawer and fished out some twenty-euro notes, which she handed to Rose. "And bundle up!" God, now she sounded like her own gran. Rose was young and healthy, and a walk of a block wouldn't hurt her.

Maura decided that she might as well go hunting for those oil lamps. She hadn't spent much time in the basement since she'd taken on the place. And it had a few bad associations, since Jimmy had taken a fall down the aged stairs just after she'd first arrived. She knew the kegs of Guinness lived down there, holding at the right temperature without any added refrigeration, but she let Mick and Jimmy wrestle those up and down the now-repaired stairs. She'd poked around a couple of times before, and the fancy coffee machine they were using now had been one of Jimmy's inspired buys—one he had lost interest in quickly. He'd gotten it cheap, apparently, but Old Mick couldn't be bothered with the thing, so it had been sent down to the dark basement. Once they'd hauled it up the stairs and polished it up, it had proved useful, especially with women patrons. But as Maura remembered it, there were a lot more dark corners downstairs that she hadn't explored—and not a lot of light. She knew the building was over two hundred years old; what were the odds that people had been dumping unwanted stuff down there for most of that time? What would two-hundred-year-old junk look like?

"I'm going to check out the cellar," she announced, "to see if there's anything we can use."

"I'll handle the customers," Jimmy volunteered generously.

Maura stopped at the top of the stairs. "By the way, Jimmy, do we have any shovels?"

"Yer after diggin' a hole?"

"No, for snow."

Jimmy shrugged. "We've seldom needed them. Might be one or two out the back."

Apparently, Jimmy was too lazy to go and look. Sometimes Maura wondered why she kept him on at the pub, but she didn't want to make life any more difficult for Rose. "When I come back, could you go check, please?"

"If yeh want," he replied without enthusiasm.

Jimmy's attitude was an ongoing problem, Maura reflected as she made her way cautiously down the stairs. Nothing like a handrail, nope. A single light bulb in the middle of the room, which didn't do much. No windows. No wonder she hadn't been down here much. She should ask Mick to explain how the connections with the kegs worked or if they were like the ones she had known at various bars in Boston. She'd left it to Mick and Jimmy to handle the deliveries and connect things, but she should know what to do.

She stopped at the bottom of the stairs and turned in a full circle, looking carefully. There were wooden shelves along some of the walls, but they looked like they'd collapse if she sneezed on them.

A jumble of rusted pots and pans was piled every which way in one corner. They looked like they'd crumble under a good scrubbing, so they should probably go to the dump. What was it they called it around here? A tip? Maura wondered if there were any newer pans in the old kitchen, which she hadn't used at all. Another shelf held a stash of old bottles, their labels peeling or gone entirely. All were empty, so any hope of finding some amazing old vintage or a cache of fifty-year-old whiskey died quickly. She poked into a few wooden packing crates holding not much of anything. Finally, in a far corner, Maura spied what looked like a few dusty oil lamps, long dry. At least they were intact and had wicks, which she seemed to recall were necessary. Two—no, three. That would probably do for a while. If they were needed. She hoped they wouldn't be.

Anything else she needed to know? The basement was cold and damp, and there was no hope of converting it into anything like usable space. Better to concentrate on the second story—no, it was called the first floor around here—and see if there was any hope for that. If there had been any cast-off pieces of furniture stuck in the basement, they'd long since rotted away. Maura sighed: there was not much help here, except for the lamps. She'd leave them where they were for now, since she knew where to find them.

She trudged back up the stairs. "Jimmy, where's the oil tank? Out back?" Another thing she hadn't kept very good track of. She'd been here long enough that she should have a grip on details like this, instead of relying on Mick and Jimmy all the time.

"In that small shed on the side, it is," he told her.

"Thanks. Good to know." No sign of Rose back from the store with food. Maybe there was none left in the village. Maura hoped that at least a few customers would stop in during the lunch hour, even if it was on their way home. As she peered out her front window, she wasn't surprised to see Sean Murphy pull up in his garda car. Sean was one of the most junior of the Skibbereen gardaí, the local police. Maura had been told that Leap had once had its own garda station, but it had long since closed for budget reasons. Now the Skibbereen officers made regular if rare passes through the town. Maura had a suspicion that Sean stopped by Sullivan's a bit more often than the schedules called for—and it wasn't to make sure the regulations were being followed. They'd been out together a couple of times, and she suspected Sean would like to see her a bit more often.

When he climbed out, she held open the door to Sullivan's for him. "Welcome, Sean. Have you come to warn us that all heck will break loose soon?"

Sean smiled at her, but his heart wasn't in it. "Nothing so bad as that Maura, but I am charged with checking that people are aware of what's happening."

"Oh, you mean that little snowstorm?"

"I wouldn't take it so lightly, Maura. I know yeh've Spent most of yer life in Boston, where there's plenty of equipment to handle what comes, but it's not like that here."

"Sorry, Sean—I didn't mean to be rude. I just don't know what to expect or how much to worry."

"Most times, I'd say you could just wait it out. But what with this global warming stuff, the storms have been growing larger and more unpredictable. I'd rather have people safe, so I'm making sure everyone knows. I know the younger folk are all about their mobile phones, but some older ones may not pay attention to the warnings on the telly or the radio."

Maura wondered briefly which category he put himself in: young or old? He wasn't more than twenty-five, but he took his professional responsibilities very seriously. As well he should when people were at risk. "What do I need to do? Before you start, we've got oil for the furnace and turf and coal for the fire. We've got kerosene for lamps if the power goes out. What else should we be thinking about?"

Sean shifted into full professional mode. "Keep your paths clear, especially in the front, before they can turn to ice. Clear off any outside grates, so the melt can run off. Try not to drive unless you have to. And drive carefully, slower than you usually do."

"Are there snowplows and sand trucks around here?"

"Some, fer the main roads like this one. Not for the lanes. People may find it hard to get home, and if one car stalls out up a hill, the others can't get by. Best to stay where you are if it looks bad."

Most of what Sean said, Maura and her crew had already worked out, except for the drains. Did she even have drains? Where would they be? "Do you guys get better official reports than we do?"

He shrugged. "The weather's unpredictable, so it's of little help. Will you be set?"

"I think so. If people stop by, what should I tell them?"

"To go home if they can. If they're the worse for drink, try to keep them here. Either they'll be a risk to others on the road, or they'll end up in a ditch and freeze to death."

That Maura hadn't considered. Was she responsible for people—most likely men—who made stupid choices under the influence of drink she had served them? "Thanks, Sean. I'll do my best. Will you be on duty throughout whatever comes?"

"Most likely. I'll be passing by now and again. Take care, will yeh?"

"I'll try."

She shut the door behind him and watched as he had to lean into the wind to get to his car.

Four

~

Mick came in a minute or two after Sean had left, shaking water off in all directions.

"Everything okay with Bridget?" Maura asked.

"As good as can be expected," he said, hanging up his not-so-waterproof coat. "She wouldn't leave if I dragged her by the hair, so I made sure she was well fixed for whatever may come. Was that Sean Murphy I saw? Did he have any news?"

"On the storm? No. Mainly that no one wants to predict what might happen. I asked about what we should do to prepare, and it seems like we've done most of what he said. Jimmy told me there might be a shovel or two out in the shed if we need them— not that he volunteered to go get them or anything—and I found three lamps in the cellar to go with the kerosene I got. And that's all I know. Oh, and Rose went out to find some food, but she hasn't come back. Should we worry?"

"She's probably sweet-talking the staff wherever it is she went to get them to check whatever they've been hiding in the back for just such occasions. She'll be fine."

It would be hard to get lost in a village that had only one main street and only one place to buy ingredients for making any food. There were restaurants, of course, but Maura wasn't quite ready to pay for prepared food, assuming there was any available at any of them. Anne Sheahan was already looking after her own guests, and Maura wanted to save her as a last resort. At least Anne had a real restaurant kitchen and should have some basic supplies stockpiled. Maura looked up at the silent telly again: the weather was still the biggest news story, and it looked like the storm had grown yet again. Of course, Maura was used to news coverage back in Boston, where the weather forecasters gleefully billed every snow shower as the "storm of the century." They'd been right about once a decade, but the most recent time was only a year or two earlier. Global warming or just bad luck?

Rose was next to return. It was such a slow day that everyone in the pub turned to see who the opening of the door would bring, and the sight of Rose—or more likely the carrier bags she brought—cheered them up. "Sorry it took me so long, Maura," she apologized, "but there was little ready-made to be had, so I had to stop and think about what we could put together here. Unless this lot will be happy with cold bread and butter?" She smiled at the group in the room, who shook their heads. "Maura, yer sure the stove in the back doesn't work?"

"I've never tried it, but it's got about an inch of grease on it, and I have no idea what fuel it needs. Sorry. I'd tell you to go check, but it might blow up in your face. Maybe Mick knows more than I do."

"No worries—I figgered as much. If we can't make the stove work, I brought things that we can warm up or even cook over the fire, if we can only find some pots and pans."

"Rose, you're brilliant!" Maura said. "I think I saw some in the cellar that might work if we scrubbed them up a bit. Jimmy, could you go down and bring up what's there? There's a stack in one of the corners—you should be able to find them."

Jimmy turned reluctantly from a conversation with one of the few non-employees in the pub. "What're yeh lookin' fer?"

How clueless was he? "Anything that doesn't have holes in the bottom, that we can use to cook in. You know, pots? Pans? Use your imagination." Or common sense, if he had any.

"Right," he said glumly, then tromped down the cellar stairs.

Maura noticed that another man had come in while she was scavenging in the basement, but she didn't recognize him, and he already had a pint glass in his hand. She wandered back to the old kitchen, where Rose was busy unpacking what she'd managed to find: bread, eggs, and veggies (apparently not a hot-ticket item in a blizzard). Rose noticed Maura's look. "If we find the pot, I thought we'd do a soup and eat it with the bread. I cleaned them out at Costcutter, but nobody wanted the vegs anyway. I even brought some spices."

Maura almost laughed. "Rose, you are a wonder. We don't deserve you."

"I like to cook," she said simply. "Even over a turf fire."

"So how does this thing work?" Maura asked, staring at the squat, lumpy but very solid-looking stove streaked with soot and grease.

"Near as I can tell, it's what they called a solid-fuel stove. It's a Rayburn—and cast iron. It's pretty simple," Rose said, opening and closing a variety of hinged doors. "You put yer fuel in here"—she pointed to one cavity at the top—"and yer oven's on this side. See? There's an indicator for the temperature. You put yer pots and pans on the top. It's not fast, nor is it easy to control the heat, but it gets the job done. You could bake something in the oven if you really wanted."

"I'll leave that up to you. You sure know more than I do," Maura said. "Can we get it going now? Or will it blow up?"

"I'll have to check the flue to see if it's clear and make sure there's not a pool of grease in the oven, but I think we could do it. Mebbe Mick could help?"

"I'll find out." Maura went out to the front room in search of Mick and found him behind the bar. "Mick? Rose thinks she can get the old stove working, but she'd like some help. Would you mind?"

Mick dried his hands on a bar towel. "Happy to take a look if it means a hot lunch." He headed back for the kitchen, and Maura took his place behind the bar.

Billy piped up, "Ah, Maura, there's many a generation that kept their families fed with no more than a turf fire. If the stove doesn't work, there's always the fireplace."

Jimmy came tromping up the cellar stairs, preceded by the rattling of metal on metal: he must have found some cookware that would work. He stumbled behind the bar and dumped his trove on the top of it with a lot of clanging. "Here's the lot of 'em, unless you want the ones with no bottoms."

Rose came out, no doubt attracted by the sound of the pans, and she bustled over to take inventory. "This is grand, Da." She pried apart the pots that had become fused with rust in the damp cellar and laid them out in a line on top of the bar. Luckily they were older pots, not flimsy modern aluminum ones, and they'd stood up well to years of neglect. Rose seemed pleased. "Would you see to scrubbing them?"

It was a treat for Maura to watch Jimmy's face when his daughter asked him to wash dishes. "And how'm I to do that?"

Rose was not about to back down. "In the sink back in the kitchen. We've soap and scrubbers here at the bar fer you to use. If you'll be wantin' to eat, you'd better get started."

Maura leaned toward Rose. "Well done," she said quietly.

A grumbling Jimmy with an armload of pans passed Mick as he emerged. "I think we're set," Mick said. "Nobody's used that relic fer years, but that's not a bad thing. I've opened the flue and cleared the vents. I'll go keep an eye on him, make sure he does no harm." He turned and followed Jimmy into the back.

Maura watched as Rose started sorting out her ingredients. "How many do you think we can feed?"

Rose shrugged. "No idea. I bought all I could. There's what—a half dozen people here now? I wouldn't expect too many more, but maybe a few. If we run out, we'll just give them the black stuff, will we?"

"I hope we don't come to that. Seriously, Rose, thanks for all this. You seem to be better prepared than I am. Have you seen a big storm before?"

Back in the kitchen, Rose was lining up her raw materials on the top of the battle-scarred table that took up most of the center of the room, taking stock. Jimmy at the sink was making more noise banging and clashing the pots than Maura thought was necessary. Rose said, over the din, "There was one storm when I was in school—they sent us all home early, and we didn't go back fer three days."

"Everybody lived close enough to walk?" Maura asked.

"They did. Most lived no more than a couple miles distant, and they walked it every day."

"Wow. Back in Boston, nobody seems to walk anymore." And half the time, the parents had fits that their little darlings were supposed to walk on the city's mean streets.

"Boston'd be a bit bigger than Leap, I'm thinking?" Rose looked at Maura with a mischievous gleam in her eye.

"Well, duh," Maura shot back. "What can I do to help?"

"You know how to peel a potato?"

"I think I can manage that."

"Then there's about five kilos that you could take a knife to." Rose pointed at the pile.

Maura set to work on the potatoes with the knife from the bar, which was far from sharp. Mick came into the kitchen and said, "I'm goin' to check on our fuels. How's the water runnin', Jimmy? How's the washing up goin'?"

Jimmy muttered something under his breath and banged more pots together.

Mick leaned closer to Maura and Rose. "Don't you dare step in fer him, either of yeh."

"No way," Maura said. "I'm busy—see?" She pointed to the pile of potatoes in front of her. She set herself to her task—her grandmother had made sure she knew how to peel potatoes from an early age—and was surprised when Mick returned quickly from his search for fuel.

Mick leaned in. "Can I have a word with yeh, in private?"

That request rarely brought good news. Maura laid down her knife. "In the back room?"

"That'll do." Mick led the way, then shut the door behind her, although not before a cold blast of air rushed out and hit her in the face. "We've a problem with the oil," he said.

"Why? I told you I paid the bill."

"No doubt you did, but I'm guessin' Jimmy's been helping himself to a bit now and again. No sign anyone's messed with the padlock to the tank, and there's few of us who know where to find the key."

"What? How does anyone get oil out? And wouldn't people on the street notice?"

"It's easy enough to siphon off a gallon or two and carry it away. I can't say how long or how often he's been doin' it, but the tank's near empty. It was half-full the last time I checked, a coupla days ago."

"Shoot, shoot, shoot! Will it last a day or two?"

"Mebbe—if we keep the heat low and use the fire. We're all right with fuel for that. And fer the stove."

"Did you tell Jimmy you knew what he was doing?"

"I will, unless you'd rather do the tellin'. He'll likely swear he planned to make it up, but that won't help us tonight."

"What do I do about him, Mick? That's stealing."

"It is that. But the decision's yours to make."

"Gee, thanks. Well, I'm not going to start a fight right now, when we're stuck here—I'll talk to him later. Maybe I can take it out of his pay. Too bad firing Jimmy would make trouble for Rose too. Look, I've got to get back to peeling the potatoes or we'll never eat. Did you get the stove working?"

"I did, with coal. It'll take a bit to heat up. And even longer to boil water to cook with, if that's what Rose is aimin' fer."

"At least it's a start. Thanks, Mick."

Back in the front room, Maura found there were new arrivals: a couple of twenty-something guys who came slamming in out of the rain. City folk, Maura guessed, because they sure weren't dressed for the weather. "This is Sullivan's, right?" one of them asked, pulling off a knit cap and wringing the water out of it. "Hard to see the sign."

"It is," Maura said, wiping her hands on a towel. "What brings you here in this awful weather?"

"We're booked to play here come the weekend. When we heard the weather might be bad, we decided to head down a bit early in case the roads were risky. Which they are already."

"Ah, so you're the Killer Lafferty brothers. Welcome," Maura said. She'd been so focused on getting through the day and maybe the next one, she hadn't even thought as far ahead as the weekend. Now she remembered the booking but not all the details. "Which of you is which?"

The taller one spoke first. "I'm Liam, the better-looking one. Me brother's Donal. He thinks he's the smart one."

"I was smart enough to tell you we should leave early, was I not?" Donal demanded.

"Where were you coming from?" Maura asked, smiling.

"Dublin. It's not so bad just south of there, but it kept getting worse the farther we went. We felt like we were flying dead into the storm. What's happening here?"

Mick answered. "You'd be right, lads. The storm's coming up from the south and west, and the harbor over the road there channels the wind straight at us. Yer lucky yeh made it when you did."

"Glad to hear it. We've got our gear in the van if you can point us where to put it."

Mick glanced at Maura. "The back room?"

"Sure, if the instruments don't mind a bit of cold. I'll show you where." Maura led the way toward the back and pulled open the double doors. It was a narrow space, parallel to the bar in front but with its own bar at one end, opposite the stage—she used it only for events or for the rare overflow crowd. A balcony ran around all four sides above, with a staircase to one side. Every vertical surface was covered with old posters, photographs, and band memorabilia—and Maura wasn't going to touch it. It was decades' worth of music history, and it made the space special.

"This is where the music happens," Maura explained, "but we don't heat it when we're not using it. We've sorted out heat and food here at the pub in front, so we should be okay for the storm, but I don't know if we can put you up. Had you made any plans?"

"Ah, don't trouble yerself. We've sleeping bags in the van—we're used to crashing wherever we can. If you've a warm corner, we're fine."

"Well, then, we're all set. Go get your instruments. Oh, and what's with the name, in case anybody asks me?"

"The 'Lafferty' we come by honestly. But we were goin' nowhere until we added the 'Killer' part. You're from America, are you not?"

"Yes. Why?"

"Because we read that the Lafferty brothers were notorious there. Mormon killers, they were. In the 1980s."

"Uh, guys, I wasn't even born then, and I can't recall anyone talking about them."

Liam and Donal did not seem troubled by Maura's ignorance. "No worries. Just adding the 'Killer' up front got us a lot more gigs."

"Okay," Maura said dubiously. "You want to bring in your stuff now?"

"Liam, you'd best go get our gear," Donal said to his brother.

"And what'll you be doin' while I'm hauling it all in?" Liam demanded. *He must be the younger brother*, Maura thought.

"Askin' fer a pint fer yeh. Go on wit' yeh."

Still grumbling, Liam stormed out the front door and back into the rain. While they waited, Donal turned to Maura. "How do yeh come to be in this part of the world?"

"My grandmother was born not far from here, and she fixed it so I inherited this pub through a relative. If you're here long enough, you'll probably hear the whole story. Mine and everyone else's. I'm guessing you're serious about those pints?"

"I am that. If yer offerin'."

Why not? Maura thought. She'd hired them, and from her limited experience, any contract with a performer included liquid refreshment, even if it wasn't spelled out. Obviously she wasn't going to make any money today. On the other hand, if she stayed open for those few brave souls who showed up, she might gain some goodwill. And where else would she go?

She started a couple of pints, and while she waited, she watched Liam stumble in, his arms full of instrument cases and electronic equipment that she couldn't identify. She tried to remember what style these guys were supposed to perform, but she couldn't tell most of them apart anyway. From what she'd seen, most musicians these days knew the entire repertory from the middle ages to last week, so no doubt they could tailor their performance to whatever audience they found in front of them. She was pretty sure they weren't a traditional Irish band.

Liam fetched a second, smaller load of equipment and dumped it all unceremoniously on the floor in the back room. "Happy now, Donal?"

"I am that." Donal moved back to the front room and gestured toward the bar. "Here's yer pint." Donal grabbed the two glasses that Maura had pushed across the bar and handed one to his brother. After a long swallow, he looked around the room. "And who might these fine people be?"

"That's Billy Sheahan by the fire there—he lives down at the end of the building. Next to him is Gillian Callanan, a local artist. Then there's Jimmy Sweeney—his daughter Rose is in the kitchen in back, working on making some soup. They both work here, along with Mick Nolan. Jimmy and Mick have been here a lot longer than I have. They keep the place running."

"While you provide the pretty face up front," Liam said, raising his glass. "*Sláinte.*"

Mick came up beside her and nodded toward the front windows. Maura followed his glance: it was snowing. Hard. Maybe the forecasters had gotten it right. It was already getting dark, and Maura couldn't remember the last time she'd seen a car pass on the road in front—and that was a main road. She couldn't even see it from where she stood—just a whirling wall of white. At least now she had a coat and boots, but Maura didn't plan on going anywhere soon.

Good smells were issuing from the back when another figure materialized from the blowing snow. At least Maura recognized him. "Seamus Burke, what the heck are you doing out in this?"

"I'd say I was pinin' for yer smilin' face, but the fact is, me tires are too worn to be of much use. Could you do me a pint?"

"Sure. But I bet Joanne isn't going to be happy that you're not going to be home any time soon." Maura started a pint for him.

"She's a strong woman—she'll make do. Besides, she's gone off to visit her sister and left me on me own. What's happenin' here? I was worried you'd have shut the doors and left."

"Well, we all got here and decided we'd rather stick together than go home again. We've got heat, light, and food. And even a couple of musicians! So we figure we're set. You're welcome to stay." Maura topped off his pint and pushed it toward Seamus.

It was maybe half an hour later when another man arrived, dusted with white, although that melted quickly in the warmth of the room. He stamped the snow off his boots at the doorway, then approached the bar.

"Well, if it isn't me old mate Danny," Seamus greeted him. "You'll do almost anything to avoid workin'."

"I had to work like crazy to get myself here," the snowy man protested.

Seamus grinned at him. "Maura, have yeh had the pleasure of meeting Danny Crowley? He comes from up the road a piece, toward Clonakilty. And he's going to tell us why he's daft enough to be out in this weather."

"Could I get a pint—Maura, is it? I don't think I've stopped in here since Old Mick passed. As for Seamus's aspersions, I was on me way home from Skibbereen, where me business took longer than I expected. It's me own fault, but I'll be glad of the company here."

Maura gave him a pint when it was ready. She'd already stopped counting and was surprised that it didn't bother her more. Still, she didn't expect many more customers to stop by.

She was surprised maybe half an hour later when the wall of white outside was broken by a figure emerging from the gloom. At first, the person was only a silhouette, but once she'd managed to pull open the door, Maura could see that it was a woman wearing a scarf pulled tight around her head. The scarf was soaked, so she pulled it off and shook it. Now Maura could see her face: she looked to be around fifty, Maura guessed. Nicely dressed, though for the city, not the country—her boots were already soaked. The woman paused and looked around the room; everyone there looked back at her, and nobody seemed to want to break the silence.

This is ridiculous, Maura thought. Why were these people going anywhere in this weather? "I don't know what you're doing out on a day like this, but you're welcome here. Can I get you something?"

"Coffee? And if I'm not going any farther, could you add a bit of brandy to it?"

English accent. Educated. What was she doing here? "Coming up," Maura said.

Five

~

The woman avoided eye contact with anyone else in the room and took a seat on a stool at the bar. She pulled off her wet coat and laid it on an adjoining stool, then shook out her scarf and draped it over the coat. Maura started a cup of coffee for her, then said, "What are you doing out in this weather? You're not local, are you?"

The woman ran her fingers through her soaked hair, trying to fluff it. "No more than you are. I live in England. I came over to settle some legal business with a solicitor in Skibbereen, and I was planning to fly back home today out of Cork airport. I guess that's not likely to happen now."

"I doubt it. You might ask those two there." Maura nodded at the musical brothers. "They just drove down from Dublin, and they said it's bad. I can't imagine any flights going out today." She turned to get the coffee and picked up a bottle of brandy, setting it on the bar. "There you go."

"Thank you. What do I owe you?"

"Don't worry about it. It doesn't seem right to charge people who risk their lives to come here for a drink. So it's on the house."

"Are these people your regulars or strangers like me?" the woman asked, darting a nervous glance at the group clustered at the other end of the room.

Maura scanned the group. "Let's see . . . the oldest one, by the fire there, is Billy—he lives in rooms at the end of the building. Mick—he's the tall one—and Jimmy and his daughter Rose work for me. Gillian's a friend—she's the pregnant one who's talking with Billy. The two loud guys are musicians who are supposed to play here this weekend, and I think they figured they'd better get here sooner rather than later. The other two—Seamus Burke and Danny Crowley—live near here, and I guess they'd rather be here than at home. I'm the owner of the place, Maura Donovan."

The woman added a healthy slug of brandy to her coffee, then took a swallow. "Ah, that's good. You're American, am I right?"

"I am, but my grandmother grew up near here, and it was a relative she kept in touch with who left me this place. What's your name?"

"I'm Diane, from London." *Was she imagining it, or did the woman hesitate a moment before answering?* "You seem a bit young to be running a pub. How'd that happen?"

Maura noticed that Diane hadn't given a last name and had been quick to change the subject. Rose popped out of the kitchen at that moment. "Sorry, but it's takin' longer than I thought. That stove is slow to heat, but I've got the soup simmerin' now. And I think I've made enough for an army. Which might be a good thing, seein' as it'll be dinnertime before it's cooked." She disappeared like a gopher into its hole.

A couple of the men groaned theatrically. Maura addressed the group and raised her voice. "Don't you dare complain, or you won't get any soup, and I'll send you out into the snow to fend for yourselves."

Seamus raised both hands. "You won't hear any complaints from me. Nor Danny, here. Right?" Danny nodded.

Maura turned back to Diane. Since Diane didn't appear to be in a mood to share, and food was a long way off, she might as well explain how she had come to be tending bar in a very small village in Ireland, she decided.

"So what am I doing here? My grandmother was born a couple of miles from here. She got married and had one son—my father—and then her husband died, so she figured she'd try her luck in Boston. They got by well enough, but my father was killed in a construction accident when I was a baby, and then my mother took off, so my gran raised me. She passed away a year ago, but she told me I had to come here to say her farewells in person. When I got here, I discovered she'd been plotting with Mick Sullivan, who owned this place. He died shortly before I showed up here, but he had no children, so he left me the pub and his house in one of the townlands. I didn't plan to stay, but I'm still here." Maura raised her voice. "Did I hit all the high points?" she called out to the others in the room.

"Close enough," Seamus yelled back.

Diane laughed. "I keep forgetting how everyone lives in each other's pocket around here."

Maura smiled at her. "You are so right. It's hard to keep a secret from anyone. I still don't know how word gets around, but it sure does." Maura debated briefly about asking Diane about her own story, but she hated to seem nosy. If Diane wanted to talk, she had plenty of time to do it: she wouldn't be going anywhere soon.

It was now nearly full dark outside, even though it wasn't yet four o'clock, and the snow, where it caught the light from inside the pub, was blowing sideways.

Rose came out of the kitchen and stopped when she saw Diane. "Oh, hello—I'm Rose." Then she turned to Maura. "You think I can ask Billy to shift away from the fire a bit?"

"If it means a meal, I'm sure he'll do it," Maura assured her. "But I thought you and the old stove had worked out a truce, and you're cooking on that. So what's it going to be?"

"Vegetable soup, and the stove's workin' fine. The fire'd be for toasting bread if anyone's interested," Rose said. "You've heard the story *Stone Soup?*" When Maura shook her head, Rose went on, "A man comes to a village and says he wants to make stone soup, see? And he has a pot and a stone, so he puts the stone in the pot and adds water and puts it on the fire. And of course the townspeople come 'round to watch. So he says, 'This'll taste grand, but you know what it could use? A bit of cabbage.' So a woman steps up. 'I have a nice cabbage at home—let me fetch it for you.' And she goes off to find it. You get the drift?"

Maura laughed. "I do, except these people aren't going anywhere, and I don't think they carry cabbage in their pockets. Did you get everything you needed?"

"All but some salt," Rose said, looking unhappy. "I forgot there wasn't any here."

Diane spoke suddenly. "As it happens, I have some salt." When Maura and Rose turned to stare at her, she said, "I was clearing out an old house, and I found some herbs and spices. Most were too old to be of much use, so I pitched them, but I thought the salt might be all right, and I liked the shape of the shaker. You're welcome to use it if you like." She fished around in her bag and emerged with a bottle of salt—far from new, but Maura didn't think that salt could get stale. Diane handed it to Rose.

Rose dimpled. "We would be delighted to have your kind gift of salt, Diane. Maura, I got the last of the bread at the store, and I'm thinkin' we could toast it over the fire. Did yeh happen to see any grills or firedogs in your search of the cellar, Maura?"

"I don't recall, but it's worth another look. And I haven't a clue what a firedog is. I'll go down and check. Excuse me, Diane."

Maura headed for the cellar stairs again. She had to duck her head to avoid hitting the ceiling beams, and of course Jimmy, annoyed at being asked to do something, had scattered rusty pans all over the floor during his search. Maura sighed. Giving orders to other people was one part of being manager that she really hated, and Jimmy didn't like to be told what to do. Jimmy was not happy working part-time at Sullivan's, but Maura wasn't sure he'd be happy working anywhere. She had no idea if he had any other jobs—on or off the record. He'd never mentioned any. Too bad Rose was stuck looking after him, but it didn't look like any woman would take Jimmy off Rose's hands, and besides, Maura wouldn't wish Jimmy as a husband on anyone.

She poked around the dark basement without much hope. She'd never made a lot of fires, and she was pretty sure the ones she had made had used wood, not peat or lumps of coal. What would Rose want for making toast? Maura's fires at Sullivan's had consisted mainly of a pile of kindling and, when that caught, some well-dried turf and/or coal. Add too much at once and the fire went out; add too little—and the fire went out. It was a constant juggling act. She had no idea how anyone could maintain a steady heat to boil something in a pot, but Rose seemed to have that part under control. Right now all she needed was something strong and sturdy enough to support pieces of bread.

She'd managed to shove the pots that Jimmy had scattered back into their corner and thought she'd spied some kind of iron grate when the single light bulb went out. Maura stood still rather than risk tripping over things she couldn't see. Blown bulb? No: from the protesting voices coming up from the main room, it was the power for the whole building that was gone, and that probably meant the town as well. Great. Could she find her way out of the basement without falling? And if she didn't find that grill, the toast would be, well, toast.

The bobbing of a flashlight—no, she had to remember to call it a torch around here—signaled the arrival of someone else: Mick.

"Rose said you'd come down here, and I know how dark it is."

"Thanks for rescuing me, Mick. But I think I saw a grill that we could use over the fire, just as the light went out. It was over there." She waved vaguely toward the corner.

"Don't move—I'll take a look." Mick shone the light along the floor, then at the pile of odds and ends stacked against the walls. As Maura watched, he reached in and grabbed something, then tried to pull it free. That resulted in more clashing of metal objects and some colorful curses from Mick, until he finally emerged triumphant with a metal grill about two feet square. It didn't look very sturdy, and it was covered with rust.

"And how is that supposed to help us?" Maura asked.

"I'm guessing you were never a Girl Guide?"

"We call them Girl Scouts, I think. No. I've never cooked over an open fire out in the woods while singing happy songs, and at home we always had a stove."

"Well, yer lucky that yer pot's taken care of on the stove upstairs, or yer job would be that much harder. All yeh have to do now is toast yer bread, and fer that, all it takes is to make the grill steady and level, once you've got yer fire goin'. And cleaned it up a bit, of course. As you heard Billy say, many's the house where the cookin's been done over an open fire before now, with a pack of children waitin' to eat. Just go with it, Maura."

"Fine. We've got a fire, and we've got bread. All we need to do is clean up the grill here and prop it up over the fire. Easy."

As she tried to get past him, Mick grabbed her arm with surprising urgency. "Wait—there's somethin' else."

Damn, she hoped this wasn't about whatever personal relationship they weren't even pursuing. Maybe some people thought being stuck in a dark basement was romantic, but she wasn't one of them, and there was a lot to be done to get the toast going. "What?"

"That woman who came in last—Diane, did she say?"

"Yes, that was it. Why? Do you know her?"

"Not personally, but . . . I might do better to say nothing, or I might well be wrong, but since we're stuck here together fer a while, I think it's wise that I mention it—between us at least."

"Mick, will you get to the point? I need to get back upstairs. What about Diane? What is it you think I need to know? She's just somebody who wanted to come in out of the storm."

"Yeh haven't been around here fer long, Maura, so you wouldn't know the story."

"What story?" Maura was getting colder by the moment, and she wanted to get back upstairs.

"Back some twenty years ago," Mick began, his voice low, "there was a murder done, the other side of Skibbereen. Surely you know by now that murder is a rare event in this country? Particularly in our part of it?"

"Yes, I got that. What's it got to do with Diane?"

"The murder was never solved, to this day. I'm not altogether sure, but I'm guessing that yer Diane up there is Diane Caldwell. She was suspected of killing a neighbor, Sharon Morgan. She was interrogated by the gardaí a time or two, but they had to let her go, for they had no evidence to hold her."

Maura struggled to process what Mick had just said. First, she tried to picture the rather faded woman she'd just met as a killer—no, that wasn't working. "So she was never arrested or went to trial?"

Mick shook his head. "There was no case to be made against her—just the suspicion."

"Here in Ireland, is it like back home? Innocent until proven guilty?"

"That's the principle, sure enough. But there were plenty ready to condemn the woman, proof or no. People talk. People then wanted to put this crime to bed, so they looked to the nearest suspect. I'm not saying they're right, but you can understand why they'd want to."

"I guess. But she said she lives in England."

"The death took place at the other woman's holiday house—they were both just visitin' at the time. Diane's house came to her through her grandparents by name of Wolfe."

"So maybe she came back now to finally sell the house—she said she was clearing up some legal business here. Wonder why she waited for so long," Maura said to herself. "Well, fine, now you've told me. What am I supposed to do about it?"

"I'm not askin' yeh to do anything. But if I recognized the woman, others might too. Jimmy, fer one. Billy. The other two local men."

"I don't think Billy would say anything. Jimmy I'm not so sure about—he likes to make himself look important, and pointing out an accused murderer in our midst might fit the bill. And stir up a bit of trouble. Should we try to shut him up?"

"I wouldn't go borrowin' trouble. If he starts in, I'll do what I can. It'll be close quarters tonight if none of us can get home, and we don't need people arguin' and takin' sides."

"Amen to that. Well, as far as I'm concerned, I don't know anything. I'll treat Diane just like any other person who walks in out of the storm. And if this does come out, I won't put up with anyone hassling her. Fair enough?"

"It is."

"And we're depending on that same fire to keep us all warm, aren't we, if Jimmy's little borrowings have drained the tank? I'd like to strangle Jimmy. What was he thinking?"

"Yeh might have noticed that Jimmy takes the easy way, whatever the case."

"Easy for him, you mean." Maura sighed. "You carry the grill. And can you grab one of the oil lamps? I'll take the other two—looks like we're going to need the light. Oh, and one last question: do you remember why Diane was the main suspect?"

"I don't," Mick admitted. "I was in my teens then and not very interested in the news, even if it was happenin' in my backyard."

As she followed Mick up the stairs, Maura wondered if she really wanted to know why Diane had been accused of murder— and if she could prevent it from coming out at Sullivan's tonight.

Six

~

When she arrived at the top of the stairs, juggling two lamps with their fragile glass globes, Maura was startled to see light in the front room. Then she realized that most people had pulled out their mobile phones and turned on their flashlight apps. That was something that had never occurred to her, since she'd seldom had the money—or the need—for a mobile phone until recently and hadn't bothered to explore the world of apps, nor did she plan to any time soon. But she figured the phones would lose their charge quickly enough, so the lamps would come in handy—and now they would have some light to get them set up and working.

Kerosene lamps were something else she was unfamiliar with. "Mick, what are we supposed to do with these things?" she asked, setting her lamps on the bar.

Mick set his down alongside hers and looked them over. "Yer lucky they've still got their wicks, but I'd guess Old Mick kept them at the ready, since losin' power is not a rare event here. Where'd yeh put that kerosene? I'll show you how it's done."

"In the back room—I don't trust the stuff," Maura told him, "and I'd probably burn the place down." She checked to see that the fire extinguisher was nearby, just in case something went wrong. Mick raised one eyebrow at that but said nothing. He retrieved the kerosene, then wiped off the very grimy exterior of the first lamp and carefully lifted the glass top from it. "This is the chimney. It's fragile, but it's necessary to protect the flame. Yeh take that off to light the wick. The wick is this woven thing that soaks up the fuel from below. Once it's wet, it won't burn itself, but it will keep drawing the fuel up and keep the lamp lit. It's also adjustable, but you don't want to turn it up too high."

"Can you just light the thing?" Danny, at the other end of the room, demanded. "Me phone's about gone."

"Just explaining to Maura here," Mick said. "Seems she's never seen one of these. And since it may be our only light until morning, it's best we all know how to use one."

"Yeah, yeah," the man muttered, but he didn't say more after turning off his phone.

"And treat them carefully," Mick added. "Here we go." He carefully filled the bottom part with kerosene and screwed on the wick in its holder, then waited until the wick was wet. Then he struck a match and applied it to the wick, put the chimney back on, and adjusted the height of the wick. "And there you have it."

The group responded with applause. Maura had to admit it gave off a pleasant light, not out of place in the old building, but she wouldn't want to try to read by it. "Good work. Where's Rose?"

"Right here," Rose said. "Soup'll be ready soon, whether it's dinner or supper. I made enough fer both. If yer hopin' fer toasted bread"—she said to the group, and a couple of men nodded— "then we'll be needin' a grill."

"Found one," Mick told her, "but we thought some light would be welcome first. Else it'll be a long, dark night."

"Well, I'll be glad for the light to cook by, but we should think about the fire now."

"That we can," Mick told her. "Jimmy, can yeh find us something to prop this thing up on? And maybe rub some of the rust off?" he asked.

"Yeh've got me on cleanup duty again," Jimmy mumbled. He didn't sound pleased.

Rose opened her mouth as if to volunteer to do it, but Maura laid a hand on her arm to stop her. "Rose, you've done your part with making us food. Jimmy, just get it done, will you? We'd all like to eat sometime tonight."

"Right," Jimmy said, biting off whatever he might have been thinking of adding. The mood in the room lightened a bit when Jimmy grabbed the grill and retreated to the kitchen in back, where he seemed once again to be making a lot of noise for what should be a simple chore.

Maura turned back to the others. "So we've got soup. Rose, how's the bread supply?"

"I managed to find a loaf or two, which will see us through tonight. How do yeh want to serve up the food? We've no bowls or cups In back. Mick never wanted to have to serve any food here."

"Mugs from the bar," Maura told her firmly. She turned back to the room and raised her voice. "We've got few spoons—you people may have to wait your turn."

Mick started doling out the sturdy mugs from behind the bar but quickly ran short of spoons. "Look in the kitchen, you lot. Guys with both mug and spoon now, line up so Rose can serve yeh yer soup."

Obediently, the younger men did, but Maura was happy to see that they carried filled mugs over to Billy and Gillian first. Two others went into the dark kitchen, and there was much clattering of metal cutlery and a bit of cursing—seemed like someone had found a knife by accident. Maura went to stand by Rose, who was ladling out the soup like she'd been doing it for years. Jimmy came stalking out from the kitchen with the still-dripping grill and ignored the dirty look that Maura gave him. "Where do yeh want this thing?"

"Give it to me, Da," Rose said. "Billy, yeh've probably got more experience than the lot of us with fixin' fires. Can yeh help me with this, please?"

"It would be my pleasure," Billy said, and he began the slow process of getting out of his seat. Gillian rose and took his arm to help, and together they moved the battered armchairs away from the fire, giving Rose a clear shot at it.

"The turf's fine fer keepin' us warm," Billy told them, "but fer cooking, the coal would be better—gives off more heat and lasts longer. How're we fixed fer that?"

"Will it see us through makin' the toast, Billy?" Rose asked him.

"It might do," he told her.

"Then let's eat first and see to the coal in a bit," Rose said firmly. Once everyone was holding a mug, Rose said, "There's a loaf of sliced bread just there, Maura. Make sure nobody takes more than one slice fer now."

"Yes ma'am!" Maura started doling out slices. "You know, Rose, if ever you decide to run a kitchen, you're doing fine with giving orders."

"Thanks, Maura." Rose turned to the line of men waiting for bread. "Don't shove. There's enough fer everyone."

Since Rose seemed to have things under control, Maura backed away to stand next to Gillian's chair. "Well, now that we've lost power, we can't get a weather report," she pointed out.

"We can with a phone," Gillian said. She pulled hers from a pocket and clicked on something, then read out the results. "Looks like snow, followed by snow, then mixed with snow for the next twelve hours, all accompanied by high winds. They won't guess beyond that." She turned off her phone again to save the battery. If there was any message from Harry, Gillian didn't say.

"If the soup's not enough for this lot, I brought back some potatoes we could bake in the coals," Rose added. "And apples. We won't starve, Maura. We're fine."

Something in Maura relaxed. Rose was right: they had everything they needed, and this weather wouldn't last forever. Maybe a day. They could manage for that long, couldn't they? No doubt the building had survived worse. "Rose, you're absolutely right. Everybody, you might want to turn off your phones in case we'll need them later. The lamps will do for now, and you don't need to be playing games or texting your friends on your phones with pictures of the snow." Maura noticed the two Dublin musicians turning off their phones, looking embarrassed.

"If it's coal yer needing, I can fetch some fer yeh," Seamus volunteered—he had drained his mug of soup.

"I'll go with you," Maura said quickly. "It's out the back, in the shed." At least, she hoped it was. She glanced quickly at Mick, who gave her a slight nod. So at least Jimmy hadn't helped himself to that too. "Follow me," she told the man, then led the way out the side door toward the sheds.

She wasn't prepared for the blast of cold, snow-laden air that hit her as soon as she wrestled the door open. Seeing the weather from inside the warm pub was nothing like standing in the midst of it, and it sucked her breath away. "This way," she yelled over the howling wind. Luckily the storage sheds lay close to the building, beside and behind it. As she remembered, Mick usually bought both coal and turf in large burlap sacks, and they were easy to find. Both appeared to be more than half-full, which was good. "So nobody's expecting you at home, Seamus?" Maura yelled into the wind as her companion filled the bucket.

"I told yeh, herself is off visiting her sister in Galway, so I'm on me own. I'd hate to miss this adventure."

"I'm glad you feel that way. I haven't done this before."

"Ah, it'll be grand—you'll see. As yer young Rose said, we've everything we need. Even a celebrity in our midst."

Uh-oh. "What do you mean?" Maura asked cautiously.

"That woman, Diane—you wouldn't know her, but time was, she was suspected of murder."

Great. Someone else knew, although Mick had warned her that might happen. "Don't say anything, okay? We're all stuck here together for the night, and I don't want anyone to start a something unpleasant."

"Would I be doin' that? I can keep my gob shut, but I won't say as much fer other people."

Maura was afraid he meant Jimmy. "How many are likely to know about her?"

"It was big news once, not so much lately. But here in Ireland, we take unsolved murders very seriously. I'd guess one or two of the others might recall. Not the young ones."

Jimmy and his big mouth worried her. "Could you try to stop the talk if it comes up?"

"Might there be a free pint in it fer me?"

"I'm pretty sure there would be."

"Don't fret yerself, Maura. I'm the last man to want to see any trouble in the pub tonight."

"Thank you, Seamus. Let's get back in there before my ears freeze off."

Seamus hoisted the heavy bucket and followed Maura back inside. Now she could appreciate just how much warmer it was inside. "We've got coal!" she announced.

Several bricks now supported the grate. Rose knelt in front of the fireplace and began adding coal to the dwindling fire. "Am I doin' it right, Billy? I've never built a fire to cook over."

Billy had lowered himself to kneel beside Rose in front of the fire. "Yer doin' fine, girl. Don't pack it in, let it breathe. And ye'll have to wait a bit for the coal to catch before yeh try to cook over it." There was a collective groan from the several people in the room. "Ah, quit yer whingin'," Billy said. "Yer warm and dry, and you've food in yer stomach. What more could yeh be looking fer?"

"A pint!" one of the musicians called out. Liam, was it? Everyone turned to look at Maura.

"Sure, why not?" How much could this small group put away, anyway? Gillian and Rose weren't drinking, and Billy stretched out a single pint for hours.

"I'll take care of it," Mick said, sliding behind the bar. The men clustered around it quickly, which forced Diane to retreat to a corner table as far away from the fire as possible. She looked cold, so Maura picked up her coat where she'd left it by the bar and took it to her.

"You look like you might want this," Maura said, holding up the coat.

Diane was so lost in her own thoughts that it took her a moment to focus on Maura. "Oh. Thanks, Maura."

"Can I get you some more coffee? Anything else? Did you get some soup?"

"No, I'm fine." Everything about the woman radiated "Leave me alone!" even if she didn't say it aloud.

So Maura did just that and went to the other end of the room, where Billy and Gillian were watching Rose set the fire to her liking. She'd got the fire going, the irregular chunks of coal glowing red around the edges. Now she was focused on placing the bricks just so to support the grill. "Will that be steady enough, do yeh think, Billy?"

"Looks grand. I'm thinkin' yer about ready fer the bread now."

Rose gave the grill one last prod to make sure it was solidly placed, then stood and dusted herself off. "All right, listen now.

If yer wantin' some toast, now's the time. I don't want to see you pushin' and shovin' at the fire. We're in no hurry."

"If we eat all the bread now, what'll we do fer breakfast?" Donal asked plaintively.

"Yeh can have a nice potato and be glad of it, Donal Lafferty," Rose said.

Maura stifled a smile at Rose's tone and dragged a chair over next to Gillian's, a few feet away from the fire now. "Any word from Harry?"

"No, not that I expected to hear," Gillian said in a dull voice. *Trouble?* "Are things all right at the house?"

Gillian summoned up a smile. "Apart from the O'Briens each looking down their noses at me all day long? As right as can be expected. Harry and I are fine, if that's what you're asking. He's glad I've been at the house to keep Eveline company, and she and I might have come to be something like friends now. Not that he doesn't trust the O'Briens to look after her, but he likes the second opinion. It all worked out fine until this past week when she took ill. She's a smart woman—it's a shame that she never had much chance to use her intelligence. But she was raised in a very different world. We've been going through old photos and the like. I track the albums down and bring them to her, and she tells me who all the people are. It'd surprise you how quick the time goes."

"Have you and Harry talked about any . . . plans?" Like what they were going to do when the baby came, or when Eveline passed away, or possibly both at once.

"You know that the Trust gets the property, right?" When Maura nodded, Gillian went on, "Eveline's apologized more than once that she has little to leave to us. She's hoping to hold on until the baby's come, but she knows she's weakening. Harry, poor lamb, alternates between complete denial and a blue funk. Either everything's fine or it's all going to hell. I never know which Harry I'll be talking to."

Maura looked around the room. The soup was ready—and smelled wonderful, but then there had been no lunch, and now it was nearly suppertime. The room was reasonably warm and lighted. The men were occupied and looked fairly cheerful. The only false note was Diane, huddled in the far corner, looking out at the snow. But Diane was not asking for help from anyone, and Maura wasn't about to shove it down her throat. Once the toast crowd had died down, Billy had reclaimed his place near the fire, and Rose had handed him a mug of soup. He seemed to be dozing, his eyes only half-open. Maura turned back to Gillian.

"Does Harry have any ideas?"

"For what? For his life? His job? Where he's going to live? Me? The baby?"

"Take your pick, Gillian. I don't mean to poke around in your private life, but you know I'll help if I can."

"I know, and I thank you for it. It's just that I don't have a plan either. No home, no money coming in, and a man who can't seem to make up his mind about anything."

Maura studied her friend's face. After a moment, she said, "If you could have anything you wanted—anything at all—what would it be?"

Gillian looked at Maura. "You're serious."

"Yes, I am. People should have dreams."

"Did you? Before you landed here?"

It was a fair question. "No. Mostly I was focused on just getting by. You know, paying the bills month to month. I didn't have much choice. Gran did the best she could, but she was getting older, and she was tired. I think she knew she wouldn't last long, near the end, and I know she was worried about me. That's how this whole thing happened. She set things up with Old Mick, and she never said a word to me."

"A practical woman, your gran. She might have said nothing because it could have fallen through, and she didn't want to raise your hopes. I'm guessing she wanted you to be strong in case things didn't work out. You still miss her, don't you?"

"Every day. She was the only family I ever knew. But back to you—you've got issues with your own family, right?"

"I do. They weren't happy with me when I said I wanted to be an artist, although I've never asked them for a penny. They're even less happy now that this has happened." Her hand drifted to her swelling belly.

"They aren't going to be thrilled by a new grandbaby?"

"They're already got a few, all nice and proper in the eyes of the church and the village."

"So what, then? You never answered my question. If I had a magic wand and could wave it and make all your dreams come true, what would you ask for?"

Gillian looked down at her hands in her lap and shook her head. "I've no idea. A home with just enough room and a place with good light so I could paint. Someone to love me, and someone to love. Well, I hope I've got that last part right, at least in a couple of months."

"And do you see Harry in that picture?" Maura asked quietly.

Gillian looked at her then. "Maybe. I'm not sure."

Seven

~

"And what about you, Maura? Where do you see yourself in the future?" Gillian asked, shifting the talk away from herself.

Exactly the type of question Maura had avoided for most of her life. "I don't know. I've never been the kind of person who worries about the future and tries to plan it because I didn't think I could. You shouldn't be surprised if you look at my family— you know the story. My gran lost her husband—otherwise she probably would have lived out her days in one of those cottages up the hill here, with a bunch of kids. Didn't work out, so she pulled up her socks and found enough money to get herself and her son to Boston. She raised her son there, and from what I know, he turned out all right. He got married, and then I came along. Then he got killed in a stupid work accident, and my mother couldn't deal with it and walked out. And Gran stepped up. We managed. But tell me, where's the room for planning in that? So I've never wasted much time thinking about things I'll probably never get."

"Do you not think of finding a man, getting married, having children of your own?"

"Not really. I've never been in love with anybody, and nobody's been in love with me. How can you miss what you've never had or even seen?" She'd known her gran only as a widow and didn't remember her father or mother at all. "And if you're asking about a biological itch, maybe I'm just not programmed that way. You and Harry have been together, sort of, for years, right?"

"We have, with no commitment on either side. It worked for us—at least for a while." Gillian's expression darkened.

"Have there been other guys?" Maura asked.

"A few in Dublin, but none that lasted."

"So you're not exactly the poster girl for relationships."

"That I'm not." Gillian looked around to see if anyone was listening to them. "It may not be my place to say, but you've got Mick and Sean sniffing around you."

"Ick—that's a terrible way to put it. Makes them sound like a pair of dogs."

"You know what I mean."

Maura sighed. "Yes, I do. And I can't exactly tell you to butt out when I've been trampling all over your love life."

"Do you see yourself with either one of them?"

"I don't know. I try not to think about it. I'm not in love with either of them, if that's want you're hinting at, but then, like I said, I've never been in love with anybody. How'm I supposed to choose? Is there a sign? Symptoms? I feel weak in the knees when one or the other is around? Do I ask them to fight a duel for me? What do I do?"

"Maura, if you don't want to talk about it, you can tell me to shut my gob," Gillian said quietly.

Maura looked around her. She and Gillian were tucked into a warm corner all but behind the fire, and nobody seemed to be paying any attention to their conversation. Mick was talking to the musicians at the far end of the room, trying to explain how they could plug in their equipment, she guessed from their gestures. No reason not to talk to Gillian now, even though it made her uncomfortable.

"I'm sorry—I haven't had a lot of women friends in my life, and I'm lousy at this sharing stuff. If I have to say this in ten words or less, I'd tell you that Sean is the sensible choice, but Mick . . . well, he's the more interesting one."

"I won't argue with that. Sean's a good man with a steady job, and he works hard. It's easy to see he cares about you, but he's letting you set the pace. Mick? Well . . . I've known him for years, but I can't say I really *know* him. He keeps a lot to himself. Kind of like you, Maura."

"Which sounds like a recipe for disaster," Maura replied quickly. "Is he hiding something? Some deep, dirty secret in his past? Why's he working at a dead-end job here? He's clearly got some brains, and he could do better."

"You'll have to ask him that, Maura," Gillian said. "I'd wager looking out for Bridget is one reason, and I'll give him credit for that. Beyond that, I can't say."

"You aren't going to tell me to follow my heart, are you?" Maura asked her, suspicious. "Because that's been pretty quiet lately."

"You've seen how well I've managed my love life, so I'm hardly the one to give you advice. But I will say this: Harry's always been special to me, even when I was with one or another different man. I've been waiting for a long time for him to grow up and figure things out. And it may be he never does. But I'll survive. So will you, Maura, no matter what you decide."

Maura nodded once, acknowledging what Gillian had said. "Well, in case you haven't noticed, I'm not encouraging either one of them. I want to sort out my own life before I get tied up with someone else. I may not even stay here in Ireland forever. I haven't made up my mind."

"I'm hoping you'll stay, even if that's selfish of me. As for the other, Maura, you're young yet. These things have a way of sneaking up on you while you're not looking."

Maura bristled in spite of herself. "Don't you go all smug on me and nod and think I'll wake up one morning and know what my heart wants. That's your baby hormones talking. What do they call it? Nesting instinct? Now you want *everybody* to nest."

"Maybe," Gillian said, smiling. "There are worse fates, Maura Donovan."

Billy opened his eyes and said quietly, "Maura, would you care to invite yer guest to join us here where it's warmer?" He nodded toward Diane, huddled alone at a table at the opposite end of the room.

Maura felt a pang of guilt: Diane did look kind of miserable. "I didn't want to bother her if she wants some peace," she told Billy. "I asked if she wanted soup, and she said no."

"If yeh leave her there, it'll be pneumonia she ends up with," Billy said. "The window on that side could do with a bit of patching—the draft is wicked."

Since Maura seldom had time to sit in her own pub, that hadn't occurred to her. "Thanks, Billy. I don't spend a lot of time at a table over there, you know."

"I do. Go on wit' yeh now and talk to the poor woman."

Maura stood up and walked across to the other end of the room. Billy was right: away from the fire, the temperature dropped quickly, and as she passed the front door, she could feel cold air seeping in. The corner where Diane sat was as far as possible from both the fire and the men clustered around the bar—keeping themselves warm on the outside with each other's body heat and on the inside with Guinness. The far corner had to be at least twenty degrees colder than the fireside, and it wasn't going to get any warmer. Maura dropped into a chair across from Diane.

"Would you like to sit closer to the fire? I think you're turning blue over here."

"I'm all right," the woman said—her statement undermined by the shaking of her hands. Diane noticed and balled them into fists.

"Look, I can understand if you don't want to talk, but I'm going to feel really guilty if you freeze to death in my pub," Maura told her firmly.

"That's not likely, but thank you for thinking of me. At the risk of sounding like some movie cliché, I want to be alone. Please?"

"Well, if you change your mind, you're welcome to join us by the fire. And for soup. It's hot."

"We'll see. But again, thank you."

Maura gave up her efforts. She felt sorry for the woman, who seemed very alone. *And she wanted it that way*, Maura reminded herself. She'd done the same thing herself more times than she wanted to count in bars and low-end restaurants back in Boston, where conversation with strangers could be annoying at best and dangerous at worst. How long ago had Mick said this crime had happened? Twenty-odd years? Surely Diane must have moved on with her life since then. Maura wondered idly why she had waited so long to sell the family property if that was indeed what she was doing here in Ireland. Had she hoped things would change, that the murder would be solved and clear her name, or at least that people would forget? Or had she been reluctant to let go of that piece of her past—the part before the death had upset things and driven her away under a cloud?

On her way back to her place by the fire—still vacant, since all the men still seemed to be happier at the bar, now that they had some of Rose's soup in their stomachs—Maura stopped and leaned over the bar. "Rose, you're a genius. Is the bread gone?"

"I've held back a bit, since this is all we've got until the storm ends. There's plenty of soup—have you had yours?"

"Not yet. How many pints has this lot had so far?" She nodded toward the cluster of men. Seamus and Danny, Liam and Donal—and Maura was annoyed to see that Jimmy had joined them and had a glass of his own in hand.

"I'm guessing this'd be their second round—not that I've been counting," Rose said. "Did you want me to?"

"No, don't bother," Maura told her. "We'll make it up somehow, and there aren't that many people drinking here. Though those who are may get rowdy after a while if they keep drinking." Maura added a mental note to herself to check that the men's bathroom was stocked with paper supplies. And maybe a light?

"Ah, Mick can keep 'em in line," Rose said with assurance. "You needn't worry. Might we ask the Dublin boys fer some music later? That'd keep 'em busy."

"Only if they've brought acoustic instruments with them. No power, remember?"

"Oh. I hadn't thought of that. But they might have tin whistles and drums," Rose said hopefully.

"I can ask 'em." Maura stood up again. She was restless, unused to just sitting and doing nothing. Well, maybe talking to people wasn't exactly nothing, but she wanted to be busy, and besides, moving kept her warm. Mick and Jimmy had the bar covered between them, serving the men in the room, except Old Billy, who was doing what he always did; Rose was cooking; Gillian was sitting with her hands over her baby bump—*What a silly term*, Maura thought—dreaming of who knew what. Maybe Harry sweeping in on a white horse with his pockets full of cash?

She approached Liam and Donal, who were standing together at the far end of the bar, on the fringes of the group of men who all knew each other. With the exception of Rose and maybe herself, they were easily the youngest people in the room. She still hadn't worked out all the details for booking of musicians yet; mostly she invited people who had been recommended, but the results had been mixed, although in general the crowds had definitely been enthusiastic. Should the pub adopt a particular style of music, like traditional or contemporary, or just go with whatever came along? She hadn't decided.

"Hey, Lafferty brothers, think you could give us some music? If you don't need electricity for your instruments?"

The two young men exchanged a glance. "What're you lookin' for?"

"What've you got?" Maura shot back. "Believe me, we won't be picky, and you've got a captive audience here."

"So we do. Liam, you up for throwin' a few songs at them and seein' what sticks?"

"Why not?" Liam said, and the pair went into the back room to retrieve their instruments. They did a bit of tuning before coming back and settling on a pair of chairs. Without any announcement, they started in on a tune even Maura recognized, although she couldn't put a name to it. After a startled response, Seamus and Danny picked it up, as did one of the strangers—and they all knew the words. Billy smiled, although he didn't sing. Maura nodded toward Rose, then toward the players, and after a moment's hesitation, Rose added a sweet soprano. They sounded great, at least to Maura's ears.

Since everyone was happily occupied, Maura decided to make the rounds of the pub. If nothing else, she could check where there was cold air leaking in, so she could fill those cracks when the snow stopped. And what the heck were they going to do about sleeping? Billy could go home, since "home" was only a matter of feet away. Heck, if the sidewalk was dangerous, the guys here could carry him home. But that still left another—she counted on her fingers—five who might want to sleep sometime, plus Gillian and Jimmy and Rose and Mick. And herself. That made ten. Where could she put them all? Maura grabbed up a torch and marched up the stairs to check out the rooms up above. Nobody seemed to notice her leaving. She could hear the music clearly even upstairs.

Damn, it was cold. Was there no heating in the rooms? Or had somebody turned it off years ago? Well, duh—why waste heat if nobody was using the rooms? But she should check to make sure everything still worked—just not tonight. She had no idea the last time Old Mick had been up here, although some of the visiting musicians had said they used to crash here. She should have brought a notepad along to make notes to herself, but it was hard enough stumbling around in the half dark, trying not to drop the flashlight. So, upstairs: three bedrooms and a bath. She knew the plumbing worked. Last time she'd looked, the rooms were filled with years' worth of discarded stuff in boxes and piles, just like the cellar. Clearly Old Mick had never thrown anything out. The only reason she could get around her house—once Mick's—was that somebody had cleared Mick's stuff out after he had died. It had been pretty Spartan when she moved in. What were the odds someone had stashed a supply of blankets up here? Slim to none. There were no beds in sight, and nobody had taken a bath in the bathroom in a very long time, although at least the toilet flushed.

The tempo of the music below picked up, which was probably a good thing. Maura prowled around aimlessly, peering into boxes and shutting them again. She wandered over to a front window, from which she could see . . . nothing. Not even the snow. All the lights, on the street and in the other buildings that lined it, were out. She thought she saw the bobbing light of a flashlight over at Sheahan's across the street, so she waved her light in that direction. Whoever held the one over there waved back. At least there was someone else out there.

Focus, Maura! What to sleep on downstairs? The musicians said they had their own sleeping bags—that was two people taken care of. Two more people could take the upholstered chairs, which meant pregnant Gillian and maybe Old Billy. That left . . . how many? Mick, Jimmy, Rose, Seamus, his friend Danny, and herself. Seven more people, which made it nine total, plus the odd stranger or two who might still wander in. No, she'd forgotten Diane, who made the total ten in need of something to sleep on or in. Would anyone share space with Diane, thinking she might be a killer? Who was likely to know about that? Mick, probably Jimmy and Old Billy for a start, and Seamus. Heck, just call it everybody, for if they didn't know who Diane was yet, odds were short that the secret wouldn't stay secret much longer. Well, it wouldn't kill them to spend a night on a bare floor with her, but nobody would get much sleep. And poor Diane would probably be left in the cold corner, just in case she might be dangerous.

Maura felt a surge of excitement when she spied some long bulky rolls shoved against the back wall of the last room. *Please be rugs!* she prayed. When she tugged at the nearest one, she smiled: rugs they were. Filthy, of course, and they'd probably gotten wet more than once, but at least they'd be softer than old flagstones downstairs—and warmer too. And they might block any drafts that swept across the floor. First bit of good news she'd had for a while, and how silly was that? Getting excited about some old dirty rugs?

She didn't see anything else that could possibly be useful, so she went back downstairs. Nobody seemed to notice because they were absorbed in the music. Jimmy was behind the bar now, obviously not singing, and looking grumpy. "What?" Maura demanded. He didn't say anything, so Maura moved on to, "Any change in the weather?"

"How're we to know? Can't see a thing out there," Jimmy grumbled.

Diane finally came over. "May I?" she said, taking an empty mug.

"Of course," Rose said. "Let me fill that fer yeh. There's plenty more for those that want seconds." She went into the kitchen and emerged a minute later and handed Diane the mug. She took it gratefully and perched on a stool at the end of the bar. Maura was reminded of a feral cat approaching cautiously, drawn in by hunger. At least she'd moved a few feet closer, and now she had some food.

Gillian still had her own mug, wrapping her hands around it. Old Billy seemed to have finished his. "Should we add more coal to the fire, do yeh think?" Rose asked him.

"Might be a few more lumps would do," Billy told her.

Rose knelt and stoked the fire and stood wavering for a moment. "Rose, sit down and have some soup," Maura told her. "You've been working harder than anyone, and you've earned a rest."

"Ah, I had a grand time. Mebbe I should think about a restaurant. Or openin' the kitchen here."

"We can talk about that now that we've got more people coming in for the music. But let's take it slow."

Seamus and Danny came back for seconds, but they were strangely polite about it. "What's fer dessert?" Donal—or was it Liam?—called out, and some people laughed.

Rose dimpled. "There's apples, and might be I brought back some biscuits, and we can make tea. If you lot wash yer dishes first, that is."

"Rose, you are amazing," Maura said with admiration.

"What time is it?" Seamus asked.

Mick pointed at the clock over the bar, which luckily was battery run. "Gone seven. You meetin' someone?" That question met with laughter.

"What're we gonna do without the telly?" Danny said plaintively.

"You're tired of singing already? You want to play charades?" Maura suggested. She wanted to divert the men from drinking, at least for a while.

Most of the men looked blankly at her. Had they never heard of charades?

Jimmy had been leaning against the back counter behind the bar, not saying much. Now he spoke, and his tone was anything but cheerful. "Seems like someone's already been playin' games wit' us," he said, his tone surly.

Maura wondered how much he'd had to drink—she'd never known him to pass up a free pint, but it might be getting to him now, and he'd been in a mood all day. Had Mick questioned him about the missing oil? That might have set him off. And then the significance of what Jimmy was saying dawned on her: Was he talking about Diane? And why? Did he just feel like making trouble? She glanced at Mick, who looked as concerned as she felt.

"Leave it be, will yeh?" Mick said to Jimmy.

"And why should I do that? Why should the likes of her"—he nodded toward Diane, who sat as still as stone on her stool—"be welcome in this fine establishment?"

Maura stepped between them. "Because I invited her to stay, Jimmy. This is my place, remember? Drop it."

He didn't. Jimmy's lip curled. "And do yeh know what kind of woman yer harborin' in yer place here? A killer, is what."

"Jimmy—" Maura began, but she was interrupted when Diane walked over to where Jimmy was standing and said, "You'd be talking about me, I assume?"

Maura stepped forward as well. "Diane, you don't have to—"

Diane didn't move from her position in front of Jimmy—a little too close for his comfort. She turned her head slightly toward Maura. "Yes, I do, Maura, though thanks for defending me. But it's clear that some of you in this room know at least some part of the story. The old house is sold, so this may be my last trip to this country. We're stuck together for the night, through no fault of mine. Do you want to hear the story? The true story, that is?"

Some people in the room looked bewildered, but it was clear that more knew what Diane was talking about. Including Maura, thanks to Mick. She stepped forward and said in a low voice, "Diane, you don't have to do this. It's nobody's business but your own."

Diane turned to face the others in the room. "Maura, thanks for trying to spare me, but just this once, I'd like to tell my story my way. The papers, the news people, they all branded me as guilty from the start. But the gardaí could never find enough to arrest me, much less take me to trial. I've kept quiet for years now, but I want someone to hear what really happened." Diane surveyed the small crowd. "Those of you who can't stand the company, feel free to leave." Diane's mouth quirked, and Maura was obscurely pleased to find she had a sense of humor.

Maura came up beside her. "I, for one, don't know the story, and I say we let her speak. You have anything more important to do?" Nobody said a word. Maura turned to Jimmy. "Jimmy, you have a problem with that?" Maura demanded.

Jimmy realized he was in the minority. "Ah, let her go on. It's nothin' to me."

"Then you'd better refill your glasses, because I'm guessing it's not a short story. Jimmy, a word with you in the back?"

Jimmy looked startled for a moment, then followed her reluctantly into the cold back room. "What're yeh after?" he said when they were sure no one would overhear.

Maura struggled to control her anger. "What you just did—that was wrong, Jimmy."

He shrugged. "I thought the others had a right to know who they were sharing space with. I'd wager most of them know the story anyways."

"You had no right," Maura hissed. "Diane is a guest in my pub, and I'm the one who gets to decide who stays and who goes. Not you. And I'm beginning to think maybe you don't belong here. How long have you been helping yourself to my oil?"

At least he looked momentarily sheepish before he turned belligerent. "So what if I've taken a bit? With the wages yer payin' me, how can I afford to keep my own place warm?"

"You're getting as much as I can afford to pay you. Feel free to look for another job if you're not happy working here."

"Mebbe I will," he said.

Wherever the talk might have gone, it was interrupted by a burst of noise from the front room: the front door flung back, loud male voices, stamping of feet. "What the hell?"

Maura muttered, and turning her back on Jimmy, she hurried out front. The room seemed filled with newcomers: two older guys and a cluster of—she counted—four twenty-something guys, clearly drunk.

"What's going on here?" Maura demanded.

One of the older men volunteered, "I found this lot in a ditch by the side of the lane while I was drivin' past. No way was I goin' to try to haul them out on this night, and so I bundled them into my van and made for Leap. Yours were the first lights I saw, and here we are."

"Nobody's hurt?"

"Nah," the other man said. "God protects fools and drunks, and these lads qualify for both. Is that food I smell?"

"It is. Welcome to Sullivan's. I'm the owner, Maura Donovan. And you're not getting anything more to drink before you've put some food in your stomachs," Maura told them firmly.

"Yer a hard woman but a fair one, Maura Donovan." The man turned to the group of younger men, who looked unsteady on their feet. "Lads, behave yerselves, and yeh'll get some food and a warm place to sit. I'm guessing we won't be going any farther this night."

"I think you'd be right about that," Maura said. "Sit if you can find a chair. Rose, find some clean mugs and give this lot some hot food."

"Coming up, Maura."

Eight

When Maura had sorted out the newcomers, she turned to find that Diane had faded into a corner again. She sidled up to her, keeping an eye on the sudden crowd. "I'm sorry."

"Why?" Diane asked.

"Because you thought you finally had a chance to tell your story after all these years, and then this bunch of drunken idiots shows up."

Diane shrugged. "Maybe it's a sign from the heavens—my time here in Ireland is done. I'll just go home quietly whenever the snow stops, and that'll be the end of it."

Why did that feel wrong to Maura? It was none of her business. Diane had come back to take care of one last legal detail, and it was purely by accident that she'd ended up in Sullivan's.

But maybe she recognized something of herself in Diane's reserve. She kept her troubles to herself, and she didn't ask for or expect help from anyone else. Had Diane always been like that? Or had being a murder suspect changed her? The event had happened a long time ago. But, as Maura had learned, memories in

Ireland were long. Maura decided to allow herself one more question, and then she'd put it aside and get back to business.

She turned to face Diane, who was still watching the crowd warily, although they paid no attention to her. "Diane, did you kill who they say you did?"

Diane turned to her, studying her face. "No, I did not. I can see why the gardaí might have suspected me, but they never found enough evidence to arrest me. Because there was no evidence to be had."

"So in the end, you just walked away from Ireland?"

"More or less. I think it was a mistake to come back now—I could have handled the transaction by post. But I wanted to see the place one last time. I don't suppose that makes sense to you—you're an American and younger than I am."

"True. But I know how my grandmother who raised me felt about Ireland, about this village and Cork. She didn't shove it down my throat because she wanted me to be an American. She never told me that she kept in touch with people around here. But I know what you mean about memories. I showed up here last March, and everybody knew exactly who I was. They knew more about my family than I did."

"And that troubled you?"

"In the beginning it did. It took me a while to realize that people meant it kindly. They weren't just being nosy. They wanted to help."

Diane turned away, looking at the blank window that reflected only their own images. "Because you were one of their own, you see. I had a bit of that since my grandparents were from here, but the people I spent time with were foreigners, and the local people didn't quite trust them. I made the choice to side with them, and when this murder happened, I paid for that. Don't lose sight of the good side of your background, Maura. People do mean well."

"I think I've figured that out. Listen, Diane—do you still want to talk about what happened?"

"It's not important. It won't change anything now."

"But it's not right!" Maura protested.

"You sound so American! It is was it is. I've come to terms with it. I have a life in England now—I just wanted to say good-bye."

Maura couldn't think of anything more to say, although Diane's attitude still made her sad. But she had a business to run, and she'd better get back to work. She turned away from Diane and slid behind the bar. The newcomers had all but inhaled their soup, and the older two had moved on to Guinness. Liam and Donal seemed to have taken the younger guys under their wing and distributed soup to them, and they were clustered in another corner. It might be a good idea to hold off on serving them anything else with alcohol until they'd gotten some food into them.

"So what's the story?" Maura asked the men at the bar. "How did you end up wandering around the lanes in the dark during a snowstorm?"

The oldest man spoke up first. He was broad in the shoulders, his hair generously silvered. His clothing was not at all suited to the country, much less to shoving a car out of a ditch. He extended a hand to Maura. "Bart Hayes is the name. I came down from near Limerick for my niece's wedding in Rosscarbery and somehow ended up looking after these young eejits, since I was one of the few sober folk left by the end."

Maura smiled. "I thought they looked a bit the worse for drink. Where were you going?"

"I've friends runnin' a bed and breakfast outside Drinagh, and they offered to put us up. It would have been an easy shot home from there. But I haven't traveled those roads for a long time, and I hadn't counted on the snow—it's worse here than to the east. I didn't know how bad the roads were when we started out—my mistake. We'd got near to Drinagh when I missed a turn in the dark and found myself with two wheels in the ditch and no way out. The lads were all for getting out and pushing, but I figgered they'd only make things worse—they weren't dressed for the snow, and they'd probably freeze their fingers off or get lost in a field. So I was working out a plan when . . ."

"That's when I appeared, like an angel from heaven," the second man said. "Joe Minahane. I'd heard a woman had taken over this place from Old Mick."

"And that's me—Maura Donovan. You're from around here, then?" Maura asked.

"I am, near Reavouler. This fella here"—he nodded at Bart— "had gotten himself lost in the dark, and God knows what his fate might have been if I hadn't happened along."

Maura wondered if Joe had started drinking a bit earlier in the day. "So you collected them and came to Leap? Why not Skibbereen or back to Drinagh? Or even to your place?"

"We've no room for five extra, and me wife would skin me alive if I brought this lot home with me, snow or no snow. I was aimin' fer Skibbereen, fer there's no place to put them up at Drinagh, and I wasn't about to turn around and try to find their bloody B and B. I thought maybe there'd be help to get the car goin' again if I went toward Skib, but the snow kept gettin' worse, so I ended up here."

Maura didn't know the local geography very well, but she guessed that Joe had gotten himself turned around more than once. At least he and the rest had landed safely at Sullivan's, even if Bart's car was still out there somewhere.

"Well, I don't think any of you are going any farther tonight in this weather. The rest of this gang is going to spend the night here, so you may as well too. I don't suppose you have any blankets in your truck?"

"And why would I have that? Well, there is the one I used last time I delivered a calf . . ."

Maura suppressed a shudder. "We'll figure something out. There's always the floor."

"No room across the road?" Joe asked wistfully. "Anne does a grand breakfast."

"At the inn? No, they were full up before the storm. I think you're stuck with me. There's hot soup if you're hungry, although I think we ate all the bread. So, Bart, did the wedding go on as planned?"

"It did. A lovely couple they made. Good thing they didn't plan to leave for a honeymoon any time soon."

"How far did you come for this?" Maura asked, mainly to make conversation.

"I'm stationed in Limerick these days."

"Stationed? Are you in the military?"

Bart shook his head. "I'm a garda. Used to be in Bantry, but my wife's people came from up Limerick way, and she wanted to be closer when the kids started coming. I've no complaints." He took a long swallow of his stout. His eyes sought out Diane in the corner and nodded toward her before asking Maura, "You know the story there?"

Oh, crap. Maura wasn't sure how to answer that to a garda, but Bart didn't look angry or hostile, and he hadn't blown the whistle on Diane as soon as he recognized her. "Only the bare outline. Were you part of that?"

"I was, back in Bantry. I was there when it happened."

Maura looked quickly at Joe, who now seemed to be deep in conversation with Seamus a few feet away. She leaned across the bar toward Bart. "Do you think she did it?"

"We had no proof," Bart said carefully.

"But what did *you* think?"

"I was younger then, and none of us had much experience with murder." He took another swallow. "But my gut said no."

"From what I've heard here tonight, the press was all over her."

Bart looked disgusted. "Ah, they're always after the story. That one had everything—money, sex, foreigners. There's still talk of it."

"Did you ever hear her side of it?" Maura asked.

He shook his head. "I was new on the job then, although we all talked. Never met the woman myself."

But you recognized her. Maura thought hard for a moment. "Listen, Bart. When you guys showed up, Diane was ready to tell the story from her side. There are some others here who remember it, even this long after it happened. None of us are going anywhere tonight. What do you think about letting her tell us what happened?"

Bart leaned back on his stool and studied her face. "And why would we be wantin' to do that?"

"Because we're all stuck here, and she's here. And I guess because based on what I've been hearing, she was tried and convicted without even being arrested. People just assumed she was guilty. It changed her life. What if she didn't do it?"

"You've been watching too many of those detective shows on the telly, Maura Donovan, where everything is wrapped up neat and tidy in an hour or less."

"I've never had time to watch television shows," she said sharply. "It just seems to me that she got branded as a killer, and that was that. It's not right."

"And you come along from America, and you're going to fix things in a night, when the gardaí and the newspapers have been tramping all over it for the better part of two decades?"

"I never said that. I just think that someone should listen to her."

"Are you sayin' the gardaí didn't do their jobs?" Now Bart seemed to be getting angry.

"No, I'm not saying that. Look, I don't know the whole story. I didn't know there *was* a story. You all just happened to end up here tonight. She's willing to talk about it."

"She might be less willin' if she knows I was a garda who was on the case then," Bart pointed out.

"So we'll ask her. And Bart? Think about it. If she didn't do it, then someone else did. Someone killed whatever her name was and got away with it for twenty years. That's just wrong."

Bart sighed and scrubbed his hands over his face. "I've been celebrating all day, and then I've driven into a ditch with a bunch of bumbling eejits, and now you want me to talk about a crime that happened a long time ago. You don't ask much, do yeh?"

"Hey, I didn't think this up—it just happened. Maybe it's a sign or something that you're all here now."

Bart drained his glass and stood up stiffly. "Yer blamin' fate now? Let me talk to the woman, see what she says. No promises. And I could use another pint."

"Coming up," Maura said.

Nine

～

Maura watched as Bart Hayes made his way over to where Diane sat. He paused when he reached the table, said something to her, and then she gestured toward the chair across from her at the table. So at least she was willing to listen to him.

What the heck did she think she was doing? Her job was to serve up drinks and make sure nobody at the pub got out of hand before closing time. Make sure they were out the door by closing time too—or close enough. But this snowstorm had kind of thrown a wrench into the whole normal pattern. Now she had her entire staff here, which didn't make a lot of sense, to take care of—she did a quick count—fifteen people. Rose had done a great job of seeing that they were fed, and Mick and she had supplied light and heat. She checked her watch: damn, it was barely eight o'clock, but with no electricity, it was pitch dark outside. Too early to tell people to settle down and go nighty-night. No way she would send them out into the storm. So now what?

Diane came back to the bar, followed by Bart. "Maura, can we pick up where we left off? Unless you have other ideas?"

"I'm willing, Diane. Bart told you . . ." she left the question hanging.

"That he was part of the original investigation? Yes, he did."

"And you're okay with him being here?"

"As I told you, I have nothing to hide," Diane said almost impatiently. "Let him ask his questions, give his facts. Let's find out what the others here think. They can be the jury—it's the only one I'll ever get."

"All right, then," Maura said. She scanned the crowd: would they want to stay to hear this? Would they veto the whole idea? "Go for it, Diane."

Diane stepped to the center of the bar, found an empty glass, and banged it on the counter top until everyone else stopped talking and turned toward her. "My name is Diane Caldwell, but I was born Diane Wolfe, from out past Schull. I know some people here have already recognized me because twenty years ago, I was accused of killing a neighbor, Sharon Morgan. Not arrested, not put to trial, not convicted. No more than accused, but people assumed I was guilty, and I've had to live with that ever since. Well, I'm sick of it. We're all stuck here this evening, and I want to tell my side of the story just this once. I'd ask if you're willing to listen, but to tell the truth, I really don't care anymore. Listen or not, and in the morning, you can all go your separate ways."

Bart stepped up beside her then. "You won't know it, but I was part of that investigation then, so I know the history. Diane here is right: we shined a light on her, but no one could prove she'd done anything, and that's where the matter has rested all these years. No one else has ever been arrested or charged with the crime. It's a blot on the record of three garda jurisdictions, and I'd like to see it laid to rest. Will you hear her out?"

If the topic wasn't so serious, Maura might have laughed at the variety of reactions from the people in the room. From their expressions, it was clear that some knew the whole story, some knew bits and pieces, and some knew nothing at all. Jimmy looked pleased by the ruckus he'd stirred up, and she really wanted to wipe the smirk off his face. Mick looked angry. The others looked confused or worried or even happy that the question of how to pass the evening had been answered: a fireside chat with an accused murderer.

Maura moved to stand alongside Diane. "You don't have to do this. You're my guest here." She turned to glare at the crowd. "And I expect you lot to be polite." Only a few looked ashamed.

"Thank you, Maura," Diane said, "but I want to. It's been twenty years since my life was upended, and the questions just won't go away. People are still avoiding me, which is why I haven't been back here often. There's no evidence, no proof, but they still assume I killed her."

"A woman died," Jimmy protested feebly. "We only want to know who killed her."

Maura turned to him. "What's it to you, Jimmy? Was the dead woman a friend? A relative? Did you know her at all?"

"It's wrong, is all," Jimmy said stubbornly. "Nobody was ever tried fer the death, see? So there's still a killer out there. All we know is that the woman didn't fall down and stab herself in the middle of the night out in the cold."

Maura still didn't understand why Jimmy could be nursing a grudge about a killing that took place when he was no more than a teenager, but maybe he was just looking for a fight. Or trying to get back at her for finding out about the oil he'd stolen. She studied the faces of the others in the room. "How many of you were here in the area when it happened and remember it?"

It was not surprising that nobody apart from Bart raised a hand. "That's what I thought. You were kids in school or maybe my age. So all you ever got was the stories passed along, and probably mangled along the way by journalists looking for a juicy story."

"Not true!" Jimmy was quick to answer. "The gardaí kept lookin' fer the killer. They took her in"—Jimmy nodded contemptuously at Diane—"for questioning more than once, but they let her go. Isn't that right?"

Maura turned on him. "So you do remember it, Jimmy."

Jimmy nodded. "I was young, in school, but it was quite a story back then. You wouldn't know, being from away, but murder's a rare thing in this part of the world—even now."

"It's all right, Maura. What he says is true," Diane answered. "Jimmy, is it? They let me go because there was no evidence—not then, not now. But people have gone on assuming that I did it—which doesn't say much for their respect for the gardaí. You think I really outsmarted them? Not just the gardaí in my backyard, but those from other stations too?"

Nobody answered. Maura considered her options. "Diane and the rest of you, we're stuck here for the night, unless one or more of you wants to freeze out there by leaving now. I'm guessing that most of us here don't know the story. Diane, you can tell us what happened from your side."

Diane squared her shoulders. "It would be my pleasure, Maura. Like I said, I'm tired of hiding and pretending, and I'm damn tired of people thinking I'm something I'm not. I've got a jury of my peers here in front of me. So let's hold our own trial, shall we? Of course, I don't have any witnesses or evidence on hand, but then neither do you—well, perhaps Bart here can stand in for all that. All you've got is rumors and what you remember from trashy journal articles, which sold plenty of papers but were a bit short on truth. So we can talk it all out. Isn't that what the Irish are good at?"

"Yer not Irish," Donal said.

"That's where you're wrong, young man. My grandparents were born here, and so was my father. Maybe I married an Englishman, but I've kept the family house all these years, haven't I?"

"Afraid to come back to it, mebbe," Danny said. Maura mentally put a black mark against his name.

"No! I loved that place. It had plenty of happy memories for me, before . . . My husband and I, we came back most summers and sometimes for short trips during other parts of the year. So don't you try to say I'm not one of you. My roots here go as deep as any of yours."

"It were Irish gardaí that took yeh in," Joe said.

"For questioning, because I was a neighbor. And they let me go," Diane shot back. "They got it wrong, and they admitted it."

"Mebbe," he muttered. He didn't sound convinced.

Maura tried to gauge the crowd. They weren't enthusiastic about hearing Diane's "real" story, but they had nothing else to do this long night. Except drink, which could get messy.

Maura was surprised when Billy spoke. "I'm old enough to remember that time. The tabloids, they were quick to jump on a headline, and the worse, the better—if you catch my drift. To be fair, mistakes were made in lookin' into the death, but our lads had little experience with investigatin' murders and no fancy equipment and the like, the way they do these days. They were caught with their pants down, yeh might say. I fer one would like to hear what the lady has to tell us. Let's see if she can convince us, like we was a jury."

"I'm with Billy," Maura told the others. "Are you in?"

"Will yeh make us leave if we say no?" Seamus asked plaintively, although there was a twinkle in his eye.

"No, because you'd probably freeze to death, and that would end up being my fault. But I might cut off your drink."

"And yeh'll be asking us to pay for it?" Seamus said in mock dismay. "While you keep us captive here?"

That at least brought a reaction from the crowd. Maura swallowed a sigh: this could turn out to be an expensive evening. "Yes, if you'll listen," Maura told them. "And be fair. Deal?" Most people nodded. Billy smiled at her, apparently pleased. "All right. Do we have enough chairs for everyone? You all want a pint, or would you rather have coffee so you can think straight?"

"I'll take the pint," Liam said. "I think better with it." Some of the others nodded.

"Fine. Everybody get what you need and settle down."

Diane was still standing in the middle of the bar, looking startled at the turn her challenge had taken. "I didn't mean to barge into the middle of it all. And I half expected them to turn me down."

"It's okay—it'll keep us all busy. I don't know if you had a plan when you started this, but now you're going to tell us your side of things the way you remember them. They're going to ask questions. Bart can back you up if he's needed. Can you handle that?"

"By now I should be able to, don't you think? I've been answering the same questions for nearly half my life. The problem is, nobody seems to believe me. They all made up their minds a long time ago."

"But you want to go ahead?" Maura pressed.

"What've I got to lose? Bart, does that suit you?" When he nodded, Diane turned toward the men scattered around the room. "Listen up. I've got one rule here: I get to tell the story in my own way. It may take a while, but the background is important to what happened. You can interrupt me, but you can't tell me to hurry up."

Nobody protested. At least she'd captured their attention.

Everyone spent some time shuffling chairs around and retrieving a few extra from the back room. Maura added some more coals to the fire; Mick filled more glasses. Jimmy sulked in a corner: if he had intended to make trouble, his plan had backfired. What was wrong with him? Billy watched, somehow resembling a wise old owl, his feathers fluffed out for warmth. Had he ever seen anything like this in his favorite pub? Maura doubted it. From what he had told her about Old Mick, the former owner had made every effort to stay out of other's people's business. It had been a man's pub, where nobody had to talk unless they wanted to. Now that she was running the place and Rose was behind the bar part of the time, some things had changed, but there were still those who came in and sat in silence over their pint without fear of interruption, and that's the way they liked it. She could respect that.

Finally, things were set. Gillian stood up. "Billy, stay where you are. But since Diane here is our guest of honor, in a manner of speaking, she should have the place of honor by the fire."

To their credit, Liam and Donal jumped up and offered Gillian a chair, and she took one with a grateful smile.

Maura realized that she was supposed to be the master of ceremonies—no, mistress—and run the show. As Diane seated herself in the upholstered chair, looking more energized than when she had arrived, Maura stood in front of the fire. "All right, guys—a few rules. No name-calling, rude comments, spitting, or throwing things. If you break the rules, you can go sit in the back room. You can't disrupt the proceedings. Let Diane tell her story and don't badger her. And keep your opinions to yourself. All she's asking for is a chance to be heard." There were a few grumblings, but nobody objected. "Then let's get started. Diane, you have the floor."

Maura removed herself to watch from a chair on the fringes of the group. She made one last check of the others. She had her doubts about the younger guys from the wedding party, but she was pretty sure they'd prefer being warm to being exiled out back, so they'd have to play by the rules.

Ten

⤬

Diane stood up and cleared her throat. "Thank you all for giving me the chance to talk—too few people have. I was born Diane Wolfe, and my people were dairy farmers out past Schull. When I left school, I decided to try my hand at finding a job in London, and that's where I met and married my husband, Mark Caldwell. When my father's mother died, she left me her cottage here in Ireland, and Mark and I kept it and used it as a second home. Mostly summers, but now and then, we'd come over for a short holiday."

"When was this?" Gillian asked.

"What? Oh, we married in 1994. That was just before the start of the Celtic Tiger. My husband was in banking, and he used whatever Irish connections he could to ride the tiger. He did well. So of course we started spending a bit more time over here at the cottage, sort of a mix of business and holiday. Most likely you don't remember those times, or maybe you might not have seen the changes west of here. Things changed quickly back then. Suddenly there were artists and writers and actors buying up the old places, throwing money around."

"The blow-ins," Mick said. "Many from Europe. Were yeh not part of that lot?"

"Yes and no," Diane replied. "I was from here, but Mark wasn't. And he had little patience for the local people—thought them slow, uneducated. He'd rather have spent his time with those others, not that they were particularly interested in him. We made a few efforts to get together with them, but nothing came of it. He wasn't happy about that. There's another side to it as well: at the same time as all those arty people were showing up, there were other people coming in and settling there—jobless people from other EU countries who thought that either they'd find plenty of work here, or if not, they'd just go on the dole, which they could do. And then there were the old hippie types." That term met with blank looks from most people. "New Agers?" Diane tried. "Back-to-nature folk? The label doesn't matter. The fact of it was, there were a lot of new people coming in, whole gangs of them, and they didn't all mix well. It changed the place, and it happened fast."

"Can yeh get on wit' the story?" Danny in the back called out.

Maura was about to step in and remind him of the rules she had set, but Diane spoke first. "You need to know this part of it. I'm setting the stage. Things had pretty much been the same for centuries, then suddenly there was lots more money and strangers coming in and taking the land. And the younger folk figured they didn't want to be dairy farmers like their fathers, so they packed up and headed for the cities for cleaner work that paid better. There were a lot of changes, and they didn't sit well with the people who'd been there all along. So things were unsettled in the nineties. Fair enough?"

"Yeah," the man muttered, then subsided.

"So Mark and I were going back and forth from England to West Cork a lot then. We had no kids, so we could come and go as we pleased. After a couple of years, we were the 'old folk,' the ones who'd been there longest. We watched as the other cottages around us were bought up. Some of the new people kept them much as they were but added decent wiring and plumbing. Others tore them down and put up fancy new places. But in a way, you couldn't really see it—like here, I gather, the houses were scattered far apart, so you needn't see your neighbors. When we first were coming, Mark and I used to joke that we knew more cows than people. Still, I was happy. I'd always loved the place, and it was peaceful. Mark had a bit more trouble slowing down because of his kind of work, so I most likely spent more time at the cottage than he did."

"Are you still married?" Maura said suddenly.

Diane turned to look at her. "We are. Going on thirty years now."

"What about the murder?" Joe called out.

Diane peered at him, then snapped, "Fine, if you're so impatient. I've painted you a picture of the way things were. A lot of newcomers, and most didn't know each other well. The longtimers resented them, even if they spent a lot of money in the villages. It wasn't the way things used to be, and that bothered them. Then, in January of 1996, right after the holidays, Sharon Morgan was found dead on her own property. Not in her house, but outside. The news stories were kind of exaggerated—half of them probably cobbled together from rumors and somebody's idea of what would sell papers. But it was pretty clear that she had been savagely attacked—stabbed from the front, many times—and left to die. She was found the next morning by neighbors walking their dog. They called the guards, and then all hell broke loose. The reporters were there before the state doctor, who had to come down from Dublin. If there was evidence, it was trampled by the curious folk who wanted to get a look at the body or at least see the scene."

"Where the lady was killed," Billy asked, "how close was her home to yer own?"

Diane turned to him. "Billy, is it? As the crow flies, maybe three miles? But there are few crows there, and by road it's more like five. And if you're wondering if I could have walked, there's a bog between the two. Nothing any sensible person would try to cross in the dark."

"How did yeh know it was dark when she died?" Mick asked.

"I was told that Sharon was seen in the stores in Schull buying her supper past five, and it was dark when she left for home. It appears that she ate her supper after she got home. And then she was killed. She was found roughly twelve hours later."

"She was married?" Billy asked.

"She was, to another London man, Paul Morgan. He was English as well."

"And where was he when this happened?"

"Home in England. As was my husband."

"So it was just you, alone in yer cottage, and this Sharon, alone in hers?"

"I was alone. I can't speak for Sharon. I never saw her that day—or night."

An awkward silence fell over the group, and Maura could hear the wind throwing snow against the large glass windows facing the street. Finally, it got too uncomfortable for her, and she stood up. "Okay, you've set the scene for us, Diane. But where do we go from here?"

"Waddayeh mean?" Joe protested. "The woman died. Stabbed at her own home."

Maura glanced at Diane. "Diane is telling the story the way she wants, and that's fine. But I'm not from here, remember? I don't know how garda investigations work—well, not a big one like this—or how they worked back then. I don't know what kind of officers were available, or how many, or where they came from. I don't know what it takes to make an arrest, and I don't know how the courts work. So somebody's going to have to fill me in along the way."

"Yeh don't know much of anything, do yeh now?" Jimmy called out.

Maura swallowed a spurt of anger—he really was in a lousy mood. "Hey, Jimmy, I'm new here. And this all happened twenty years ago, when I'm guessing it was a pretty different place, and I have to take that into account, which you don't because you've lived here all that time. So, what does that mean? No mobile phones, for one thing. Not everyone had a television. How many channels were there? What were the newspapers, and how many people had a chance to read them?" Everyone was now staring at her, which she found kind of annoying. She didn't think she was being unreasonable.

But this was her pub, and she had a right to speak. "What I have learned since I got here is that memories are long around here. People then knew each other—except for the blow-ins you're talking about. And people talked to each other back then. You know how that works: a story starts spreading, and by about the fifth time around, people have added flying saucers and an army of thugs. Maybe the truth was simple, but it wouldn't have taken long for people to muck it up and fill in the blanks however they wanted. And that's what stuck."

Mick spoke up suddenly. "People felt safer back then. Like yeh said, everyone knew his neighbor and could count on them to help—look after the herd if there was trouble, keep all the kids in line, that kind of thing. And then, all at once, like Diane said, there were all these new people comin' in without any history with the place. Nor did they want to build a life here, for the most part. People who'd lived here all their lives were unsettled—and rightly so. And then this murder in the midst of it all—it scared people. They didn't know who they could trust anymore."

"I can see that," Maura said, wondering how much things had changed. At least she'd been welcomed, but it hadn't happened overnight. "But tell me this: why was everybody so willing to point the finger at Diane? She had a history here. Plus, she was a woman. How many woman killers have there been in Ireland?"

"How many killers have there been at all?" Seamus asked. "It was said at the time that Sharon Morgan's killing was the first such in West Cork since Michael Collins was cut down in 1922. And people are still arguin' about who did that one."

"Can we save that story for another night?" Maura asked, softening her comment with a smile. "One thing at a time. Diane was accused of the murder of Sharon Morgan during a January night in 1996. She was questioned by the local gardaí for it."

"Twice," Diane volunteered in a wry tone.

"Twice, then. But the gardaí didn't hold her because they had no evidence. They do still need evidence to arrest people in this country, right?"

"They do," Mick said. Bart nodded but didn't speak.

"Look, guys—and Gillian and Rose—I don't know how many American television shows you get here, or if you watch them, or if there's the same kind of thing made in England or here, but these days everybody thinks they know how to solve a murder because they've seen it all before. And all those murders are solved in an hour. People seem to believe there are magic machines that can identify evidence and DNA and make facial reconstructions, and they can check phone and Internet records and bank accounts and credit cards in minutes. Of course that's not true—back in the States, these things actually take months or sometimes years. Or so I've been told."

"Yeh, and yer Bulger fellow was hiding in plain sight for, what, fifteen years?" Bart commented. "And nobody noticed?"

"I never said American cops or the FBI got it right all the time," Maura shot back. "Some things don't get looked at, or somebody jumps to the wrong conclusion when they do look. Mistakes get made. Now, you can correct me if I'm wrong, but back in the nineties, things were still pretty simple here, right? At least in this part of Cork. From what I've heard, most crimes around here were for drunk driving or petty theft. The gardaí didn't have much experience with homicide and not much in the way of labs for the science part, either. Have I got that right?"

Nods from most people, including Diane and Bart.

Maura wondered just what she thought she was doing. She knew nothing about what had happened—but maybe that was a good thing, because she could be objective. The most she'd hoped for was to keep these people entertained until they all fell asleep, and maybe in the morning the snow would have stopped, and everybody could go home. Then Diane had walked in, carrying with her what had to be one of the more notorious stories of the past century, and based on how Mick and Jimmy had reacted it was still a sore subject. Of course people both had opinions and wanted to hear more once they knew she was here. And Diane seemed willing to talk about it. So Maura was willing to roll with it, but they needed some sort of order or structure. "Okay, we've got the star witness right here. We're going to give her a fair trial."

"What're yeh talkin' about?" Joe asked.

"Forget what you see on the telly. You all know this part of the country. We'll look at the facts. We look at the evidence that we know about and ask if there might have been more, if anyone had been looking, and if anybody saved it or if it's gone forever. We talk about the whys and hows and whens. We ask Diane the hard questions." Maura glanced quickly at Diane, who didn't object. "What reason would she have had to kill Sharon Morgan? And if she didn't do it, who else might have had a reason? Unless you want to say there was some random crazy person roaming the bog after dark, bashing people without leaving evidence behind." That brought a muffled laugh. "You'll answer questions? All of them?"

Diane gave her a long look before answering. "Yes, I will. I've got nothing to lose." She turned to look at the rest of the group. "Do your best—or your worst."

Seamus grinned—he seemed to be the most invested in this, among the people in the audience. "Then we'll give you your trial," he said. "We'll poke holes in what everyone thinks they know based on those dumb stories like 'Where Are They Now?' that pop up now and then."

"Will we be choosing sides, then?" Donal asked anxiously. "Like, maybe, for and against?"

Maura had no idea. "Has anybody here actually been to a trial?" The question was met with silence. "Well, maybe that's a good thing—you're all law-abiding citizens."

"Or we haven't been caught," someone said. Several men laughed.

Maura turned back to Diane. "What do *you* want, Diane? Do you want someone to speak for you? Like a solicitor or an advocate or whatever the heck they call them around here?"

Diane shook her head. "I don't think so. No one else knows the story or what questions to ask—well, maybe Bart here, but he'd serve me better as a witness. I'd be better off on my own. We need a moderator, though, to keep you all in line. You can do that, Maura. You have no stake in this and no wrongheaded ideas about what happened."

"Fair enough," Maura told her. She checked the clock. It felt like twelve hours had passed, but it was still only nine o'clock. She hadn't seen any headlights passing outside the building for quite a while. Maybe other people had had the sense to stay home. "Okay, then. Everybody comfortable? You need another drink, get it now. Because it's not fair to stop and start."

"And should we all visit the loo, mammy?" Seamus asked.

"If you need to."

A few people bellied up to the bar; others drifted toward the back, where the lavatories were. Maura studied the way the chairs were laid out and decided a circle made sense, open to the fire at one end. Billy had his seat and Diane hers on the other side of the fire. The rest could fend for themselves.

"You're sure you want to do this?" she asked Diane again.

Diane smiled. "Stop asking me that, will you, Maura? I know my own mind. I can handle myself, you know. I've been living with this for years, and I've probably heard every question they could throw at me more than once."

"You say you didn't kill Sharon Morgan. Do you have an idea about what really happened?" Maura asked softly.

Diane eyed her, maybe trying to assess her motive. "God's honest truth, I do not. Let's see what a batch of fresh minds can come up with."

"You've got it," Maura said, then raised her voice. "All right, everybody, let's get this thing rolling."

Eleven

Most people found themselves a seat, while a few remained leaning against the bar. Maura was surprised when Liam and Donal approached her, followed by the sheepish lads who still looked half-drunk. "If it's all the same to you, Maura, we were thinkin' we might rather sit in the back room—or the kitchen if it's too cold there. This old case means nothin' to us. But yeh'll still let us have our pints?"

"Sure, fine, whatever. Just don't freeze your buns off. And take one of the lamps with you—we've got the two others." Maura pointed them to the bar and nodded at Mick when they asked for another round. Jimmy was nowhere to be seen, and Rose was sitting near Gillian. Billy looked half-asleep, but then he often did at this time of night. They were ten—eleven if Jimmy came back in from wherever he was hiding. How big were Irish juries?

"Everybody set? In case the Guinness has gone to your heads, we're here to try to figure out who killed Sharon Morgan. Most of Ireland, including the gardaí, think it was Diane here. How many of you agree with that?"

Joe and Danny raised their hands, and Jimmy, now lounging in the doorway to the kitchen, added his. Rose just looked bewildered. Gillian kept her opinion to herself, looking speculatively at Diane.

"Okay, that's a start—three of you. How many of you think she was railroaded?"

"Are you sayin' falsely accused?" Billy asked.

Maura nodded. "Yes. The gardaí really wanted to point their finger at her, but then they couldn't find anything to prove it."

Billy and Mick raised their hands. *Interesting*, Maura thought. Billy's response she could understand, since he had a soft spot for women, even if he'd never managed to marry one. Mick's reaction was more surprising. Did he know something? Seamus slowly put his hand up as well. Three to three now. Bart hadn't chosen a side.

"And what about yerself, Maura?" Mick asked.

"I have no opinion. I've been here in Ireland for about three minutes, and the first I heard about this murder was today. So I'm going to stay neutral for now. Somebody has to convince me one way or the other."

Billy leaned forward in his chair and looked at Diane, and Maura was absurdly reminded of a talk show host. "You've set the scene fer where it happened, Diane, but before yeh go on, what can yeh tell us about the woman herself?"

Diane settled herself more comfortably in her chair and seemed to be collecting her memories. "I can't say I knew Sharon Morgan well. As I told you, she and her husband were strangers to the area. She was about my age. Attractive, nicely groomed.

Not too tall, not overweight. Just kind of, I don't know, ordinary. They had a late-model car but nothing too showy—I'd see them driving to Schull now and then. We might cross paths in town when we were food shopping, and we exchanged a few words, most often about the weather."

"Did yeh not share a meal now and then?" Billy asked.

"Not that I can recall. Remember, this was just a second home for both of us, and we didn't come and go on any kind of regular schedule, so it was hard to plan ahead. If you're wondering, there was no animosity between us. We just didn't happen to see each other often."

"Did they have a dog?" Bart asked suddenly.

"No, not that I remember. It's hard to keep a pet when you're moving between two houses."

"Did she have any hobbies? Gardening? Painting? Writing, mebbe?"

Diane shook her head. "Not that I know of."

"Did she drink?" Jimmy's voice came from the far end of the bar.

Diane glared at him. "Now how on earth am I supposed to know that? I've already told you that I'd never seen the inside of her house, and she'd never been in mine. My husband and I rarely went to pubs around here. I never noticed her stumbling around the pastures singing or cursing or anything like that. And why do you think it would matter?"

"It's a fair question," Seamus said. "Seems like the two of yez were like ships passing in the night. Did you even know when the two of 'em were there?"

"I couldn't see lights from their cottage from ours. Usually I knew only when their car went by. There's little traffic on that lane."

"Did they have a field?" Danny asked.

Diane appeared confused by the question. "I have no idea. Why?"

"Might be they rented it our fer the grazin' when the season was right. It would have nothin' to do with them, but there could have been someone coming to check on the cattle now and again."

"Ah." Diane stared at the ceiling for a long moment. "I don't remember seeing any cattle back then, but there could have been some. My family owned the land just next to our cottage, and I don't think anyone ever asked if they could use it. It wouldn't have been a problem—I grew up with cattle in those fields. I'm not sure what my husband would have thought about it. He'd never lived on a farm."

"So why did they buy the place, then?" Bart said.

"For the same reason we held on to our cottage. It was quiet, and there weren't many people around. It was a good place to come and relax when the city got to be too much."

"Unless someone's lookin' ta kill yeh."

Maura spoke up. "Hang on. Before we go any farther, can we dump the random stranger theory? That somebody just showed up looking for someone to kill, and Sharon was handy?"

Several of the men looked at her with disgust. "And why would we be thinkin' that, Maura?" Seamus asked.

"Well, it's possible, isn't it?" she said stubbornly. "So it should be crossed off if it couldn't have happened." *Could it?*

"Easy. Yeh live up at Knockskagh, am I right?" he said.

"Yes, about two-thirds of the way up the hill."

"Do yeh know yer neighbors?"

"Only Bridget Nolan, I guess. The houses right next to mine have been empty for a long time. Most of the ones up the hill farther are empty too. Closer to the road, there are some others that are newer, and there are people living there, but I wouldn't recognize them if I met them on the street. Why?"

"Does anyone walk by yer cottage? Or drive?"

Maura shook her head. "Not much. I hear Mick's car when he comes to visit his grannie. Some of the other owners have jobs, I guess, so I hear them leave in the morning and come back after work if I'm around, which I'm usually not. What are you getting at?"

"Yeh'd notice a stranger's car, would you not? The sound of an unfamiliar engine?"

"I guess, but like I said, I'm not there a lot, day or night, so people could be going back and forth all the time and I wouldn't know it. What's your point, Seamus?"

"If there was someone who knew the lay of the land, say, and knew when the people who lived there would be comin' and goin', it'd be easy enough to slip in without bein' seen."

"So?" Maura said. "That doesn't eliminate a stranger."

Seamus raised one finger. "But at night, he'd have to know his way around to cross the land."

"Exactly, Seamus," Diane said quickly. "A torch would show up a mile away at night, save on a night like this. I wouldn't risk crossing it in the dark, and I know the place. Too easy to twist an ankle or worse."

"Yer sure Sharon was killed in the night?" Mick asked.

"That's what the gardaí believed then. And she'd eaten her supper," Diane said. "But without sounding like I'm trying to defend myself, mistakes were made on their part from the start."

"And they'd be?" Bart asked, trying to keep his tone neutral. Maura wondered again what he really thought.

Diane looked at him squarely. "You know them. First, Sharon was found in the morning by a neighbor. But the gardaí had to call in the state pathologist from Dublin to take a look at her officially, and it took the man over twenty-four hours to arrive, so you can guess what state the physical evidence was in by then, after the body had sat out that long. As a result, the gardaí really weren't sure when she died."

"Wait," Maura interrupted. "There's only one person in the whole country who can examine a body?"

"That's right," Bart said. "The state pathologist who investigates anything related to foul play. Yes, there's only the one, although there may be a couple of assistants. This case was big enough to bring in the chief."

Maura resisted the urge to shake her head. No forensic evidence for how long? What on earth had the pathologist been doing all that time? "Walk me through it again. Sharon shops for supper in Schull and heads home sometime after five, which was the last time anyone saw her. Or admitted to seeing her. She's found the next morning at the edge of her own property by a neighbor—out for a walk? Who was that, and why was he there?"

"Married couple, lived the next farm over," Seamus volunteered. "They were walkin' the dog early—a King Charles spaniel, female. She'd gotten loose before and gotten herself in the family way, so they kept a close eye on her after that because they'd hopes of breedin' her fer pups they could sell."

Maura stared at him. "Seamus, why do you know all this?"

"I've followed the case, and every time I think it's done, there's another interview on the telly or something. They always repeat the same facts—not that there were many to be had."

Was that ghoulish of him? Maura wondered. *To keep thinking about a twenty-year-old murder?* "What did these neighbors do next?"

"Well, like yeh said, there was no mobiles then. They'd've had to walk back to their own cottage to make the call to the gardaí. If they had a phone."

"Why no phone? No phone wires? Or no money?"

"One or the other."

"What do we know about those neighbors?" Maura demanded. "Were they locals or blow-ins? Old or young? How did they get along with Sharon and her husband?"

"Yer gettin' ahead of yerself, Maura," Billy reminded her. "We've only just found the body in the tale. The call's been made to the gardaí by those neighbors, and the gardaí have to work out who's in charge and who else should be told and then who to send."

"It was the Bantry station sent a man out to keep watch over the body," Bart said levelly. "He put a tarp over the victim."

"So it's already a day since Sharon died, and the investigation really hasn't started yet?" Maura demanded. Diane gave her a sad smile but said nothing. "All anyone really knows is that the woman is dead, on her own property, outside."

"Right so."

The group fell silent, thinking. Diane had been right: there were problems with the investigation from the start. Maura felt more and more sorry for her. But it still wasn't clear to her how the gardaí had come to focus on Diane as their prime suspect.

"Did any of you ever meet any of the people involved?" Maura began again. "See the inside of their houses?"

When nobody said anything, Bart asked, "This all happened over past Schull. What would these people be doin' over there? Yer thinkin' like an American again. Most people there—and here as well—kept cows. Cows take a lot of tendin'. Dairy farmers don't just take themselves off joyriding. Am I right, Seamus?"

"You are," Seamus agreed. "Cows won't wait when they need milkin'."

"Just asking," Maura said, trying not to sound whiny. "So all we have to work with is what was in newspapers and whatever stories people have told you," Maura said, almost to herself. Well, it couldn't be helped now. "All right, back to the scene. There's a garda standing watch over the body, waiting for the pathologist and maybe more gardaí to show up. Did the local gardaí—from Schull or Bantry—take a look at Sharon's house? There could have been another body there—or a real messy scene that might tell them something."

"They did, right enough," Bart said.

"What can you tell me about it, then?" Maura said. "Seamus, you seem to know a lot of the details."

"So does Bart there," Seamus pointed out.

"True, but he was part of the official investigating team, and we aren't sure we believe them. Sorry, Bart."

"I take no offense, Maura," Bart said. "After all, we never solved it, did we now? Seamus can tell us what the average person heard about it."

Seamus shut his eyes, the better to remember, Maura hoped. "She had no keys on her," he said slowly, "but the door wasn't locked anyways—people didn't do that much then, nor do they now. But it wasn't standing open. It was closed nice and neat."

"Was there a back door?" Maura asked.

The man cocked his head at her. "Now why would she have gone out the back to run toward the front? That's daft."

"Humor me," Maura retorted. "Okay, the place was wide open, and she went out the front door. She kept going for a while, because she wasn't found close to the house. The gardaí arrived, took a look at the body, figured pretty fast that it was murder, and went inside. What did they find?"

"No mess. She'd left a plate and a glass by the sink in the kitchen—just the one of each—like she'd had her supper but hadn't washed up. The lights were on. The radio was playin'. Upstairs, her slippers were by the bed, but she was wearin' a pair of boots when she was found. She hadn't changed out of her nightclothes."

"Which were?" Maura wondered if a guy would remember that detail.

"Clothes she'd wear to be comfortable in, like an old shirt and—what do yeh call 'em?—pajama pants. No fancy negligee, if that's what yer thinkin'."

"But nothing was broken or messed up inside the house?"

"No more than usual."

"How would anybody know what 'usual' was? Like, was she a neat person or a slob?"

"I'm only sayin' that a woman alone, with no callers expected, wouldn't much care about how tidy the place looks. It looked . . . ordinary, I'd guess. Mind you, nobody said."

Maura thought briefly of her own cottage, which would probably look a lot more messy if she owned more than her clothes and a few pots and plates. And unless there was a real mess at the house, why would the gardaí, who most likely were all men back then, have even thought about the victim's housekeeping details, much less included them in a report? All they'd reported, apparently, was that nothing looked unusual inside the house. "Okay. So bottom line—nobody had been fighting inside the house, right? Nothing broken, no blood? And she'd already eaten her dinner that she'd bought earlier in Schull."

That produced nods from the audience.

"So either Sharon opened the door to whoever it was," Maura pressed on, "or the intruder walked in quietly and surprised her. But she didn't fight, and she didn't run." She'd taken the time to put on boots? Did that make sense?

"That sounds right," Joe said.

Maura was surprised to find that she had somehow taken on the role of interrogator, but she was horrified by how the case had been handled from the beginning. She had to remind herself that that was hardly fair: Ireland had few murders, and most gardaí had little or no experience with serious crime back in the 1990s and little access to technology that most Americans now took for granted. She shouldn't let herself jump to conclusions. It seem like at least they had asked the logical questions, like had the dead woman shared a meal with anyone? Was the bed disturbed? Was anything broken?

She surveyed her small group, most of whom looked mildly interested but sleepy. The pub was warm and dark, full of the odor of burning peat and unwashed woolens. "Who would Sharon have opened the door to? Did she have any friends? Diane, do you have any ideas?"

Diane had been oddly silent so far, even though she had started this. "I didn't know her well. I can't say," she said.

"Didn't the gardaí talk to the husband? Where was he, anyway?"

"England," Diane said flatly. "With a boatload of witnesses. He was nowhere near the place."

"So he had a solid alibi. What kind of work did he do?"

"Construction and the like," Danny said. "He was a manager, a planner—didn't get his hands dirty any longer, though he had once at the start. He was having a grand ol' time with the Celtic Tiger and all, puttin' up buildin's all over. I worked with him a time or two back then."

"Did Sharon work?" Maura had been a child in the 1990s, so she had little idea how many women, with or without children, held down a job in Ireland—or anywhere else. Apart from raising the kids and helping out around the farm, of course. To make it worse, she knew only what Boston women did; here in West Cork, jobs might have been hard to find unless you were a farmer, which most of these newcomers weren't, although they might put a cow in the garden as an ornament. She knew of one house near hers that kept a goat tethered in the front, although she couldn't guess why. Goat as lawn ornament? She straightened up and rotated her head, trying to get the blood flowing to her brain again. She was getting punchy.

"I couldn't say, but it might be in the records," Bart said. "She might not've needed to, since her husband's business was growin' fast, and he'd hired plenty of people from all over the county. And she took a fair number of holidays with or without her husband."

"Was he ever a suspect?"

Some men in the small group exchanged glances. "Like Diane said, he could prove he was somewhere else. So the gardaí fixed on her there"—Jimmy nodded at Diane—"from the start."

"Why?" Maura asked. Her question was met with silence. Maybe the people in the room were uncomfortable talking about it with Diane sitting there, although she hadn't objected. In fact, she'd she said she wanted to talk about the old—if unfinished— story, to give her side of things. Did the others really have no idea what had happened, or did they know something Maura didn't? Or had they all made up their minds two decades earlier, and nothing was going to change that? "Why would Diane have killed her?"

The men in the room shuffled their feet and shifted their glances, avoiding looking at her or Diane. That was odd. Didn't motive matter in Ireland? Or was the supposed motive something that people here—particularly men—didn't like to talk about? Had Sharon been in a lesbian relationship with someone? With Diane? In the 1990s, that whole subject would have been pretty much off limits, Maura guessed. But how would that provide a motive? Maura glanced at Diane, who was sitting as still as stone. Was she hiding something now?

"Diane?" Maura said. The woman turned slowly to look at her. "You must have a guess after all these years."

Diane looked at the faces around the room. "The killing was an awful thing, and I'd be the first to say I want to know why Sharon died and at whose hand. If this fine crowd here at Sullivan's comes up with a new idea about the killer, I'll be over the moon."

"Diane, you didn't answer the question," Maura said. "Why did the gardaí look at you first?"

Diane went very still and took her time answering. Finally, she said, "Because my husband was having an affair with Sharon."

Twelve

Maura could have sworn that time stood still. Had nobody heard that piece of news before? Back when it happened? Since? Or were the men in the room reluctant to say it out loud? She glanced at Bart, and he nodded silently.

She needed time to think. "Okay, everyone, I think this would be a good time to take a break. If you want another round, get it now." She checked with Mick and Rose to make sure they were ready. "And if you need to use the loo, now's the time." That was met with a few sniggers. It also seemed to loosen the tension in the room, to Maura's relief.

She turned to Diane. "You knew? About them, I mean?"

"Yes."

"The gardaí knew?"

"I told them then. I never concealed the fact. But Mark had an alibi, which left me."

Maura shook her head. "I need some time to think."

"Do you think less of me now, Maura?" Diane asked softly.

"I'm not judging you, Diane. I just need to work out how this fits. Excuse me."

Mick seemed to have the bar under control as several men leaned against it, waiting for their pints. Rose, on the other hand, had disappeared into the kitchen in back, judging by the clatter of dishes back there, so Maura decided to follow her. She found Rose washing glassware by candlelight.

"Did you hear that, Rose?"

"You mean, the part where Diane says her husband was fooling around with the dead woman? Before she was dead, I mean?"

"Yeah, that. I guess it makes sense in a way. The two couples didn't socialize—at least not as couples—according to Diane, although there might have been other things going on. Anyway, it would have been easy to slip around without anybody noticing. And it sure does provide a motive."

"Do yeh think Diane cared enough about her husband to kill the woman?"

"Oh, Rose, how should I know? I don't know these people. I know plenty of people fool around, and most of them don't end up dead. But I don't know Diane well enough to guess. Apparently the gardaí grabbed on to that as a motive and never let go." Maura looked around the dark room, lit only by . . . "You found candles, Rose?"

"I did, under the bar."

Maura vowed to take closer stock of what she had in the pub—something she had apparently neglected. "You don't have to do the dishes," Maura said.

"I think I do, if you count what's been used and us with no dishwasher. It's no problem fer me."

"Well, thank you. I'll dry." Maura searched in the dim corners until she found a towel that looked clean and started polishing glasses. She sneaked a glance at Rose. "What's up with your father? He's been in a lousy mood all night, even before the snow started. Is something bothering him? Things all right at home?"

Rose's expression was hard to read in the dark, but Maura thought she might be smiling. "He's got a lady friend."

That was an odd way to put it, Maura thought. "He's seeing someone?"

Rose nodded.

"Doesn't that usually make people happy?"

"Well, for most it might," Rose said, then stopped again.

"So what's the problem?" Maura demanded. She'd never heard Jimmy mention any woman in his life, although she'd known him less than a year, and she wouldn't say they were exactly close. She knew that Rose's mother had passed away a few years earlier, and Rose had been keeping Jimmy fed and their home clean since she was old enough to do it. Jimmy seemed to think that he deserved her services, although Maura had been pushing Rose to think about her own future and what she wanted to do with her life.

"Depends on who you ask," Rose said. "I think she's grand. She's a widow from up near Drinagh. She came into a nice dairy farm from her husband. She's me da's age, maybe a coupla years older. She's nice to look at and easy to talk to. We get on fine."

"And? Come on, there's got to be more. Why is Jimmy biting everyone's head off?"

"She wants to change him, of course. And he's not having any of it. He's had it easy these past few years, what with me lookin' after him. Suits him fine. But Judith—she wants him to pull his own weight, help her with the farm."

Jimmy was still shy of fifty, so he must have had women along the way. Maura hoped that at least he'd been discreet for Rose's sake.

Rose glanced at her and giggled. "Ah, Maura, yer tryin' so hard to be . . . tactful. I'm not a child, and I know what's what. Me ma's been gone fer a few years. Me da's been seein' other women for a while now, and I've no problem with that. I'd love to see him settled with someone—with or without marriage."

"So you can get on with your own life?"

Rose nodded. "And I'm a bit put out over me bein' his excuse. 'Ooh, I'd love to spend more time with yeh, dear, but I've the child to think about, and I'm all she has in this world.' Handy if he wants to keep his distance, if yeh know what I'm sayin'."

"So he likes, uh, to keep his options open?"

Rose nodded, her hands still deep in soapy water. "That's one way of puttin' it, and a kind one. But there's not many women around here who might be interested in him fer a husband now, and he's run through most of 'em. Sorry, that sounds a bit . . ."

"I get it, Rose. What's different about this one? What's her name, by the way? Do I know her?"

"She's Judith McCarthy, and she's not one fer the pubs. She's a strong woman any way yeh look at it, and she's set her mind on finding a new husband who's young enough to be of use to her. Why she's landed on me da I cannot say. But I've told her she has my blessing, no matter what Da says. I won't be his excuse any longer."

"Good for you. Does she have children of her own?"

"One son at university and a daughter who's a teacher over at Bandon. So they're not at home, save for the odd holiday. And she's not plannin' on adding to the family. She's a bit past that."

Rose was one smart girl. "Rose, what would you do if you could do anything you wanted?" Maura asked, not for the first time. But she'd already asked Gillian the question, and she might as well collect everyone else's.

"See a bit more of the world—or at least of Ireland. Dublin, mebbe. Go to cookery school."

Finally, someone with a plan! "Great," Maura said firmly. "Let me know if I can help. Oh, and would Judith have a problem with Jimmy working here if they end up getting married?"

Rose shrugged. "I think she'd rather he helped with the cattle, but she's been managing on her own fer years now. I'm guessing he'd like to keep something fer himself, like the job here, even if it is only part time. If she has her way and they end up married."

"Well, I wouldn't mind, as long as he's a bit less angry all the time. That's not going to bring in any customers."

"That's true." The glasses were all washed and dried, and Rose drained the basin she'd been using for them. "What're you hoping fer out there?" Rose nodded toward the front room.

"I have no idea, to tell the truth. I mean, I've never heard about this murder, and then Diane walks in. Everybody else in the place knows more than I do about her. I thought it might be interesting to talk through what happened, and Diane seemed to want that. Everybody assumes she killed this woman Sharon, and she just dropped the motive in our laps. But there was never enough to take Diane to court, right? Was that fair? That people judged her without evidence? Did the gardaí back then do a good job, or did they get it wrong? And don't forget—if Diane didn't do it, someone else did, and he or she is still out there."

"Why do yeh think there's anything left to talk about so long after it happened?"

"I don't know that there is. But from what I'm hearing, people *are* still talking about it. It's kind of like a sore tooth that you can't stop poking your tongue at."

"That's because it wasn't ever solved. Murder is a rare thing in Ireland, Maura. Not like in yer country—or Boston, even."

"Are you going to help me out with this thing?" Maura asked. "You haven't said much until now, but I know you've been busy with the food."

Rose cocked her head. "What is it you think I can do? This happened before I was born."

"Then you can be impartial. Like me. Listen to whatever evidence there is, and hear it with fresh ears. Gee, that's a bad way to put it, but you know what I mean."

"And what if yeh do find somethin' new? What're yeh goin' to do?"

Maura hadn't considered that, and she realized she had no answer—yet. "If—and that's a big if—we find something new, I'd tell Sean about it when the roads are clear. Let him handle it."

"What is it yer thinkin' he can do?"

"Rose, I don't know! He's a garda, and he'll know what to do, okay?" Maura realized she hadn't been paying attention to whatever was going on in the front room for too long. "We'd better get out there before that lot drinks us out of business." And Diane had no defenders in the room, as far as Maura knew. Except maybe Bart. What was he thinking?

"I'll bring the glasses, then, shall I?" Rose said.

"Fine. Thank you, Rose."

Maura strode back to the main room and paused in the doorway for a moment to let her eyes adjust. The room was still
dark, lit only by the oil lamps and the fire, and there was only
blackness outside the plate-glass windows. The smoke of the
fire eddied around the room, particularly near the ceiling, so
the wind must still be strong out there, forcing the smoke down the
flue. No sign of the storm ending any time soon, from what
she could see.

People had arrayed themselves again in the chairs facing the
fire—*Kind of like jurors filing into a courtroom*, Maura thought
irreverently—and most were holding filled pint glasses. Billy
was still in his usual seat to one side of the fire, and Gillian
had moved herself to his other side; Diane had reclaimed
her place in the other chair by the fire so she could face the
group. Everyone in the room turned and looked at Maura
when she walked in, which was unsettling; she felt way out
of her element here. She glanced to her left and saw Mick
was still behind the bar, and Rose had joined him and was
setting the clean glasses below the counter. Mick gave her a
small nod.

Maura faced Diane. "You ready?"

Diane shrugged. "Let's get started."

"All right, then," Maura said with more assurance than she
felt. She turned to the group. "Remember, we're just talking.
Rose and I are the only ones who weren't around back then, so
we may have the most questions. The rest of you, pretend it's the
first time you ever heard all of this. Feel free to ask questions, but
be polite. Everybody okay with that?"

The men nodded.

"Before we start, did anybody here have any personal connection to the original investigation? Except for you, Bart, I mean. Like, were you a garda or related to one? Or did you hang out in any local pubs with one? Or were you friendly with any of the people involved?"

"What's that matter?" Danny asked.

"Because you might think you know more than some people here. Maybe you do, but you have to share what you know. And share whether you think that source was reliable, not just drunk and showing off. Deal?"

More nods.

Quit stalling, Maura! she told herself. *If you're going to do this thing, just do it!*

"All right," she began. "Let me state the facts that we know. Sharon Morgan was murdered on her own property in West Cork in January 1996 by someone unknown. Her body was found the next morning by neighbors, and the gardaí were called. They arrived and began their own investigation. The pathologist arrived from Dublin later that day, and the body was removed for examination. The gardaí sorted out who was running the show and began collecting evidence and interviewing people. Anybody know how many people they talked to?"

"I'd heard it was more'n a hundred," Seamus said. "Not just neighbors, but anybody who might've been drivin' by in the night or seen or heard something they thought was suspicious. I have to say, most of those came to nothing. Except fer Diane."

"Thank you, Seamus—that's a lot more than I expected," Maura said. "Diane became a suspect because someone, or maybe a lot of people, knew her husband was seeing Sharon and thought that was a motive. But Diane was never arrested. Nobody else was either. And that's kind of where things still stand today."

Joe stood up. "Can we ask questions when we want? Should we raise a hand or just stand?"

Maura swallowed a smile. At least Joe was taking this seriously. "You can just raise your hand if you have a question. Do you?"

"I do. Seems I don't know the details as well as some here. Let's start with, how did she die? I mean, was it violent? Cruel?"

"I don't know the details beyond that she was stabbed," Maura told him. "Diane, can you give us the details?"

Bart spoke before Diane could begin. "Sharon Morgan was stabbed multiple times in the chest and neck area. More times than were needed to kill her. This happened outside, and the ground under her was soaked with her blood. She bled to death where she was found."

Maura glanced briefly at Diane, whose expression was stony. She'd heard this before.

Danny waved his hand and asked, "Did she put up a fight?"

"There were few defensive wounds on her," Diane said in the same level tone. "A shallow cut or two, but nothing to show she fought hard with the attacker. Most likely she was surprised by the first blow, and then she had no chance."

Danny sat, but then Joe jumped in again. "Was she messed with?"

"Do you mean, was she sexually assaulted?" Maura asked. Several men looked uncomfortable at her choice of words. Had all the gardaí who had originally investigated been men? Had they felt squeamish about asking questions like this? Joe nodded.

Diane responded in the same neutral tone. "No, there was no sign of any recent sexual activity, willing or not."

Billy spoke for the first time. "We've been thinkin' of the poor woman as a body, but can you tell us a bit more about her? You knew her, did you not?"

Diane turned to him. "I've said this before. Yes, I knew her, but not well. I wouldn't call us friends, exactly—more like casual acquaintances. But if you're asking if she was strong or fit, I'd say she was kind of a medium-size person. Not short, not tall. Not frail nor heavy. Could she have put up a fight against someone in the middle of the night, someone she trusted? Maybe. I can't say."

Billy went on, "Did she walk much?"

"You mean hike? She wasn't a health fanatic or particularly athletic. Or did you mean, did she walk into town?"

"How far was her house from the town?"

"A couple of miles, I think. I think she did walk if the weather was good. Some people said back then that she would bring them parcels or stop by with a cake or something if she was passing by on foot. But she was not particularly athletic. I think—and I admit I'm only guessing, based on what was reported after—that she came to Cork to relax, slow down. She didn't make a point of socializing, not with the local people or with visitors of her own, and there were relatively few of those. She was polite and pleasant enough, but she wasn't looking to make friends. I guess you'd say she was kind of a private person."

Maura decided to step in. "You said earlier that there was no sign of a forced entry or a struggle at the house. Would she have let just anybody in?"

Diane turned to Maura. "Isn't that how it is around here? Most people are trusting, or at least they used to be. If someone comes to your door, you chat with them. You invite them in for a cup of tea. That doesn't mean that these people are the best of friends, only that they're friendly by local standards."

That matched what Maura had seen around Leap. Maura gave a short nod, then turned to the group. "I'm the new kid here. Do you agree that's how things are around here?"

No one objected. Maura turned back to Diane. "So the fact that she let this person in really doesn't tell us much, does it? Only that she was following the local custom, although it was kind of late. It could have been someone she knew, or it could have been a stranger. All we can say is that she wasn't afraid of him. Right?"

"I'm afraid so," Diane said. "It could have been almost anyone."

Thirteen

~

Maura realized there was one big question that no one had asked yet. It was time to get it out on the table. "Diane, you kind of hinted that the gardaí focused on you because of your motive—that your husband and Sharon were having an affair. Did other people know? Did somebody make that public? See them together? Was there gossip at some pub in Schull?"

Diane didn't answer right away. She looked over the small crowd, where the men outnumbered the women. "Let me put this in perspective for you. In 1996, the local gardaí were almost all men. Even now, I've read that women make up less than half of the force in this country, though I can't guess which depart‑ ments. Gentlemen," she said with a touch of sarcasm, "will you admit that men and women see things differently?"

Several men raised their glasses.

"And they'll ask different questions as well. Am I right?"

Nods all around.

"So, back then, a reasonably attractive woman, not yet forty, was found dead outside of her home. No sign of robbery or assault before the vicious stabbing that killed her. Nothing was stolen or disturbed in the house. No one nearby—not that there were many—saw or heard anything out of the ordinary. If you toss out the random homicidal stranger, as Maura suggested, and aliens from space, there's nobody who wanted to kill the woman. So the male police force jumped to the conclusion that this was about sex."

That statement met with stony silence. "Didn't anybody have a better idea?" Maura asked.

Diane shook her head. "Not that I heard. The problem was, nobody would say it out loud. Sure, it was a different time, but this was an official investigation, not just some sniggering in the pub."

"Okay," Maura replied, "I can see why that wouldn't fly in the press. Was there censorship then? Things that the papers couldn't say or print?"

Diane sniffed. "The journalists had a grand time dancing around the subject, and everybody knew what they meant. They stayed within the letter of the law. But it made a better story and sold more papers if there was a whiff of scandal."

Maura considered her options. Clearly the men, most of them not young, were uncomfortable talking about this subject, even though they had probably thought of it before in connection with the murder. "Why your husband? Was there nobody else around that was a good fit?"

Diane shrugged. "There's a whole handful of reasons—take your pick. Our house was closest. We all knew that stretch of ground, so it would have been easy. We didn't have children to get in the way. And as Seamus pointed out, someone else coming by regularly would have been noticed. No one was."

Maybe she should come at it from a different direction. "Okay then, let's take another tack," Maura said. "Sharon was married, right?"

"She was. But as I've said, her husband was a few hundred miles away, drinking with his mates. Unless he had a twin brother, he couldn't have done it."

Maura looked around at the group. "Anybody know of a twin? Or someone who could be mistaken for him? Six cousins who all look alike?" Nobody answered.

She turned back to Diane. "What was their marriage like?"

Diane shrugged. "I can't say. I've told you that I didn't know Sharon well. When we did see each other, we talked about simple things, like the weather or airfare or some such. I might have met her husband once or twice, but I can't recall if I ever had a conversation with the man. Of course the gardaí covered all that with me. I'm not sure they believed me when I said I didn't know either of them well. They seem to have assumed that the entire English crowd spent their time together."

"Did she and her husband usually travel here together?"

"Sometimes. Not always."

"How did they come to buy the house in this area? You said you had family connections, but did either one of them?"

"Maura, I never gave that much thought," Diane replied, looking bewildered. "I think she told me once that she and her husband had driven through once, years earlier, and she'd always thought it looked like a pretty, peaceful place. But I can't say if that was their reason for returning. He was a property developer— maybe he thought it was a good investment."

"There were and are a lot of people from other countries out that way, aren't there?"

"There are—we were considered 'blow-ins.' For a time, it was fashionable in certain circles to own a country house in West Cork. There were English, then Germans. I'm told the Belgians have moved in more recently, but I haven't spent much time around here in the past few years, so things could have changed again."

"The area's been popular fer a while," Bart answered. "Mostly because it's pretty, and the land was cheap, at least compared to other places. Not much use fer more than the scenery, unless you want to graze yer cattle. Which the blow-ins did not. They liked to tell their city friends, 'Oh, I have a cottage near the coast in Ireland.' Trendy, it was, fer those who could afford it."

"Did these blow-ins and the local people hang out together?" Maura asked, trying to find a different angle.

"Yer askin' us?" Joe said. "We weren't exactly invited to their parties, yeh know. They might buy a load of turf off of us if they hadn't already put in the central heating."

"Yeah, I get that. But did one person arrive and buy a place, and then tell all his friends back home, and then they all showed up and bought places? So they sort of knew each other?"

Mick stepped in. "Maura, we wouldn't know. It's a ways away from here."

Maura swallowed a comment about how a place ten miles away could be considered unknown territory to the local men. They might know the townlands nearest to their home down to the last rock, but someone from the next town over would be said to come "from away." "How many people are we talking about?"

"Maura, what're yeh gettin' at?" Mick asked.

"I want to know how big the suspect pool was. Ten people? Fifty people? And how far away was considered too far to be on the list? Did people drive? Walk? Ride bikes? A horse? Look, it comes back to my question: were there no other suspects?"

"When the gardaí learned that my husband was having an affair with Sharon," Diane said quietly, "they thought they had their answer."

Maura took a deep breath. "Who told them?"

"It wasn't me, although I confirmed it when they asked me. So someone else told the gardaí," Diane said.

"Did *you* know?" Danny asked. "About the two of 'em?"

Diane turned toward him. "I knew but I didn't, if you see what I'm saying. We came down to Cork for a mix of business and holiday. My husband Mark had started making money with investments. Paul's construction company was doing well, and he had local clients. In fact, he may have remodeled some of those houses the newcomers were snapping up. For all I know, they may have done business together—I never asked."

"So why did you say you thought you knew that he and Sharon were . . . you know?"

Diane smiled without humor and looked at the others in the room. "Shall we pick a term to use? I don't want to offend anyone here with my language. Would you prefer 'getting it on'? Shagging? Sleeping together?"

"Let's stick to havin' an affair," Bart said. "It was physical, was it not? Not just longing gazes across the bog?"

"As far as I know, it was. But I wasn't looking for proof. It was easier to turn a blind eye."

Diane's bald statements were not making her popular with the people here. Had she used the same line with the gardaí, originally? If so, it wouldn't have been surprising that they'd held it against her.

"How did they manage to carry on an affair?" Maura asked suddenly. "I mean, you were married, Sharon was married. You both lived somewhere else, not here. You both came over here when you felt like it, not on some regular schedule. Sometimes alone, sometimes with your husbands. So when and how did they find the time to carry on? Did they meet up back in England? Somewhere else? Weekends in Paris or Spain? How did this work?"

Diane and several other people were staring at Maura now, but she went on, "I mean, seriously, how many 'meetings'"—Maura made air quotes—"does it take to make it an affair? One a year? Once a month? And were they in love, or were they just scratching an itch? Or messing with your head or Sharon's husband's?"

Now people were gaping at her, and Maura was getting frustrated. "Oh, come on, people. You must have thought these things at some point. Somebody died. Have you heard anything that tells you that anybody involved felt strongly enough to kill that person?"

"I can only speak for myself, Maura," Diane began. "My husband and I were not in love at that point, but we had a decent enough relationship. If he was carrying on with Sharon, I have no proof, as I said. I never came upon them together doing anything suspicious. And this was not the first time or the last for

Mark. We're still together. I know that may be hard for most of you to understand, but it works for us."

"Did yeh stay with him fer the money?" someone asked.

"I've worked most of my life, and I inherited a bit from my parents. I didn't need his money. And if I'd wanted that, I could have killed *him* rather than Sharon. He had plenty of insurance."

"Yer tellin' us that you didn't care that he was seeing another woman right under yer nose?" Danny asked, his tone incredulous.

"Well, it wasn't exactly under my nose, but that's what I'm saying."

"And had you had . . . flings of yer own? As payback, say?"

"No, I did not. Not here, and not in England."

"Did anything change for your husband or both of you when Sharon died?" Maura asked. "Did he stop catting around? Was he depressed? Angry?"

"I'd say he was relieved."

Maura stared at her. "Why do you say that?"

Diane looked down at her hands in her lap. "As I said, I don't really *know* the facts. I'm only guessing. I think Mark enjoyed the hunt, the secrecy, the drama of an affair. He enjoyed the company of women—in all ways. But he also had a short attention span, if you will. Once he'd made his conquest, he got bored quickly. He had Sharon, he tired of Sharon, end of story."

"So yer sayin' he didn't care enough fer the woman to kill her?" Billy asked.

"That's about it. I'd say she cared more than he did. It would have been more likely that she would have killed him—not the other way around—if he left her."

"Who's to say she didn't try, and he ended up turning the tables on her?" Danny asked.

"I told you, he was in England when Sharon died. The gardaí did check that."

"Can we go back to where we started?" Maura said. "Diane, you're saying the gardaí decided you were their favorite suspect *only* because your husband Mark was having an affair with Sharon?"

"Yes. For them, it appeared to be the easiest answer. They boiled it down to: my husband was having an affair with Sharon, I found out and got angry, I killed her in a fit of rage, hence all the stab wounds. That was enough for them. That and the fact that they had no one else to look at after interviewing everybody else in the area."

Billy asked suddenly, "Diane, would yeh be kind enough to stand?"

After a confused look, Diane stood up.

"Maura, could yeh come stand by her?" Billy went on.

Maura moved closer to Diane until they were side by side.

"Maura, how tall would yeh be?" Billy asked.

"Uh, five seven, maybe?"

"And Diane here's a bit shorter. How tall was Sharon, do you recall, Diane?"

"About my height. And we weighed about the same."

"Ta. Gentlemen, can yeh picture this lady grabbing up a knife and inflicting the kind of wounds we know Sharon suffered?"

The men stared for a long moment, then a few shook their heads.

"Mebbe one blow to the heart, but many?" Billy pressed on.

"What happened to the knife?" Joe called out.

"It was never found," Diane said. "Plenty of bog there, so it would be easy to throw it away."

"How did the gardaí describe the weapon?" Maura asked. "How big? What kind?"

"They thought it could be a medium-size kitchen knife with a blade about an inch wide," Bart said.

"And they assumed that would be a woman's weapon? If it was from a kitchen?"

Diane shrugged. "They might have done."

"You and Sharon both had knives in your kitchen at your cottages?"

"I assume. After all, we both cooked for ourselves and for our husbands. For guests now and then."

"Were they in sets?" Maura asked. Then she realized she couldn't remember ever buying knives for herself at all. She was still using whatever Old Mick had left behind—not that she cooked much anyway.

"No. Look, this was a holiday cottage. We didn't exactly outfit the place for show. There were probably three, four knives in the kitchen, large and small. I don't recall that any went missing, but things were a bit unsettled at the time, so I couldn't say for sure. And after Sharon's death, after the investigation, we never came back."

"Until now," Maura reminded her. "You didn't have to, you said. You could have let a lawyer handle everything."

"Yes. I suppose I thought enough time had passed . . . Oh, I don't know what I was thinking! But I do know that once I was happy there, and ever since Sharon died, I've been angry that someone took that away from me. I did nothing to deserve that, yet people still assume I had something to do with her death. It's not fair."

"No, it's not," Maura said. "So let's do something about it."

Fourteen

❧

Maura looked around the room. She was surprised to see that some of the younger guys had crept in from the back room. Cold? Looking for another pint? Or just bored? Whatever the reason, she didn't mind. Fresh eyes on the cold case if they stuck around.

"Diane, let's back up a sec," Maura interrupted. "You said your husband was in England when the murder happened, right? And so was Sharon's. How long did it take them to show up in Cork?"

"You're thinking of their alibis? I don't remember the flight schedules back then, and there were ferries, too. But neither ran often—maybe twice a day?" Diane appealed to the rest of the crowd.

"Could be right," someone answered. A couple of others nodded. Maura guessed that few of them had done much traveling back then.

Maura started again. "So Sharon was killed late at night. Her body was found the next morning. The gardaí were called in, and it took until afternoon to sort out who was in charge. When did they notify Sharon's husband?"

"How would I know?" Diane protested. "They knew who she was, and they would have found quickly that she was married. I assume there was a phone number for the man somewhere in her cottage. But I can't say for sure."

"How quickly did you call *your* husband?"

"I . . . I'd have to think. The word of the death didn't go out immediately, you know."

Is she avoiding answering the question? Maura wondered. Had she been afraid to give bad news to her husband—or afraid that he wouldn't be where he'd said he would be? Or was she just waiting for garda approval to tell anyone else? "How did *you* find out that Sharon was dead?"

"You mean, who told me? I think it was my nearest neighbor, Mrs. Foster. Her house was on the larger road, a couple of fields over, and she would have noticed the garda vehicles passing by— that was a rare event then."

"So *she* decided to spread the word? Without checking with the gardaí?"

"Well, at first she wouldn't have known what the trouble was, only that there was something going on down the lane. But her sister's son was a garda over at Bantry, so she may have called her sister to find out what was going on."

Pretty casual communications for a major case, Maura thought. "When?"

"Maura, what are you goin' on about?" Mick asked.

She turned to him. "Look, the gardaí didn't know what they were dealing with for a while. They certainly wouldn't have been making public announcements until they knew who was in charge. And remember, this was before mobile phones. So who would have announced that Sharon was dead, and who would they have told? And when?"

"It coulda happened the way Diane said—that Mrs. Foster found out from her nephew or someone at the garda station in Schull," Mick said.

"So what did Mrs. Foster do?" Maura shot back. "Did she start running around the fields telling everyone she could?"

"The woman was past sixty!" Diane protested. "With arthritis."

"So did she get in her car and drive around to tell people?"

A number of people were now looking at Maura as if she had gone crazy. "What?" she protested. "I'm just trying to work out a timeline. In January, it gets dark like at four thirty, right? What time did Mrs. Foster arrive to give you the news, Diane?"

"I really don't recall," Diane said apologetically.

"All right, how about this?" Maura rushed on. "When they heard about Sharon's death, did your husband or Sharon's husband take the ferry or fly over?"

"My husband caught a plane," Diane said. "I can't speak to how Paul arrived."

"And the Cork airport is what, an hour by road from your place?"

"A bit more."

"When did Mark arrive?"

"The next morning."

"Ah," Maura said.

That made Diane angry. "Ah, what? I called him at our home once I knew that Sharon was dead. Yes, I reached him at home, if you're wondering. He hadn't planned to come over here then, but he caught the first plane he could. Which wasn't easy, since it was the end of the holiday season. He arrived at our cottage about mid-afternoon. The day *after* Sharon was found."

"Wait—you hadn't spent the holidays together?"

"No, we didn't. Mark had a son by an earlier marriage. He wanted to spend the time with his son. I was fine with that. I never minded being at the cottage alone. So, if you're asking, we hadn't had a fight, nor were we separated or anything like that."

Maura wondered if that was the real reason or only the public one. Once again, she wondered what kind of impression Diane had made on the West Cork gardaí when they'd first talked to her. She came across as cold. She traveled alone and didn't seem very close to her husband. The question of whether she knew about his affair—or multiple affairs—must have come up in some interview sometime after the first frenzy, and Maura doubted that the young Catholic men who made up the gardaí had been particularly sympathetic, especially since Diane was English, not local. Had that colored their opinions? Or worse—their official reports? Maura didn't want to think that Diane had been considered a suspect merely because she wasn't particularly likable, but her attitude might have tipped the scales.

"How long did all this take?" Maura asked.

"What, the whole investigation?" Diane asked.

"No, just the time between when the gardaí knew they had a murder on their hands and when they decided on their suspect—you, Diane."

"But she was never named," Seamus said. "She was never arrested or charged. It was only that she was brought in and interrogated more than once."

And somehow everyone had known that. Communications in Cork still mystified Maura. "And other people weren't?" Maura demanded.

"Not so often as her."

"Okay, what was the process?" Maura felt she was talking in circles. "The gardaí have a body, clearly murdered. They know more or less how and when she died. Then they start asking questions and interviewing people, right? How many people did they interview?"

Some of the men exchanged glances. "A few hundred, mebbe?" Seamus volunteered.

That stopped Maura. "Wait, how many?"

"Told you—hundreds," Seamus said, sounding irritated. "Can't say they weren't doin' their job." Bart nodded in agreement.

"But, but . . . Look, I don't pretend to know that part of the county, but it can't be more crowded than around here, can it?"

"About the same," Billy said. "Lots of pastureland. Cows."

"So where the heck did the gardaí find that many people to interview?"

"Well, they'd have started with the near neighbors and worked their way outward, wouldn't they?"

"Okay, sure. That'd be, what—fifty? Then what?"

Joe joined in. "They woulda talked to the husband—Sharon's— fer sure. They woulda talked to the people what gave him his alibi. They woulda talked to his friends back in England or in Dublin or Cork city. 'Was he the kind of man who could kill?' they might ask. In the heat of anger, or would he make a plan? Was there any money involved? Had he put insurance on Sharon? Was she planning to leave him? Or he leaving her? They'd talk to her friends as well, wouldn't they now?"

"And the local gardaí talked to all these people?" Maura asked, incredulous—and wondering if Joe had been in trouble with the law at some point, to know so much. And why was he suddenly so talkative?

"They did indeed," Seamus said. "Why d'yeh think it took so long? The lads wanted to get it done right. The whole country was watchin'."

Maura had to remind herself that she shouldn't underestimate the gardaí—certainly not now, since she'd seen them at work, and not those in the past either. Many of them might be young, and they might not have the experience in investigation that came with working in a big city, but it would be wrong to assume they were stupid or lazy. And what did she think she was doing now? Proving that they'd failed back in 1996? Did she really think she could sit down with a bunch of random guys who had fuzzy memories of something that had happened two decades ago, and they'd figure out exactly who had killed Sharon? Like that was going to happen! *Maura, this was just a way to pass the time while we wait for the snow to stop*, she reminded herself. *We're only talking*. Diane deserved a fair break. It seemed wrong that she should have to carry this load of suspicion around for the rest of her life if she hadn't done anything.

The problem was, if this group couldn't figure out someone to point a finger at, then nothing would change. What were the options? One, Diane had in fact killed Sharon and gotten away with it, or two, she knew who had and wasn't talking. Or three, Diane was as innocent as she claimed she was, and someone *else* had killed Sharon in a violent and bloody way—and gotten away with it. *Which do you like best?* Maura asked herself.

What she would prefer was to be in her own bed at home right now. Well, that wasn't about to happen. She was stuck here along with her customers, and Diane had dropped into their laps. Maura checked the clock: almost ten. It wasn't even near closing time.

She turned to the curiously silent Bart. "You agree with what Joe said, Bart?"

"Close enough. The gardaí did their jobs. Like he said, a lot of people were watching."

"What was your part?"

"I was new to the job. Mostly I typed up other officers' notes. Sure, I read them all. I can't say they missed anything."

No help there. Maura checked the room again—after all, that was her job. "Hey, guys? How about we take another break, stretch our legs?"

"Another pint?" someone called out.

"Yeah, fine. But if anyone wants to chip in to the snow pint fund, all contributions welcome."

Gillian pried herself up from her chair and made her way over to the back of the room—headed for the loo, no doubt, before the guys realized they needed to make room for that next pint. Maura drifted in that direction, then leaned against the wall to wait for Gillian to emerge. By the time she did, there was a line of guys waiting in the narrow hallway.

"You doing okay?" Maura asked Gillian when she came out.

"As well as I can hope. Don't worry, I'm not about to pop this child out now—we're months from that."

"Well, it would be a different way to entertain this lot for the evening."

Gillian laughed. "I can see them making a run for the door! If they have to choose between helping deliver a baby and braving a snowstorm, I don't think there's much question which they'd choose."

"I hear you. Any word from Harry?"

Gillian glanced around, then moved toward the back room. Maura followed reluctantly: the boys hadn't lit the fire in there, and it was icy. The lone oil lamp was burning low, so Maura located the flashlight she knew was kept behind the bar before gesturing to Gillian to shut the door. Then Maura asked quietly, "What's wrong?"

Gillian leaned against the bar. "Harry's been texting me. He says Eveline won't last the night."

"I'm sorry to hear that—she's sort of the last of her kind. But it's not exactly unexpected, is it?"

"No, of course not. She's well past eighty. But I don't know what Harry will do."

"About what? You?"

"Where he'll live. Where I'll be living. With Eveline gone, Harry and I will be kind of orphans, do you know?"

"Oh, you mean you've got no place to live?"

"Exactly. Harry's got a flat in Dublin, but it's not big enough for two and certainly not for three, no matter how small that third one might be. Nor do I really want to raise my child in the city."

"So what are your options?"

Gillian stood up straighter and stretched her back. "I don't know. With a baby, I can't work or even paint, and there's no way I could pay for a childminder on whatever little I made."

"Won't Harry help?"

"As much as he can, but that may not be much. Whatever his family name and history, the money's pretty much gone now, and he lives on his salary. I don't know how far that will go. Though he won't be paying the O'Briens to look after Eveline. I wonder how they're fixed . . ."

"The O'Briens are not your problem. Uh, you're welcome to stay with me, you know."

"I wouldn't ask, Maura. You're kind to offer, but you haven't lived with a baby. No, this is something Harry and I have to sort out between ourselves—and sooner rather than later."

"Have you talked about it?"

"No, because Eveline's been so ill. I haven't wanted to add to his troubles."

"Tell me this: do you want to be together?"

"Now? Forever?"

"You're ducking the question, Gillian. If you ask me, there is no such thing as forever when it comes to people. Put it this way: do you want to try to make a go of it, the two of you plus one?"

Gillian knotted her fingers together. "I think so. I think the last few months have really shaken Harry, and now he knows he has to grow up. And I have to accept that there's no way I can go it alone, without some financial support, even if I want to. It simply doesn't work."

"Well, at least you've figured out what the problems are."

"But Maura, I have no solutions. Not that I expect to arrive at any tonight."

And she had no ideas to offer, either. After a moment, Maura asked, "How do you think it's going out there?"

"You mean, your trial? Or rather, Diane's? It's been interesting, I have to say."

"How much did you know about any of this?"

"Not much. I'm only a few years older than you, Maura, so I was still a child when it all happened. To make it worse, there were parts of it that the adults wouldn't talk about in front of the children back then—probably the sex-related bits. They didn't want to have to explain. So I'd say that the facts were in short supply, and some of us probably made up a lot of bosh to fill in the gaps, and then those parts became the facts. I admire what you're trying to do, to sort it out now, but what do you hope to take away from it?"

"I guess I started because it seemed like a good way to pass the time, since we can't leave here tonight. I do think Diane got a lousy deal—she had no way to fight back against rumors and gossip. But now that we've been talking about it for a bit, I have to wonder what really did happen and if the whole mess was handled right."

"You think the gardaí messed things up?"

"No, not really. They did their best."

"Do you think Diane did it?"

Maura shook her head. "No. She says not, but then she would, wouldn't she? But apart from that, I don't think she's angry enough. And I don't think she could have done it physically."

"You might be surprised. But if not Diane, then who?" Gillian asked.

"I have no idea. And nobody else's name has popped up so far. Should we go back now and see if anyone's had a brainstorm?"

"Let's do. Better than worrying about Eveline and Harry."

Fifteen

Back in the main room, people had gathered in clumps—many armed with a fresh pint—and were talking with a lot of gestures. It looked almost like an ordinary night, except that it was darker. Nobody seemed to mind. Gillian went to the bar for something nonalcoholic to drink, so Maura made her way over to Billy and sat down. "What do you think?" she asked him.

"Are yeh talkin' about yer brilliant idea to stir up old troubles?"

"I guess. You might have noticed that I'm one of the few people in this room who knew nothing about the murder, but even I've heard it mentioned on the telly now and then since I got here. How on earth does something like this hang on in the news for so long?"

Billy smiled. "Ah, Maura, fer all that you were raised in the city, yer still a bit of a wide-eyed innocent when it comes to crime here. I know it's hard fer you to put yerself back in that time, but even now things are simpler here than in America."

"Yeah, I kind of get that, Billy. Is it because it was murder? A messy violent murder of a woman? An outsider? Because there were hints of scandal? Were people angry at the gardaí? What I don't understand is why everybody seems to know about it now, this much later, and have an opinion about it—and why Diane has always been the villain."

"All good questions, m'dear, and there's a bit of truth in all of 'em. Why the lady ended up in the middle of it, I can't tell you."

Did people blame her because her husband was fooling around? Or because she knew about it and did nothing? Which was kind of the same as approving? One more strike against the outsiders. Maura leaned closer to Billy, not that anyone else in the room was paying attention to them. "Were there really no other suspects?"

"Many or none—who's to say? The woman was dead, no question. She had few friends in the area—no one knew her well. That left the door open fer a lot of guesses. But there was little to work with—the husbands were elsewhere and could prove it. So without any true evidence, Diane was the easiest choice because of the husband. People jumped to the likeliest conclusion, and it stuck."

"I suppose you'd have to say the least *un*likely, right? Who knew about her husband's carrying on with Sharon? And do you believe that Diane felt strongly enough about it that she would kill for him?"

"I can't answer yer questions, Maura," Billy said sadly. "I can only guess at what folk might've thought back in the day."

Maura sighed. "So now she's sold the house, and she's going back to England, and that will be the end of it. Except for the stories. You Irish sure love your stories."

"Are you not counting herself amongst us, then, Maura Donovan? Did yer gran not fill yer head with tales when you were no more than a child?"

"I . . . can't remember. She was always working, and I was in school, and there wasn't a lot of time to sit around and tell stories. Or maybe I just wasn't paying attention." Maura felt a wave of sadness that came out of nowhere. Gran had been the only parent she had known, and while she had moved on with her life, sometimes she missed Gran fiercely. That was one reason she had stayed on in Leap: people around the village had known her. Fewer and fewer of them now, but they were Maura's last link to her grandmother. It hit her suddenly that Gran would have known about the murder. She'd already have gone to Boston, but Maura knew now that Gran had kept in touch with a number of her Irish friends. If anyone had written to her once she was settled in Boston, would they have mentioned it? Gran hadn't been a saver, and she had kept few letters, so Maura would probably never know.

It was a double-edged sword, this long Irish memory. Maura reaped the rewards, as the people who had known her family long before she was born had made her new life in Leap possible and were still helping her along the way. But the downside was that nobody ever let anything go—like this old murder. She had to admit that she felt very young and very American now that she was trying to figure it out. She didn't want to suggest that the gardaí had messed up the original investigation. Most likely they had done the best they could at the time. But they had been inexperienced, which was both good and bad—good because there was little violent crime in Ireland and bad because when they were confronted with that kind of crime, they weren't sure how to deal with it. *Boston should be so lucky!* Maura thought irreverently.

But Maura was forced to admit that there didn't seem to be much evidence to go on. One body, stabbed with a lot of anger. A weapon that was never found—but plenty of bog close by to dump it. No one had known the woman well: she was a foreigner and was pleasant but reserved and mostly kept to herself. Many of the near neighbors fell into the same category as foreigners, outsiders, blow-ins; they hadn't spent a lot of time in West Cork and hadn't necessarily crossed paths with each other—much less with the local people. No wonder nobody had arrived at an answer.

If she was honest with herself, Maura wondered if she could possibly add anything now. There was still too much they didn't know, and maybe nobody did. She was an outsider herself, although in this case, that was probably useful: she had no preconceived ideas. She probably had more knowledge of current forensics than most local people in this group, except Bart, although most of that came from what little television she had watched. But that wasn't much use if there was no physical evidence to examine. Had anything been saved? Were Sharon's bloody clothes preserved somewhere? Had DNA analyses had been done at the time of the murder? Would they have shown anything useful after the body had sat out for a full day?

Sharon had not been raped and had not had sex recently. Had that ever been stated publicly, apart from the official report? Had the papers and the gossips kept quiet about it because it was a taboo subject—or at least distasteful? Could they talk more freely about Sharon's sexual activities now than they could have twenty years earlier? But was there anything to talk about? Did it matter?

Maura checked the clock again: the hands were creeping up on eleven. The people in the room might be good for another hour or two of talk, tops. Two hours to arrive at a conclusion about a crime that had remained open for nearly two decades. Was this the time to give up, tell everyone to settle in for the night, and forget about it? Maybe Diane should have a say in that decision.

During the lull, Diane had been nursing a cup of coffee in the far corner, looking out the window even though there was nothing to see. Maura crossed over to where she stood. "Are you okay?"

Diane turned away from the view of whiteness. "Nice of you to ask, Maura. I don't think I have many friends in this room." She took another swallow of her coffee, which must be cold by now. Maura waited. "Am I all right with my life? Maybe. I'm going home to England as soon as I can, and then all this will be behind me. My husband will be waiting, and we'll get on with our lives. Or were you asking, am I okay with what's happening here tonight? Maybe. It feels good to talk about it, to get it all out in the open, and most likely this will be the last time. Do I think all this talk with prove anything? Probably not, but I guess I need some official end to it all. Back in England, nobody knows, or maybe they just don't care. I was never arrested. I have no criminal record. I have a different life there."

"I can see that."

"Can you? You come from a very different place." Diane eyed her curiously but without hostility. "If you don't mind, I think I'd like to finish this. It's interesting to hear what people have been saying about me all these years. Actually, it hurts less than I expected. I know I didn't do it. I guess I can see why people might think I did. But as we've all said, if I didn't do it, someone else did. Someone lured Sharon out of her house and stabbed her and left her bleeding in the dark. I don't know who or why, but I would like to know why this person made a mess of my life. Did they even know me? So let's finish this." With that, Diane rose and strode across to the fireplace, where Billy was busy adding more fuel to the fire.

Maura followed and turned to the group. "Diane wants to keep going. Do any of you want to quit? It's getting late, and you can make yourselves comfortable and go to sleep if that's what you want."

"This is better than the telly," Seamus said, grinning. "Our own reality show, like. I fer one want to know more. I want to hear the rest of the story. Youse guys, are yeh with me?" He looked around the room. Most people nodded. Rose, still behind the bar, flashed Maura a smile. Jimmy still looked pissed off at something, but Maura wasn't going to take it personally.

"All right, then. Where were we?"

Diane cleared her throat. "May I say something?"

"Of course—it's your show."

Diane started pacing in front of the fire. "Look, I understand why the gardaí—and a lot of other people—looked to me as the killer. Really, I do. I was an outsider, even if my grandparents did come from around here. I had more money than most people. I was independent—I didn't always travel with my husband. And that last point matters. My husband was having an affair with

Sharon. I knew that. Maybe calling it an affair made it more than it really was. Let's just say they got together when the opportunity arose, which wasn't all that often. I don't know who else knew they were involved—as I'm sure you know, it isn't easy around here to see who's going where when."

Diane swallowed. "Sharon wasn't the only one, for that matter, although she was the only one here, as far as I know. But to tell the truth, I was debating about leaving my husband that winter. That's another reason he wasn't here with me on that trip. I told him to stay home because I wanted to think. By myself."

"Were yeh angry with Sharon?" Joe called out.

Diane faced him. "No, I wasn't. Don't believe me if that's what you want. As I said, she wasn't the only one. She wasn't the first one. My husband was—and is—a jerk."

"Yer still with him, aren't you?" Danny asked.

"I am. It's complicated. How many of you are married?" About half the people in the room raised a hand slowly. "Okay. The rest of you, have you been married in the past?" A couple more hands came up. "So most of you know what marriage—or at least a long-term partnership—is like, right? We didn't have children together. We both had jobs that we liked. We had plenty of money. We took a hard look at our lives and decided it wasn't worth splitting up." Diane held up a hand. "Before you judge me, I know that isn't a decision that you'd like. We weren't madly in love, and I don't think we ever were. He'd been married before. We were adults when we got together, and we had a more or less happy life. I knew he slept around. If it matters to you, I didn't. I wasn't out to prove anything, to get some kind of payback. I just never met anybody I was that interested in. So Mark and I muddled along, and I ignored his affairs, and eventually they ended. Sharon was nothing special. Mark wasn't planning to leave me to marry her."

"Why are yeh tellin' us this?" Joe asked suddenly.

"I'm telling you I didn't care what Mark did with Sharon—or anybody else—because that means I had no motive for killing Sharon. She wasn't that important to me. Why would I lure her out in the middle of the night and stab her however many times? It makes no sense. But the gardaí had trouble believing that— they thought I should be angry."

"Why should we believe yeh?" Danny asked.

Diane shrugged. "Because it's the truth. Think about it, will you? The gardaí found no evidence on which to arrest me. If I'd been in Sharon's house that night, if we'd shared a cup of tea or a drink or whatever, wouldn't I have left something behind? Fingerprints? Hair? Spit? Anything?"

"You coulda cleaned it all up," Bart said.

"When?" Diane shot back quickly. "Okay, say I was there, and we were chatting. How would I have convinced her to go outside with me? She was in her sleeping clothes, for God's sake. It was January and cold. Did I say, 'Hey, let's take a walk, shall we? Admire the stars?' Does anyone even remember the weather that night?"

"It was rainin'. A soft rain, mebbe, but no stars," Bart said.

"Fine, no stars. You're saying I convinced Sharon to take a walk—in the rain, in the middle of the night. Somehow I concealed a large sharp knife, and when we reached the fence, I faced her and stabbed her. Again and again. Can you imagine me—or any woman of my size—doing that? Not one single blow, but blow after blow. While she stood in front of me and never even fought back."

"You'd have surprised the woman, would you not?" Seamus said.

"Well, yes, I'm pretty sure she wouldn't have guessed I wanted to kill her—if I was even there. But hear me out. You'd have me standing there in the pitch dark, with the knife in my hand and Sharon dead at my feet, yes? And there would have been blood, wouldn't there? All over myself. So then you'd say I turned around, got rid of the knife somewhere, in the bog, maybe, and walked home to clean myself up, and I concealed anything that might have had her blood on it. And then after that, I went back to Sharon's house and made sure to remove any fingerprints or anything else I might have left? Do you really believe that?"

Nobody spoke.

Diane went on, "The gardaí went over that house: no blood inside anywhere. The only blood was where she died. And they looked at *my* house very carefully, and they found no blood there. They looked at my clothes and my shoes and my drains and anywhere they could think of, and there was *no blood*. I'm not that good a cleaner, I promise you. There was no evidence. The gardaí never arrested me. They talked to me, yes, that very day, and they found nothing. And whatever you may think of me, it's not possible that I could have brutally murdered a woman I knew and left her out in the rain, then run home and cleaned myself up, then run to her place and cleaned *that* up as well. It couldn't be done. Just think about it, will you? All of you? Not possible."

Maura almost smiled. Trust a woman to think about how long it took to really get something clean—and all the investigators had been men.

Sixteen

～

A sudden thought hit Maura. "Is there a map for this? I mean, something that shows whose house was where? Remember, I've never seen the area."

Diane looked at her as though she'd gone nuts. "I don't carry one around with me. There may be a map in my car, which is now buried out there under the snow, but I doubt it would show the kind of detail you want, I'm guessing."

"Can you sketch one from memory?"

"I suppose, since I've just been over the details with my solicitor for my property. But why does it matter?"

"Because I don't know who lived where or how far apart. Anybody here know?" Maura asked the crowd. Most of them looked blank. "That's what I thought. For years, you've been hearing that So-and-So was the closest neighbor, or What's-His-Name lived too far away to be part of it. But what does that really mean? Hey, I grew up in a city. I know city blocks and how long it takes to get from one place to another. But we're talking about country, right? Fields and fences and hedgerows. Bogs. Cow and cow pats. Sheep. We've already said that it was dark and raining. A stranger would have had to stick to the roads, right? And people would have noticed a car."

Liam finally spoke. Had he been napping? "It was dark and cold. People's windows would be shut. They might not have heard nor seen a car passing."

Trust a musician to think of the sound of things, Maura thought. "Good point. If we're doing a map, we need to show how close the houses were to the lanes and if anyone could have seen anything outside. Diane, can you at least get us started?"

"I'll need some paper, I guess. Do you have a big sheet of it?"

"Uh . . ." Maura said.

"There's a roll of drawing paper in my car," Gillian volunteered. "If someone could go out and get it."

"I'll go," Jimmy said abruptly. "I can use the air. Where's the car?"

"Just by the bridge," Gillian told him. "It's not locked. The paper would be in the back seat."

"The blue car, yeh?"

"Yes."

Jimmy grabbed his coat from a peg by the door and stomped out, slamming the door behind him. From the brief glimpse outside, Maura could see only more blowing snow. The storm didn't seem to be stopping.

She turned back toward the room. "Okay, we'll need something flat for Diane to draw on. Let's push a couple of tables together. Will that work for you, Diane?"

"Sure, why not? And some light, please. I can't do this in the dark."

A couple of the men leapt up and starting moving furniture. Others set about rearranging the chairs. Billy remained in his usual seat, watching, a half smile on his face. Maura went over to his side, mostly to stay out of the way.

"A smart idea, that," Billy said quietly.

"I just wanted to get a picture of the layout in my head, you know? I've never seen the place. I'm still getting used to how places around here relate to each other. I can look at a map, but that doesn't tell me about some ancient right-of-way or the path that everybody uses that's not on the map. Sure, maybe it was five miles to the nearest neighbor from Sharon's house, but if there was a shortcut, who would know about it?"

"Yer thinkin' that this had to be someone local, are you not? Else they would've gone bumbling around in the dark, makin' a lot of noise and fuss—or fallin' into the bog."

"I guess that's what I'm getting at. Someone who knew the cottage and how to get there, anyway. I'm going to make a big leap and say that there wasn't somebody from somewhere else staking out Sharon, looking for the right moment to kill her— that seems kind of ridiculous. And wouldn't the gardaí have found someone who had seen a stranger lurking around? Anyway, if we assume it was a local person who knew the land, that can't be a very big group."

"Are yeh thinkin' the gardaí didn't have the same idea?"

"I hope they did. But didn't someone say they came from more than one station? So not everyone would have known the layout of that specific townland or thereabouts. Or the people who lived there."

"That's a fair point, Maura." Billy nodded with approval.

If they had had Internet handy, Maura thought, they could call up the newspaper reports from 1996—there might have been a map. Maybe. But there was no laptop and no power. Funny, wasn't it, that they were looking at the evidence now the way it might have been done when Sharon died? No fancy tools, just personal knowledge and common sense.

Jimmy slammed back in, clutching a thick roll of paper. "Sure, it's desperate out! The wind would skin you alive." He shook himself like a dog to get the snow off, then crossed the room to hand the roll to Diane.

"Thank you, Jimmy," Diane said sweetly. She laid the roll on the bare table and unrolled a piece about three feet long, then tore it off. "Could you nice fellas find a way to hold it down?"

Several men all but tripped over themselves offering ways to fasten the paper so it wouldn't slide around. Maura decided to stay out of it—let them sort things out. Eventually the paper was attached more or less securely to the tabletop.

"All right, then. Diane, will you do this?" Maura said.

"I can try. But don't hold it against me if I get the distances wrong. Anyone have something to write with?" Diane looked around. "Pencil? Pen? Marker?"

Bart fished a felt-tip marker out of a pocket and presented it to her with a flourish. "There yeh are. And we're only after setting out the relationships of the places. It doesn't have to be perfect."

"Thank you." Diane took the marker that Bart held out toward her, pulled her chair closer to the table, and leaned forward. "Where do I start?"

"Schull," Maura said. "That's the nearest town, isn't it? And most people here know where that is."

"Right." Diane made a circle about an inch across in the center of the paper and labeled it. "Now what?"

"Where was Sharon's house?"

"Let me think," Diane said, then pointed to the Schull circle.

"The N71 here runs as far as Ballydehob to the east. Then you take a smaller road to Schull—I forget the number. Once you've passed through Schull, it's maybe another five miles south to Sharon's place, maybe a bit less. Toward the water but not in sight of it."

"Are there many roads?" Maura asked.

"No more than here, I'm guessing. Mostly farm lanes. I can draw you the main roads, but not all the small ones."

"Fine. Put in the ones you know, and then show us where the properties were."

Diane thought again and then sketched in a road running roughly from northeast to southwest. "Sharon's place was about here." She made an *X* on the map, maybe six inches south of Schull on the paper. "Mine was here." Diane made another *X* about six inches from the first, farther west. "The Laytons, who found her in the morning, lived here—their land abutted Sharon's." She made a smaller *X* between Schull and Sharon's house.

"Were there other neighbors?"

"Some. Mainly farther out. The ones who'd been there for generations, who were still farming. Like the Fosters that I mentioned. You want me to add those?"

"Can you make a guess? How many different places?"

"Five or ten, maybe. Things may have changed since. They were pretty evenly scattered about." After another moment, Diane added a few more *X*s and labeled them with names.

"All right, what about bogs?"

"There was a bog that lay between my property and Sharon's," she added. "I've told you that you wouldn't want to try to cross it at night. Sharon put up a fence there so no animal would stray into it. Although animals are usually fairly smart about things like that. But she hadn't been raised in the country, so she wouldn't know." Diane crosshatched an area near the X for Sharon's place.

"Was that the only bog?" Maura asked.

"The biggest one, certainly. There were patches here and there, depending on the weather any year. Even upland bogs."

"What's that?"

"You can run into a bog on a hillside—they're not all low-lying. They're not usually deep, but they can surprise you if you walk into one."

"If you were walking, how long would it take you to get from one house to another?"

"By the road? Maybe ten minutes from the closest houses. Across the land, it could vary widely."

"Or if someone was to come by water?" Donal said suddenly, breaking his long silence.

Diane peered at him in the dim light. "You mean, if they arrived in a boat and walked to the house?" She sketched in a shoreline to the south.

"Could it be done?"

"If you knew where you were going, maybe. Might take half an hour once you got off the boat." Diane studied the map for a moment, then pointed. "Here's the closest beach where you could land a small boat. And of course, there's Schull—they have a good harbor. But again, it was a miserable night, which would have made it harder for anyone on the water."

"Say the husband went to his party or pub or whatever back in England to set himself an alibi," Donal said. He seemed to have finally gotten into the spirit of the discussion. "And then he ducked out and found someone with a fast boat to take him across. How long would that take?"

Diane stared at him. "I have no idea. I think it would have to be a very fast boat."

"Did yer man know boats?" Bart asked.

"Barely. He'd been out with friends, I think, but he couldn't manage one on his own."

"Could the man have rented a plane?" Seamus asked.

Absurd though the question was, Maura felt a small thrill: now the guys were thinking outside the box, which at least meant they were willing to consider someone other than Diane as the killer. "Diane, did he have the money or the connections to do that?"

Diane turned to her. "I have no idea. I don't think Mark would have had the cash, but I can't speak for Paul. I saw Paul only a few times, and we certainly didn't talk about money. Sharon didn't flash any around."

"He was a property developer, though, so it's possible?" Maura pressed.

"Two problems with that, even if he had the money fer the plane," Mick said suddenly. "One, where could he have landed the thing that would be close to the house? And two, that would have meant involving other people—a pilot and someone with a car to get him from the plane to the house and back. Somewhere there would have been a record—a charge to his account or a lump of cash he'd taken out. Something. The gardaí would've looked."

"But would the gardaí have looked that hard?" Maura demanded. "Would they have looked at his business accounts? Remember, the gardaí were local. They were thinking it was a local crime involving people in West Cork, not flying in from who knows where. They weren't looking at international connections, were they? At least, not after they'd talked to the alibi witnesses in London. They wouldn't have seen the need to."

Mick looked exasperated. "Maura, yer tryin' too hard. Say he did hire a plane and paid the pilot enough to shut him up. And he knew where to tell the pilot to land. The timing would have been tight. Both Paul and Mark were seen in London at eleven. Sharon died sometime between supper and when the neighbors found her in the mornin'. I don't know much about air speeds and the like, but I'm not sure it's possible. When was Paul seen again in London?"

"Sometime the next day," Diane said. "Once Sharon's body was found and identified, the gardaí called him and found him at home. Nobody thought to look at the time between."

"His motive would have been the same as yer own, right?" Mick said. "If he knew his wife was seeing other men behind his back."

"I wouldn't know about that. She and I didn't exactly share that kind of information, and I was too far away from the house to see who was coming or going."

"And what of yer own husband?" Seamus demanded. "Could this Sharon have gotten it into her head that Mark was her true love, and she wanted to be wit' him ferever, but he wasn't having any of it?"

"You're suggesting that he killed her because she wanted him for herself?" Diane asked.

"Yer after tellin' us that yer lifestyle suited you both. Mebbe he didn't want to see it changed, and Sharon was going to mess things up, and she wouldn't hear 'no.'"

"But to kill her?" Diane shook her head. "My husband may have the morals of a tomcat, but he's no killer. He's too lazy, for one thing. He couldn't have planned this whole thing, and having lived with him for years, I can tell you he would have left some trace. Plenty of trace. He probably would have left his shirt behind or taken off his shoes."

"Great marriage yeh've got there," Joe muttered.

"I won't defend it, but it works for us. And he's not the kind of man who could have put such a mad plan together quickly."

"How'd he react when you were suspected of killing Sharon?" Maura asked.

"When the gardaí first brought me in for questioning, he laughed. He thought it was a joke. He never thought it would come to anything, and I suppose he was right about that. It's still a bit of a joke between us—'my wife, the murderer.'"

"Do you think it's funny?" Seamus asked in a more quiet tone.

"No, but it seldom comes up any more. As I said, my friends in England don't know much about it. I lead a different life there."

"Let's get back to the map," Maura said. "Was there any back way from Schull to where Sharon's house was?"

"There might have been, but I didn't use it. As I'm sure you all know, there are a lot of lanes, many of them barely paved. I hired a car when I visited back then, and I didn't want to get stranded in the middle of a field somewhere because I'd torn out the muffler or the transmission or whatever on some rocks."

That was something Maura could sympathize with, since she often felt the same way. But she still had questions. "Didn't your grandparents know the back ways?"

"Probably. But they've been gone a long time. Some of those lanes, if they're not used, they get grown over fast—in a few years. They all but disappear. I don't remember any in the 1990s."

Maura noticed that some eyelids were beginning to droop and decided she'd better shift the conversation to a higher gear. She stood up. "Okay, folks—let's assume for the moment that Diane is telling the truth. So if Diane didn't kill Sharon, who did?"

Seventeen

~

"Say the husband hired someone else to kill her," Jimmy said suddenly. He'd helped himself to a generous glass of whiskey and was standing behind the bar savoring it.

"Which husband?" someone called out.

"Either. Both," Jimmy replied.

"Hang on," Maura interrupted. "Are there hit men in Ireland?"

"Not quite like the Mafia, Maura," Mick said, looking faintly amused. "But it could be that someone was hard up for the money, and somehow either Mark or Paul found that person and made him—what do they say? An offer he couldn't refuse? All he had to do was sneak out to Sharon's house, kill her, and disappear. Coulda been a local man, so he'd know the ways."

"But, but—" Maura sputtered, questions crowding in.

Luckily other people had the same questions. "Which husband are yeh lookin' at, Mick?" Seamus asked. He seemed to be having a very good time.

"Sharon's husband is the likeliest, is he not?" Mick told him. "The killer is usually someone close to the victim, and he'd have reason to want her dead."

Maura found her voice again. "But why? Because she was sleeping around? Was that so important back then? Important enough to kill over, I mean? I could see it if Paul had killed her in the middle of an argument, if she was throwing it in his face, or if Paul walked in on Sharon and Mark together, but if Paul hired someone to do it, that would have taken planning and time. He would have had plenty of time to cool off."

"Maybe she'd told him she was leavin' him fer Mark and that made him angry," Liam said. "Or maybe he'd put all his assets in her name and he couldn't afford to have her leave him."

"That's an interesting idea," Maura said. At least it was new. "He was in construction—what was his reputation like? Did he cut corners? Take bribes? Drag his feet in finishing his projects unless a little more money came in?"

"He's not dead, you know," Diane said wryly. "He's done well for himself, although he doesn't do much work in Ireland these days. But back home, I haven't heard or read anything against him."

"Do you follow the news about him, then, Diane?" Mick asked.

"Not deliberately. I'm not stalking him, if that's what you're asking. But his name comes up in the business section of the journals now and then, and I can't help but notice, can I?"

"Sharon's death did him no harm?"

"Well, since he was never a suspect, why would it? He no doubt got a lot of sympathy at the time, which wouldn't hurt."

"So you and your husband didn't see Sharon and him when you were at home in England?" Maura asked.

"No," Diane said impatiently. "As I've said before, we weren't friends before it happened. We just happened to cross paths in

Ireland now and then. You can't think that we'd bond over a shared murder. That's ridiculous."

"What if it was the both of 'em?" Jimmy asked eagerly. He seemed to have gotten interested in the conversation now. Maybe the whiskey had helped.

"What, they planned it together?" Maura asked.

"Why not? Say Sharon is mad fer Mark, and she throws it in Paul's face. But Mark doesn't want any part of it—he was just in it fer a bit of fun. Paul tracks down Mark to tell him to back off, and Mark tells him he wants no more to do with Sharon. But now Paul doesn't want her either, so the two of 'em sit down and start lookin' fer a way to get her off both their backs. In a manner of speakin'," Jimmy finished triumphantly. "And the two of 'em work it out together, like."

"Well, that would have confused the gardaí," Maura said. "But I'm having trouble picturing these two guys, who barely know each other, sitting down in London somewhere and saying, 'Okay, let's get rid of Sharon—you have any ideas?'"

Diane snorted. "I can't see it either, Maura, although I'd bet Paul would be the brains behind it. But isn't this far too complicated? You've got two people conspiring to hire a hit man and have him kill someone in another country. It would have been a hell of a lot easier just to divorce Sharon and be done with it. I think my husband would have made it clear he wasn't going to step into Paul's shoes, or at least not until after he'd spent a while consoling Sharon," she said wryly.

"What if she'd come to you and told you she wanted Mark? What then?" Bart asked.

"Wouldn't have done her any good. I've already told you, I knew what she and my husband were up to, and I didn't really care. I would have said as much to her."

"But she still wanted him, so she pitched a fit and grabbed a knife and attacked you, and you got the thing away from her and turned on her, and she ended up dead!" Liam said, almost bouncing in his chair with enthusiasm.

"Seriously?" Diane said, her tone amused. "And where did this happen? At her house? At my house? The gardaí and their scientist people checked both: no blood at either house. Neither of us was missing a knife. Do you really think she invited me over for a drink one evening and told me she wanted my husband, and would I please step aside, and then I went berserk and dragged her outside—all the way to the front gate—and stabbed her? Please!"

"Sorry." Liam hung his head.

It did sound ridiculous if you put it that way, Maura thought. But Sharon had died, viciously stabbed by *somebody*. "Anybody want to go back to the hit man theory?" Maura asked the group.

"There were often strangers in Schull, although fewer in winter than in summer," Joe offered.

"So a hit man who arrived by boat might not have been noticed?"

"Right."

"But if he wasn't local, how would he know where to go?" Jimmy demanded. The whiskey had definitely warmed him up.

"Okay, so he arrived early, then, and checked it out," Maura suggested.

"Seems like finding a local fella would make more sense," Bart said.

Maura wondered briefly if he was playing devil's advocate or if he knew something. "But how would Paul or Mark have known who to ask?" Maura said. "They were pretty much strangers to the area—they didn't know the people around there."

"True enough. But if Paul was a big man in the buildin' trade," Bart said, "he could have known someone who knew someone, if you see what I'm sayin'."

"Maybe," Maura said, unconvinced. "But that would be a big risk for him, wouldn't it? You can't just ask one of your construction foremen, 'Hey, I want to kill my wife—you know anyone who's looking to make a little extra money?'"

That brought a muffled laugh from a couple of the men.

Billy spoke suddenly—Maura had thought he was asleep. "Yeh've a sayin' where yeh come from—KISS, is it?"

"You're right, Billy. 'Keep it simple, stupid.' You're saying we've kind of left 'simple' behind?"

"Yeh might say that. Over the past while, yeh've suggested a boat, a plane, a hit man, a conspiracy between the two husbands, and more than one other man to do their biddin'—and all of 'em didn't leave a trace behind. Sounds a bit daft to me."

Billy was right—this was getting ridiculous. Maybe the gardaí back then had considered all these possibilities and rejected most of them quickly because they were silly and completely absurd for Ireland—much less rural Ireland. Which left only the main parties involved and the local people. No wonder they had focused on Diane: she was the easiest answer. She was there on the scene, she knew the victim, and she had a simple, basic motive that most people would understand.

But Diane said she hadn't killed Sharon. Was she telling the truth? It all kept coming back to that.

Maura scanned the crowd: after the last brief flurry of excitement, most people were beginning to droop, and it was getting late. "How about we take another break? It looks like we're all going to have to sleep here. Why don't you all clear the floor to make room? There are some rugs and stuff upstairs that might make the floor feel a little softer, but I can't offer you anything better. And Gillian and Billy should get first choice."

"Ah, don't worry yerself about me, Maura," Billy said. "Many's the time I've fallen asleep in my chair and slept until mornin'. I'm fine where I am."

"You wouldn't rather go home to your own bed, Billy?" Maura asked.

"There'll be no heat there. It's warmer here."

"Your saying there's a real bed that's not bein' used?" Liam asked.

"Down at the end, at Billy's place. You want it? Or should we all draw straws or something?" Maura asked.

"We've got our own sleeping gear, so we won't mind if there's no heat," Donal pointed out.

Maura looked around again. "Anybody object?" When no one did, she told Liam, "I guess it's yours. And Billy's got a couch, right?"

"That I do. You boys are welcome to the both of them."

"That's fine, then," Maura said firmly. "Gillian?"

Gillian smiled ruefully. "In my state, it's hard to get comfortable in any position. I guess I'll follow Billy's example and take the other stuffed chair, if you don't mind. Maybe put my feet up."

"Great. The rest of you, sort things out. You can go upstairs and scrounge for anything you like, but I don't think you'll find much."

"Will there be a pint in it fer us?" someone asked plaintively. Maura wondered just how much of the stout she had left. It was past closing time, but who was going to notice? "Sure." She turned to Mick. "Can you make sure we have enough wood or turf or whatever to see us through until morning?"

"No problem. With all these bodies packed together like sprats, it'll be warm enough. What is it you call it in the States? A slumber party?"

"So I've heard." Next, she asked Rose, "How're we fixed for breakfast?"

"There's a bit of bread I've held back, and butter, but little else," Rose said dubiously.

"Well, nobody's going to starve. Coffee?"

"Plenty. And tea as well."

"Well, there you are. And the sun will come out in the morning and melt all the mess by lunch. Right?"

"We can only hope," Joe said.

Having something practical to do seemed to have energized the men, and there was much banging and crashing going on as they armed themselves with torches and went up the rickety stairs to explore what there was above. At least they sounded happy.

Maura made her way over to Diane, who was leaning against the fireplace surround, her arms wrapped around herself. "I'm sorry I brought all this down on you, Maura," Diane said.

"Hey, I'm not. It's been interesting, at least for me. We could have gone on, but I think everybody's tired, and this seems like a good point to stop. Like Billy said, we're kind of getting out into left field with the theories about what really happened."

"Nothing I haven't thought of myself, sad to say."

"Do you mind my asking—what's your husband like?"

"He's not a bad man. Weak, self-indulgent, irresponsible, maybe. He's been a decent father to his son, though he hasn't seen him often. Since we were both older when we married, I guess we didn't expect or demand much from each other. Someone to go to events or places with. To share the bills. That kind of thing. I know—not very romantic, is it?"

"I'm not the person to ask, Diane," Maura said. "I don't do romance."

"Maybe that's best. But in all fairness, I cannot see Mark killing anyone. He doesn't have it in him. Any more than I do." She cocked her head at Maura. "Do you still believe me after what you've heard?"

"I think so."

Diane nodded once. "What about the others?"

"If we put it to a vote now, I'd say you—or we—have raised some reasonable doubt. But I don't think they'd all support you."

"That doesn't surprise me. I'm not angry at the gardaí, you know. I can follow their reasoning. I was the logical choice. But they failed to make their case because they had no evidence.

Because there was no evidence to be had. Nobody goes away happy."

"Why don't we see what happens in the morning? If nobody brings it up again, we can let it rest."

Diane sighed. "Let them talk if they want. As I said earlier, this may be the only trial I ever get, and if they can find a killer who isn't me, I'll be forever grateful to all of you."

"Fine. I'll go pretend to supervise, I guess. Not that there's much to do. Help yourself to the warmest corner."

Maura slid behind the bar, mostly to keep out of the way as the other men hauled down things she didn't even know she had. Someone had taken the stools and most of the chairs to the back room, out of the way. Billy and Gillian were enthroned by the fire, looking like contented cats. She could see Billy as a judge—wise and fair. Gillian was harder to categorize. At least she looked comfortable.

Funny what a mixed lot they had collected here this evening by random chance. Billy, who had never married but appeared to enjoy the company of women. Gillian, who hadn't planned to marry but now seemed to be backing into some kind of long-term relationship. Jimmy, who'd been married before but who seemed to be reluctant to return to that state, if Rose had it right. Mick? Well, he was the wild card. Maura had no idea what his history with women was, and she wasn't about to ask. He never mentioned relationships apart from the one with his grandmother. And he'd kissed her—a definitely noncasual kiss. As for the rest of the men? Most had signaled that they were or had been married. Probably a good statistical sample.

Diane was the odd person out. Her marriage was not the center of her world, and she claimed she'd looked the other way when her husband had slept around. That didn't win her any points with the guys in the room. Maybe they all secretly wished for something like that, but that didn't mean they wanted to hear it said—much less by a woman who was also a suspected killer. The whole situation was weird all around.

By the time the men were done, the floor was strewn with coats and rugs and other odds and ends, and the guys were bellying up to the bar again for that promised last pint. Maura turned her attention to filling glasses. When everyone who wanted one had a pint, it was close to midnight, but nobody showed any sign of slowing down. Decision time.

"Hey, everyone," Maura said loudly. "You ready to call it a night, or do you want to keep talking?"

"Let's finish this thing!" Seamus called out.

"Everybody willing?" Cheers all around. "Okay, then let's go. Settle somewhere, and there's no penalty if you fall asleep. Now where were we?"

Eighteen

❦

Billy smiled. "Yeh were out in the far field huntin' down crazy theories. Good thing we got rid of the little green men early in the night. Now look for a simple answer, will yeh?"

"But where've we got to go fer it?" Danny complained. "Diane sez she didn't do the deed. Her husband and Sharon's husband were in another country, fer God's sake, and not in possession of a plane or helicopter or hovercraft to make the trip. Can we be sure that Sharon didn't stab herself to death?"

"Twenty times?" Seamus said to him. "Once, mebbe. And if she'd wanted to do herself harm, there were easier ways to do it. Warmer and drier ones as well. Don't they say that most women turn to poison? It's far neater—no mess to clean up."

"That's as may be," Danny protested, "but the woman died, and it was a bloody death. No one saw or heard anything, for it was a dark and stormy night, eh?"

"So let's go back to the basics, okay?" Maura said firmly. "Someone wanted her dead. Why here, in West Cork? Who knew she was at the cottage?"

"Her husband. Some shopkeepers in Schull. Maybe some friends back in England? Some of the neighbors—the gardaí talked to them all, so there'd be a list of 'em somewhere. Diane—and most likely her husband as well," Joe said. Maybe he'd been quiet, but he'd been paying attention.

"Do we know of any other lovers who might have come calling that night?" Maura asked. Nobody had anything to say. "Can we rule that out?"

Diane spoke up for the first time. "For what it's worth, I think she stuck to one man at a time. If you think there might have been another man, that kind of rules out some of the earlier theories, like Sharon being infatuated with my husband. And in case you're wondering, he didn't have enough ready money to be worth blackmailing."

"True enough," Maura admitted. "You know, we never decided whether she had a job when she was at home. Diane, did she ever mention anything like that?"

"She said she came to Cork to forget about the rest of her life. If I recall, it came out during the investigation that she was some kind of counselor or psychiatrist, and she worked with troubled people. It had never come up the few times we'd talked."

"That's what she told the gardaí," Bart agreed.

"Now that's interesting," Maura said, pleased to have any new piece of information at this late hour. "Could any of them been stalking her? Followed her here?"

"I'm pretty sure the gardaí looked and didn't find anything or anyone," Diane told her. "But as we've already said, the gardaí were a bit slow to get started, so someone could have returned to England before they thought to ask. And no one would have known of their connection unless they went through all her patient records back there."

"The gardaí would have interviewed local people, but what would they have done about strangers just passing through?" Maura said, almost to herself. Another example of bias? The gardaí had believed from the start that it was a local crime. She eyed the rest of the people scattered around the room. "Didn't anybody follow this up?"

"You mean, if the woman was a shrink, whether a patient might have pursued her here?" Mick rephrased Maura's question. "It's possible, but it would be all but impossible to check now, twenty years after. And how would he know all the details of the place?"

"Maybe he was obsessive. Maybe he did a lot of research—or stalked her," Maura said stubbornly. "Maybe he contacted her somehow and said it was an emergency and he really, really needed to see her right away. Sure, an ordinary person couldn't have worked it all out, but the information is out there if you look for it."

"A fair point. We'll leave that on the Possible list."

"Damn, I wish we had a whiteboard or something," Maura muttered. "I can't keep all this straight in my head."

"But we do have the drawing paper, Maura," Gillian pointed out.

"So we do. Here, turn a table on its side and attach the paper to it, and then we can make a list of the suspects, with categories like, 'Crazy,' 'Possible,' and 'Likely'? Everybody okay with that?"

"The little green men go in the crazy column?" Seamus asked, grinning.

"Yes, they do. And so does the CIA and the KGB." Damn, she was getting punchy. She watched as a couple of men set up a makeshift whiteboard in front of the bar. Maura filled in the headings. "Okay, does the psycho patient from England go in the Possible column?"

"Until we know otherwise," Mick said.

Maura added "Patient" to the list, then scrawled "Little Green Men" under the Crazy heading. "What now?"

"Put me at the top of the Likely column," Diane said. "I did have motive and opportunity and could certainly have had a knife."

Maura did so, then added Paul Morgan and Mark Caldwell. "But they have alibis!" Danny protested.

"Yes, but they did have motive. And either one of them could have done it under the right circumstances." Then she added "Hired Hit Man" under the Possible heading. "His only motive would be money from whoever wanted Sharon dead. Or maybe someone was holding something over him and made him do it."

"Sharon might have stiffed a local shopkeeper or hired someone to fix up the place and failed to pay him," Bart said, his tone neutral.

Again, Maura wondered if he had information that hadn't come out. "Good point. But would that be enough to kill for?"

"You wouldn't think so, but if it was a good amount of money, and the man was desperate, and she was rude to him or blew him off, he might have done it," Danny said.

"Do we have any reason to believe she was having money troubles?" Still, Maura added "Shop Owner" under Possible. "Anyone else?"

"Mebbe she was being blackmailed?" Joe suggested.

"Someone threatened to tell her husband about her affairs? That assumes he didn't already know. And why kill her, then?"

"She stopped paying out, and the blackmailer was angry?" Joe persisted stubbornly.

"Angry enough to follow her to Cork? Maybe." Maura added "Blackmailer" to the Possible list, but with two question marks. "You know, everybody here has been saying the killer was a man. Apart from Diane, are there no other women to consider?"

"An angry wife?" Liam said.

"But Sharon had moved on to Mark by the time she was killed."

"A disturbed, angry wife with a grudge?" Liam insisted. "Doesn't have to be logical, except in the mind of the killer."

Maura wasn't convinced, but it might be worth considering. "Can we at least agree that a woman could have the strength to kill her with a knife?"

"My wife would!" Seamus called out. Several men laughed.

Maura smiled. "Seriously, Sharon might have been willing to follow a woman out of her house, thinking she wasn't a threat. Even if she was wrong." Something nagged at Maura's memory, but she couldn't pry it loose. "There was no sign of a struggle in the house, right?"

"That's what the papers said."

"And only the one cup and plate by the sink? So she wasn't entertaining anyone. Or if she was, he or she didn't eat or drink anything."

"Right. So?"

"And she was found outside wearing what might be considered nightclothes—or at least clothes she'd wear around the house, not if anyone was going to see her. She cared about her appearance, didn't she, Diane?"

"I would have said so. She always looked nicely dressed when we crossed paths, even when we were only out walking. Not fancy but good quality."

"So she hadn't invited anyone in and hadn't planned to see anyone that night. She expected to be alone. Do we all agree on that?"

"Why's it important?" Danny asked.

"Stick with me a bit longer. When she was found, she was wearing her ratty old sleep clothes, with a sweater or something pulled over it. And boots." *Ah, that was what had bothered her,* Maura realized. "Boots! Okay, she was a woman alone late at night. I don't care how safe West Cork is—this was a woman used to living in a city, and you get into habits if you live like that. You don't trust strangers. You lock your doors, and you make sure you have a peephole or something so you can look out and see who's there before you open it. You watch other people on the street, stick to lighted areas, don't walk alone down dark streets."

"It's not like that here!" Gillian said.

"You're right, it isn't. But habits are hard to break. So picture the scene. Sharon has a nice supper on her own, maybe reads for a while, then goes up to her bedroom and gets ready to go to bed. She's all tucked in when she hears someone knocking at the door. She's not expecting anyone. What would she do?"

"Go down and ask who was at the door," Seamus said promptly.

"Okay—although she'd probably check to be sure the door was locked, just in case. But say she asks that, and she knows who it is, so she opens the door. Or—and here's the catch—she may not know the person, but she doesn't think she has any reason to fear this particular person, and she still opens the door. Are you with me so far?"

"But how does that help us?" Bart asked. "Most of the people on yer list there would fit that description. Her husband, clear enough. Diane or Diane's husband. A garda, looking fer something or someone. A patient, like you suggested, come from England to see her. Some friend we don't even know about, come fer a surprise visit. We're no more forward than we were."

"Except for the boots!" Maura crowed. "She wouldn't be wearing boots to go to bed or to open the door. Everything points to her being upstairs with a book. Then someone comes to the door, and she puts on her boots—and they were lace-up fancy boots, from what I've heard, not just something she could have pulled on fast, like farmer's boots—and she *goes outside with this person, and then she dies!*" Maura finished triumphantly and waited for reactions.

Maybe everyone was stunned or just sleepy: no one said anything. "Oh, come on," Maura said, frustrated. "Not only did she answer the door, but she took the time to put on her boots and went out in the dark and rain with this person. Why would she do that? Who would she do it for?"

"Somebody's kinky idea of fun in the rain?" Jimmy suggested. "They'd tried it on everywhere else they could think of?"

"Get yer mind out of the gutter, Jimmy," Billy said sternly, surprising Maura. "You've made a point, Maura. Had she been found with her feet tore up from the path and no shoes, yeh could see someone surprisin' her at the door and draggin' her out. But the boots put a different face on things."

"Why did nobody ever put this together before?" Diane asked. "I mean, it's just common sense. Why didn't the gardaí see it?"

"Maybe they all sleep in their boots?" Maura quipped. God, she was getting tired.

"But what—and who—could have drawn her out at night like that?" Bart asked.

"Someone in need of help? Sharon wasn't a doctor, now, was she?"

"No, not a medical doctor," Diane said. "But maybe she knew more than the average person or was nearer than any doctors. If someone had been having a heart attack or had OD'd on drugs or there'd been an accident, a person might think Sharon could help if there was no one else to be found quickly. And it must have been an emergency if she didn't take the time to put on her clothes but just grabbed up the boots, which she probably left close to the door."

"Wait—what about her car?" Maura asked eagerly. She was beginning to get excited by this idea. "Did she have one? Was it there?"

"She had a hired car," Diane said, "and it was found next to the house, locked, so she didn't use that. No fast trip to a local hospital—which would have been noticed anyway."

"So if someone had come looking for help, he or she must have driven there—or must have lived very close and walked over."

"No one else took sick or died that night," Seamus said. "The gardaí did check that." Bart nodded in agreement.

"That you know of! If things went really wrong, whoever it was might not have gone to a real doctor or a hospital. Say someone was harboring a fugitive that they didn't want the world to know about. Or they were holding someone captive. Or they were hiding a child they'd been abusing for years. But something bad happened and they panicked, and Sharon was the first person they could think of."

"Maura, yer soundin' like this is an old movie—and a bad one," Mick said. "Mebbe it's time to let it go fer now. We're all tired, and we're not thinking straight. Mebbe things will look clearer in the mornin'."

Maura wanted to protest—*But we're so close!*—but Mick was right. They were all exhausted. But in an odd way, she realized, that let her brain roam more freely, even if it zigged and zagged along the way. Maybe the gardaí had thought of everything she'd brought up—or maybe they hadn't. Why had Sharon carefully laced up her boots in the dead of night and gone outside with someone? What kind of story could that person had given her, knowing that he—or she—planned to kill her? What would Sharon have believed? And why had no one identified that person?

Nineteen

❧

"What if it was a child?" Maura said suddenly. "Lost? That would have attracted Sharon's attention, wouldn't it? She wouldn't know how many children went wandering around in the middle of the night, so she'd believe the story."

"All the children there were accounted for, and there were few enough of those nearby, not that Sharon would know that," Seamus said. "Most of the blow-ins didn't have any children or mix with those who did."

Well, that must have been a strike against them right there, Maura thought. *No wonder they weren't popular.* "Okay, if it wasn't a child, maybe a horse got loose or cows who got onto the road? Or . . . a lost dog?"

"Maura, you'd be askin' us to recall who had a dog the other side of Schull back then? Most farmers then and now had a dog or two, and a cat to keep the mice down," Seamus said, incredulous. "If a dog went missin', like as not it didn't stay missin'. Farm dogs didn't get lost—they roamed about. Nobody's gonna go lookin' fer 'em, much less askin' the neighbors to help find 'em."

Maura hated to give up on her idea. She said stubbornly, "But guys, think about it. What would make a woman get out of her warm bed on a lousy night, open the door to someone, then pull on her boots and go out with that person?"

"The little green men?" Danny asked.

Maura struggled to swallow her frustration. Yes, it was late and they were all tired. And in truth, there was no reason anybody in the room, apart from Diane, should be taking this seriously. Even Diane seemed resigned to whatever happened, and she was on her way to leaving Ireland for good. While the official case might never be closed, it would eventually be forgotten. Why did she care?

Diane seemed to sense her mood and stood up. "Maura, I thank you for what you're trying to do here, but even with your interesting theory, there's not much to be done now. And we're all getting too tired to think straight."

So now Diane wanted to give up too? "Do you think that theory makes sense? That she opened the door to someone she knew, for what she believed was a good reason, never thinking that this person might want to hurt her?"

Diane hesitated, then nodded. "Based on what little I knew of the woman, I agree with what you've said. I'll go along with your idea of someone luring her out of her bed with a story intended to call up her sympathy—a lost animal, a sick child, whatever. But what difference will it make now? And how could it be proved if nobody came forward then?"

Diane had a point, Maura knew. The part about what it would take to get the woman out of her house—that was just logic based on how she thought she herself would react. Had the gardaí thought it through? Hard to say. But it was after that that things got murky. Maura would be happy enough if it turned out to be an outsider who'd done it—but that person would have to have known an awful lot about the place and how to get around and what would work as a story for Sharon. After eliminating Sharon's husband and Diane, that meant it almost had to be a local person who had all that information—and who had an issue with Sharon that they couldn't see a way to resolve without killing her. And it wasn't a real professional job, because the killer could have taken the body away or dumped it in a handy bog where it might not have been found for days or weeks or ever—not just left her outside in a pool of blood. Maybe whoever it was had killed her and then lost his nerve and run away. It would have been messy, with lots of blood.

Billy spoke up suddenly, startling Maura—she'd thought he'd gone to sleep again. "What happened to the land, Diane?"

"Sharon's place?" Diane stopped to think for a moment. "Well, her husband hung onto it while the investigation was going on, which took a while—I think he had to, until he was cleared of her death. But he didn't come back after the gardaí had finished with him. I think he always saw it as Sharon's place, and after she died, maybe he wanted no part of it. At some point, I think he sold it. I can't really say, because I didn't come back myself, and I never saw the man in England."

Billy nodded, digesting that information. "Those neighbors who found Sharon in the morning—what was their name?"

"They were the Laytons—Denis and his wife Ellen, I believe," Diane told him.

"And how was it they came to find Sharon? Was their house near?"

"The next property over, but the houses were half a mile or more apart, I'd guess," Diane said. "You couldn't see from one house to the other. I think they were in their forties then—not young—and his family lived there for generations. They raised dairy cattle, but they always seemed hard up. On the day, they were out early in the morning together. Walking their dog."

Diane stopped abruptly, realizing what she had said. "They had a dog, a spaniel—we mentioned that earlier. It was a female, and they hoped to breed her and sell the puppies. I think they needed the money. The dog had gotten loose once before and came home pregnant, and they were careful not to let that happen again, which is why they stayed with her."

"Why do yeh know so much about their dog, then?" Danny asked.

"I'd see them walking often, usually together. We'd spoken now and then if we passed on the lane. The husband's parents had known my grandparents, and they claimed to remember me when I was young and spent summers there. I can't say that I recalled them, but there was no reason I should. Now and then we'd stop and chat, and they'd tell me about the past. I even thought about taking one of their puppies if they'd ever produced any. But nothing ever came of that."

"So they were out walking that dog early in the morning, and they just happened to find Sharon's body?" Maura asked.

"They'd gone that way before, I'm sure. As we've said, there aren't that many lanes in the area, and they wouldn't have gone across a bog."

"Could Denis Layton have been a lover of Sharon's?"

Diane laughed. "You'd know the answer if you'd met the man. He was a farmer raising cattle. I don't mean to be unkind, but he wasn't much to look at, and he didn't smell very good. Unless Sharon had a mental lapse, I can't picture the two of them together."

"Could Mrs. Layton have suspected such a thing, even if it wasn't likely?" Maura pressed.

"How'm I supposed to answer that?" Diane protested. "I exchanged no more than a few hundred words with either of them. In my judgment, the answer is no."

"But they did have the dog."

"Yes, they had the dog. It was a pretty little thing, but it yapped a lot. Sometimes you'd hear that across the fields."

"Ellen Layton . . ." Billy said out of nowhere. Every time Maura thought he was asleep, he'd come up with something that showed he was following the talk. "Was she a Dempsey before she married?"

Maura swallowed a laugh. There was probably no one in the room who could answer that question except Billy. To her surprise, Jimmy spoke from his corner. "Ellen Dempsey, yah. The Dempseys lived up the Drinagh road, near Minanes. I think my folks went to Ellen's weddin'. Me mam kept saying that Ellen was marrying beneath her. But then, she said that about most women who were marrying then, including Rosie's mother. We married a year or so after Ellen."

Billy nodded. "That would be right. The Dempseys had a nice piece of land, did they not? But when the parents passed, none of the sons wanted to take it on, so they sold it and divided the money. Ellen was married to Denis Layton by then."

"Sounds about right," Jimmy agreed.

"But the Laytons' land," Billy went on, "their grazing was poor, and the fields were smaller. Seems like Denis Layton's father had sold off a field or two to make ends meet before Denis took it on."

"Why do you know that, Billy?" Maura said in spite of herself.

"I know Ellen's ma and da. His folk as well," Billy told her.

Of course—Billy knew everyone who had ever lived nearby. But he'd known about the Layton place only through the local connection. Maura struggled to connect the dots. What were the odds that one of those plots was the one that Sharon and her husband had bought? That would have been in the late 1980s or early 1990s, about the time Ellen and Denis had married. And the Laytons were already struggling then. She looked at Billy, and he returned her look steadily. Challenging her to put the pieces together?

"How did the Morgans come to buy that piece of land?" Maura asked of no one in particular.

"Most likely because the Laytons were sellin' when they were lookin'," Billy told her.

"Did Paul Morgan build his own house? I mean, was there none there before?"

"It was a new house when I knew it," Diane added. "I don't recall if there was anything there in my grandparents' time."

All right, Maura thought. It was a pretty shaky equation, but this wasn't a court of law, and the proof could come later. What did she need to know or confirm?

That the land the Layton family had sold had been bought by Sharon's husband, who had built the holiday house on it early in his construction career. The place where Sharon had been murdered. Obviously Ellen and her husband would have known the land well.

But why kill Sharon? Okay, say the Laytons had struggled financially for years, with poor land, as Billy had hinted. Their dairy business was not particularly successful. Maybe there had been some major expense that nobody knew about, like a health crisis. They were trying to breed some puppies to sell for a little extra cash. But how did that add up to murder?

Still, it might be possible . . . Maybe they'd realized they couldn't manage to graze their cattle on what land they had left, but they'd already sold off a piece to the Morgans. But what if Sharon died a horrible death on that plot of land, and her husband wanted nothing more to do with it and would sell it as fast as he could? Maybe at a reduced rate? And there would be Denis Layton, waiting with an offer in hand, hoping to get his land back cheap. And that timing could be proved—there would be property transfer records somewhere. And if they'd gotten it back, maybe the Laytons had rented out the house—if in fact they'd bought it, after Sharon's death, to bring in a little more cash—that would be easy to check. Win-win for them. After all, Sharon hadn't died in the house, and most tourists wouldn't know the history.

She looked again at Billy. "You think . . . ?"

"I may do," he said. "But that said, the Laytons were and are decent, hardworking people."

"What are you talking about?" Diane asked, bewildered.

Maura scanned the room: everyone looked to be nodding off. She'd already thrown enough off-the-wall ideas at them, and there was no point in tossing this in now. Morning would be time enough, and she needed time to think. She leaned toward Diane. "I've got an idea, but it'll keep until morning. There are still a lot of holes in it. What we all need now is sleep."

Diane gave her a long look, then shrugged. "If you say so."

"For now," she replied. Then she turned back to the group. "I think we've taken this about as far as we can go for now, and you all look wiped out. I know I am. We could all use some sleep, if you can get comfortable on the floor here. We can come back to this in the morning if you want to."

There were some grumblings, but nobody objected. People started sorting themselves out and choosing what they hoped would be the warmest corners.

Bart came over and said softly to Maura, "A word with you?"

Curious, Maura said, "Sure. In the kitchen?"

Bart followed her there, unnoticed by the rest of the people, who were busy trying to get comfortable on a stone floor. "You've done well in there, Maura Donovan."

"Thanks. But you've been pretty quiet, especially since you know more facts about this than anyone else in the room. Do you have a reason for that?"

Bart sighed. "I was new to the gardaí when it happened, as I've said, and heard only bits and pieces at the time. I never did make up my mind who'd done the deed, but I didn't fix on Diane then or now. I think she deserved a fair hearing. But if I open my gob now, people will give what I say more weight than it might deserve. I'm still a garda, and that commands some respect still. So I've held my tongue."

"I see. I appreciate that you've let this go ahead. But if you do know something that goes against what anyone here says, you'll speak up, won't you?"

"That I will. I'd best go find my own space on the floor now before all the good ones are taken."

Maura followed him out to the main room, where the floor was covered with what looked like bundles of old clothes. "Billy, you okay there in the chair?" Maura asked.

"I'm grand. Liam, Donal—yeh've claimed the bed and chair in me place at the end?"

"We have, and many thanks. Is the door locked, then?"

Billy waved his hand. "I've nothin' worth stealin'. But yeh might bring back any food yeh find in the mornin' fer our breakfast."

A smart idea that hadn't occurred to her. Maura opened the front door for the two and pointed to the end of the building. "Think you can make it?"

"No fear we'll get lost. Ta." The two trudged the twenty or so feet to Billy's home, laden with rolled sleeping bags, kicking up snow as they went, like a pair of kids. They disappeared quickly into the snow.

Maura stood a moment outside and breathed in cold, clean air. Was it wishful thinking, or was the falling snow less dense now? Still no lights visible and no sign of any cars or trucks passing on the road. But they had warmth and food, so she couldn't complain.

She was surprised when Mick came out and joined her. "Yer not freezin'?"

"Not yet. It's kind of a relief—I hadn't realized how smoky it was inside."

"Yeh think yeh've figgered something out," Mick said flatly.

"Maybe. Something Billy said . . . No, I'm not ready to talk about it. It may fall apart by daylight."

Mick peered at her between the swirling flakes. "Why is it yeh care so much? Yeh don't know Diane, nor anybody the far side of Skibbereen. What's it matter to yeh?"

Maura wrapped her arms more tightly around herself, staring at the snow blowing across the road. "I'm still working on that. When Diane showed up and I heard her story, I guess I thought two things—assuming, of course, that you believe her when she says she didn't kill that woman, which I do. One, why couldn't the gardaí find a single vicious killer in an area where everybody knows everybody else and watches out for them? And two, why are people still talking about it?"

"The second one's easier to answer. This place isn't filled with violence, like Boston, or even like the North. People do know each other. So when someone dies the way Sharon did, they're troubled. Fearful. Angry. They need to know what happened so they can feel safe again. They need to trust the gardaí."

"Did the gardaí screw up?" Maura asked. "I don't mean any disrespect," she added quickly.

"I think they did the best they could. They weren't prepared for something like this, and then all the press came trampling over the place, which made it harder for them to do their jobs. There were a few problems with who would take charge, as you may have noticed. Not to mention the press keeps draggin' it out again every few years to poke at it. The gardaí would be more than happy to see an end to that."

"Even if it turns out to be a local crime?"

"Someone from the townlands, you mean? It might embarrass them, but they'd want to know. What about that first question of yers? What're yeh thinkin'?"

Maura shook her head. "If the gardaí did their jobs as best they could, how did this one person slip through? I'm not ready to say. We can talk about it in the morning. Right now I need sleep, even if it's on that dirty floor."

Twenty

❧

Maura found a corner without drafts, the one that Diane and Rose had already staked out nearest the kitchen, which after Rose's efforts was still faintly warm. Did that make it the ladies' corner? Maura stoked the fire one last time, then retreated to join the other women. The floor was hard, but they had their coats, and the men between them and the door blocked some of the cold. Unfortunately, more than one of the same men snored, sometimes in chorus. It didn't seem to disturb any of them.

She woke suddenly the next morning, and it took a moment for her to remember where she was and why. She checked the clock: it was nearly eight and growing light outside. It was the light that had awakened her, after too few hours of broken sleep. Not just the ordinary light of dawn, but light reflected off a world that had turned white. Before climbing out from under the coat that covered her, she took stock: most of the men hadn't stirred, nor had Gillian in her chair or Diane. Rose was missing, but Maura assumed that the clattering from the kitchen came from Rose making breakfast. Such as it was—they didn't have a lot to work with.

She tried her best to extricate herself from the pile of bodies without waking anyone, then tiptoed over to the fire to add some more logs. Billy hadn't stirred, but he opened his eyes, then winked at her. "Well done, Maura Donovan," he whispered. "Yeh've kept us warm and entertained, and now the sun's come out."

Maura smiled at him. "I can't take credit for the sun, but thanks for the rest. I'd better use the loo before everybody else wakes up." She picked her way across the floor to the bathroom, where she was pleased to see that the toilet paper supply was holding up. But the tap water was icy, so she settled for splashing her face. She'd only just come out when Liam and Donal, who had taken advantage of Billy's home, surged in through the front door, triumphantly waving bread and butter and some eggs, as if they'd foraged them themselves rather than raiding Billy's pantry. That was enough to wake everyone else. Maura waved at them and pointed them toward the kitchen, then heard Rose greeting them cheerfully.

Pulling her sweater more tightly around her, Maura stepped out the front door and looked around. There were a few tire tracks on the road, although she hadn't heard any vehicles passing. She had no idea what, if any, road-clearing equipment existed in West Cork. Given how rare this kind of snowfall was, as everyone kept telling her, she figured there probably wasn't much. People would simply wait until it melted. Maura could already hear water trickling in the gutters, so maybe it wouldn't take long. Well, at least in town. It could take a lot longer up in the hills, and she wondered when she would be able to get home.

She went looking for Rose in the kitchen. She appeared to be quite happy boiling water for coffee on the back of the stove, which was radiating heat again, and slicing bread. "Shall I scramble the eggs, do yeh think?" she asked, smiling.

"If you want—your choice. What about the bread?"

"There's a bit left, and there's some from Billy's place. If the boys are mad fer toast, let them do it themselves. Let's hope they figgered out how to do it last night, fer there's no room on the cooktop here. At least the coffee will be hot, and if they ask fer tea, I'll hand 'em a tea bag."

Maura laughed. "I think you've got it covered, Rose. You know, you really are amazing, the way you managed the food for everyone."

"Ah, go on," Rose said, clearly pleased.

"You know, we've kind of talked about doing more food here, but I was waiting until I figured out how the pub worked before I decided anything, and I never really looked at the kitchen. But after what you did with so little during the storm, I'm beginning to wonder if it might work. I'm pretty sure there's licensing and inspection stuff to think about, but I wanted to get an idea of what it would cost to set up a real kitchen, not just a collection of semi-antiques. What do you think?"

"Are yeh serious?" Rose looked around the room before answering. "Yer stove there is an antique, but it was enough fer us. You'd have to get a real one, though, if yeh want to think about makin' meals. Electric or gas or whatever. The cooler's old, and it'd be simpler to replace that as well. Yeh've got the sink and water laid in. Would you be wantin' a dishwasher right away?"

"I . . . don't know, Rose. I don't really cook, and I have no idea how a kitchen runs. Could one person handle it all?"

"The right person, mebbe. Who's willin' to work hard. And knows a bit about cookin'."

"You have anybody in mind?" Maura smiled.

"Are yeh askin' if I'm interested?" Rose responded with a smile of her own.

"I might be. If you wanted to move out of your father's house and get a real job."

"It's somethin' to think about. I won't say no. Let's see how long it takes Judith to tie me da down."

"No rush. I'm just trying to look at my options. Of course, I have no idea if it would make any money or even pay for itself."

"There's books you can get that'd tell you how to plan fer yer costs and such," Rose said quickly.

"And you might happen to have one of those?"

"I might," Rose admitted.

Maura nodded. "Well, then, maybe I could borrow it one of these days. Just to look at."

"I'd be happy to lend it to yeh," Rose said.

"We'd better be getting back," Maura said. "At least we all made it through the night without freezing."

In the front room, people were starting to stir. Seamus, Danny, and Joe looked none the worse for a night on the floor. The four wedding boys resembled young chickens, kind of rumpled but cheery. Billy cracked one eye open at her and smiled.

"I'm hopin' the folk up in the hills have fared as well."

"From what I've seen, a lot of the older houses are more ready to handle power failures than the newer ones as long as they have fuel handy, and most of them do."

"That's a fair point. I'm sure Mick'll be wantin' to see how his grannie's doin'."

"I don't blame him. There aren't a lot of people in walking distance up on that hill, so it's hard to ask someone to check on her. But she's probably been through this before, many times."

Mick joined them, so Maura asked, "How long before the lanes are clear?"

"When God decides," he said, and Maura wasn't sure he was joking. "There'll be no school today—the buses can't get up the lanes."

"No snowplows, huh?"

"In Skibbereen, maybe. Not off the main road here."

"What'll I do with this bunch?" Maura waved vaguely toward the front room, half of whom were still cocooned in their coats and whatever else they had scrounged to sleep on or under.

"Yeh've plenty of fuel—you should add some to the fire. If it's food yer worried about, Rosie's got it in hand, what with Billy's supplies. Rosie, yer doin' a grand job with little to work with."

Rose beamed at him. "Thank you, Mick!"

"You're right—she is," Maura said firmly. "You make it look easy, Rose. I'd love to see what you could do with a real kitchen."

Rose blushed and turned her attention to slicing bread. "Ah, go on with yeh. I'm just doin' what I do fer me da every day, except for ten times the number."

"Well, thank you for pitching in. Which is more than I can say for most of the guys out there. Mick, do we need to clear the walk in front or just wait? And do we have to worry about opening hours?"

"Yer plannin' to serve 'em pints fer breakfast?" Mick quirked an eyebrow at her.

"No, of course not. Normally we'd be opening at ten thirty, but I don't think today is exactly normal. Maybe I'm more worried that whatever license I have covers serving food. Not that I've read it or anything."

"I'm thinkin' the gardaí may have bigger problems than worryin' about you servin' toast. If they come pokin' around, tell 'em it's a private party and yeh forgot to get the special license."

"I will. It's more or less true anyway. Can you remember a storm like this?"

"As a kid, maybe, but they all seemed bigger then. Not often, fer sure."

"Coffee's ready," Rose announced, "and I've sliced all the bread. If the guys want it toasted, they're on their own."

"Fair enough. Go on and tell them—I'll be out in a minute," Maura told her. She watched as Rose juggled a plate stacked with bread and a large aluminum coffee pot she'd found who knew where, then was greeted with cheers in the front room. Then she turned back to Mick. "You think it's worth going on with what we started last night—with Diane, I mean—or should we just let it rest?"

Mick didn't answer right away. Finally, he said, "Yeh've raised some good points, I'll admit. Like who'd the woman open the door to. And the boots. That kind of says that she went out by choice, but she didn't expect to meet her death. Why not leave it to Diane? It's her life, after all. She's sold the old farm, and she's ready to close the door on all of it."

"Fair enough. It's not really my problem, is it?"

"Yeh seem to have made it your own, Maura. Why would that be?"

"If Diane is innocent, if the gardaí got it wrong, I think that should come out, I guess. Nobody's managed to prove she did it, but it's screwed up her life anyway. That doesn't seem right. And I guess I have to wonder if that's because she was an outsider. Like me."

"She's no more or less an outsider than yeh are—both of yez have grandparents from here."

"That's true—I hadn't looked at it that way. Look, if she says no to it, I'll let it go. We've got enough to worry about today."

She headed into the front room, where most people were now upright and looking busy. Several were seated along the bar with coffee mugs in their hands—Rose had apparently managed to wash all those up the night before. Someone had added plenty of fuel to the fireplace. Billy was still in his favorite place, and Gillian had reclaimed the matching chair on the other side of the fireplace. Rose looked like she was having a good time managing the guys who wanted to toast their bread, making them line up and be patient as she doled out long-handled forks.

Diane too had a coffee mug in hand but was standing in the corner, watching warily. Did that signal that she was retreating again? Maura decided that she might as well find out what she wanted now, before someone else brought it up. She made her way over to the woman. "How you doing this morning?"

"Stiff, I guess. Thanks for the coffee. You have any idea when we'll be able to get out of here?"

"If it was Boston, I might be able to guess, but this is my first winter here. Mick says it doesn't happen often, so probably most people don't have a clue about what to do."

"I guess I wouldn't either," Diane said. "Listen, Maura, about last night . . ."

"Look, Diane, if you don't want to talk about it anymore, that's okay. Or if you'd rather talk just to me or someone else instead of to the whole group, that's fine too. Your call."

Diane hesitated. "I'd have to say I'm of two minds about going forward. I've spent a lot of my life trying to put this behind me, and if I'd had any sense, I probably could have found a solicitor in Schull or Cork city and sold the place without leaving England. Instead, I chose to come back. Maybe it was a silly, sentimental choice, but I remember being happy on the farm when my grandparents were alive. I guess I wanted to see for myself if I could call up anything like that again."

"And you decided to sell," Maura said.

"I did, but it doesn't make me happy. The thing is, even if my name was cleared—if the real killer was found and convicted—I'm not sure it would change anyone's mind around here. I've been their favorite suspect for nearly twenty years. That's a whole generation."

Maura chose her words carefully. "I see what you're saying, but that cuts both ways. I've been here less than a year, but people remember my family—the good things. They've helped me a lot from the day I arrived because of who my grandmother was. I wouldn't still be here if they hadn't—I'd never planned to stay."

"And how does that apply to me?" Diane asked.

"Because you do have roots here. People knew your grandparents and the history of the land, right? Were they good people? Honest, hardworking, all that stuff?"

"They were, I'd say. You're telling me that's what people will choose to remember, rather than the fact that a lot of them believed I could kill someone I barely knew?"

"Maybe. Like I said, I'm the new kid here, so I'm not going to guess how those people out there feel. It's up to you to find out which side they'll land on. You walk away, you close that door. What have you got to lose by wrapping up what we started last night?"

Diane smiled. "Ah, Maura, I wish you'd been here back when it all happened. You would have cut through all the fuss."

Maura smiled back. "I'd have been six years old and totally useless to you. But I know what you mean. You want to kick this off?"

"Why not?" Diane stepped out of the corner and stood in front of the fire, waiting until she had the attention of most of the room. "Folks, last night we all took a long, hard look at Sharon Morgan's murder, the one people think I committed twenty years ago. With Maura's help, I think you all came up with some new ideas, things that weren't seen back then. It looks like we'll be stuck here a bit longer, until the roads are cleared, so I'm asking you now—do you want to see this through? Or maybe I should start with the question, how many of you still think I did it?"

There were some furtive glances exchanged, and a couple of the men raised a hand.

Diane pressed on, "How many of you think I didn't?" Three or four hands went up, including Rose's and Gillian's.

"How many of you haven't decided?" At least half the hands went up.

"Fair enough—and that's better than it was when we started. Okay, last question: how many of you want to see if you can figure out who else might have done it, if it wasn't me?"

After a long moment, a majority of the hands crept up. "If it don't take too long," Danny called out.

"It's been an open case fer close to two decades," Mick said. "Now yeh want an answer in an hour or two?"

"Hey, we did all the hard stuff last night," Maura informed him. "There's not many suspects to choose from."

Diane smiled. "Thank you, Maura. You want to summarize what we've figured out so far?"

How had she gotten herself into this? She was lousy at civics and hated public speaking, and now she was defending a suspected murderer. Had she skipped that page in the pub owners' handbook? She cleared her throat. "Okay, guys, don't throw things at me—I'm not good at this. I think what we figured out last night was a couple of important things that a woman might think of but not a man."

A couple of the men in the room booed, but they were smiling.

"Give the lady a chance," Billy said, and the noise subsided.

"Thank you, Billy. One, Sharon wouldn't have opened the door to just anyone—a stranger in a ditch, say. She wasn't a very friendly type of person, and she was a woman alone at night, so she would have been cautious. You all buy that?"

Most people nodded.

"So for her to open the door late at night, she would have to have trusted whoever was at the door. Either it was another woman, which didn't frighten her, or it was someone she knew."

"Diane fits that, right?" one of the naysayers called out.

"Yes, she does, but we're looking at other possibilities right now, okay? So this person comes to the door, and Sharon opens it to him or her, and the person tells her a story—there's some kind of trouble, and can Sharon help? So Sharon puts on her outside boots—and that's a big red flag for me. She's in her at-home grubbies and she doesn't change, which to me makes it look like she's in a hurry, but she stops long enough to sit down and pull on her high boots and lace them up before she goes out. What does that tell you?"

"She was going somewhere mucky?" Bart suggested.

"Yes, or at least on uneven ground. She had a car—why didn't she take that?"

"It wasn't far? Or whatever the emergency was, it was someplace a car couldn't go?"

"Right. Maybe both. Someone came and asked for her help and needed it fast. This person couldn't handle whatever it was by himself. Or herself. Sharon was the closest person to ask. She said yes, she'd help. So she puts on her boots and goes out with this person into the dark and rain. And she only makes it as far as the end of her property, close to a regular path where somebody was likely to find her. She's stabbed many times. She doesn't seem to have put up a fight. Nobody found the knife. Nobody could give any reason she would be where she was found."

"What about the mystery lover?"

"If there was a lover. Look, she was home alone. Wouldn't it have been a lot easier to invite him in, where it was warm and dry?"

"Maybe he liked to do it in the rain?"

There were a few sniggers at that comment. "With the woman wearing boots?" Maura shot back. "Let's keep it clean, boys. Seriously, what reason would a lover have had to take her outside? No, I think somebody made up a reason to get her out of the house. Someone who knew she was there alone. Someone who knew what her soft spots were and what she would be willing to help with. Someone who was angry enough at her to stab her over and over again, after convincing her that someone needed her help. Someone who planned this whole thing." Maura looked over the crowd: everyone seemed to be paying attention. "The question is, who was that person?"

Twenty-One

~

"Yeh know," Jimmy said suddenly, "it still comes back to the motive. Why'd this person do it?"

"You're right, Jimmy," Maura said, trying to encourage his participation if he was going to be serious about it. "We haven't given him one yet. Is there something about Irish law that says motive doesn't matter? Or can't be considered?"

Jimmy waved a hand dismissively. "We're not in a courtroom here, are we now? What's important to most ordinary people is knowing *why* someone would do such a thing. Even if the reason only makes sense to whoever done it, and they're seriously messed up in the head—it has to make sense to someone. Nobody is sitting in front of the fire and suddenly sez, 'I do believe I feel like murderin' someone.' There's got to be a reason. And some time to think about it. So this guy makes up his mind, 'I want to murder Sharon or whoever because . . .' and once he's worked that out in his head, he goes on, 'And the best way to do it would be . . .' Am I right? It's not like a fight in a pub that gets out of hand, and one guy grabs up a chair and whacks his mate over the head with it. Somebody had to give this murder some thought. And he had to have a reason," Jimmy finished triumphantly.

It was possibly the longest single speech Maura had ever heard Jimmy make—and he had boiled down the situation pretty well. Motive might not be a legal issue, but it certainly was a human one. People wanted to believe that most killers had a reason to kill, not just a random urge to end a life. And this particular murder didn't offer many options for motive. Maybe in the beginning of the investigation somebody—garda or journalist—had hinted that it was all about sex, and that had made people uncomfortable, and they hadn't looked any harder. "Oh, right, it was all about the adultery, enough said." Since the two husbands had solid alibis, Diane had been next in line as a target, as the wronged wife. They might have assumed that her husband's affair would have made her angry if her husband was really messing around with Sharon, and that was enough motive. At least nobody had tried to manufacture evidence—it could have been worse.

"So where's that list we made?" Diane asked. "I seem to remember we eliminated quite a few people. Who's left that fits with this new point of view?" She sounded no more than mildly curious, rather than eager.

Billy fished around behind his chair and pulled out the slightly rumpled piece of paper. "Would this be it?" he asked.

"It is, Billy." Maura smoothed it out and laid it on a table. "So last night—possibly under the influence of drink—we decided that the two husbands were the most likely suspects if we set aside Diane, but they both had alibis, and even though we tried really hard to put them in two places at once, it didn't work. Our Possible list has a former patient of Sharon's, over from England; a hit man hired by one or the other husband; a local shop owner that Sharon hadn't bothered to pay; a black-mailer of some sort; and a neighbor with some kind of emergency. Remember that the gardaí never found a stranger that fit the bill. Anybody want to add someone else?"

"Who was it that said, 'The simplest solution is usually the right one'?" Bart asked.

"Sherlock Holmes?" Liam called out.

"Nah, some ancient philosopher or somethin' long before Sherlock," Bart replied. "Don't they teach you kids anything in school these days?"

Maura ignored Bart's comment. "And which of these candidates is the simplest solution?"

"The neighbor with a problem," Jimmy said.

"Right," Maura said. "But the gardaí talked to all the neighbors, didn't they?"

"Of course they did," Bart said, sounding a bit defensive. "Many times over. The local gardaí did, and then those from the other stations as well."

"And nobody the gardaí talked to looked likely to them," Maura said. "There were no accidents reported, no medical emergencies, and no missing kids or even a cow. How many of those neighbors had dogs?"

Men looked at each other and shrugged. "Like we said last night, if it was a farm, there'd be a dog or two," Joe said.

Maura refused to be discouraged. "The Laytons lived closest. We know the Laytons had a dog, and they walked their dog near Sharon's house a lot of the time. That's how they found the body."

"That's right," Seamus agreed. "But why would they kill the woman and then just happen to find the body?"

"You tell me," Maura challenged. "What did the Laytons tell the gardaí?"

Seamus stretched and looked up at the ceiling. "Seems I remember Ellen Layton had hysterics and had to be put to bed. It were her husband called the gardaí, back at their house."

Which left Sharon's body unguarded for a while, Maura realized. But then, it had been unguarded all night anyway—what was another hour or two? "Did the gardaí stop first at their house to talk to them?"

"Must've done, wouldn't they?" Seamus said. "If Ellen was too gutted to hang around near the body. So Denis got her calmed down at the house, then showed the gardaí where to find Sharon."

"Did they talk to Ellen that day?"

"Not much to be told, is there? They were walking the dog, like they often did. They found Sharon, dead. Ellen went to pieces, and Denis took her home and made his call. Her story never changed, nor did her husband's. What's it matter when they were asked?"

"Think about it," Maura said impatiently. "Who could be better to report finding Sharon? They had every reason to be there, since they lived next door—they often walked their dog past Sharon's house. If their footprints and stuff were found on the scene, they had the perfect excuse. And if they had carried away any evidence from the killing, like blood on their clothes or shoes, they had plenty of time to clean it up or get rid of the clothes or whatever. And plenty of time to sort out their stories."

"But they were nice people!" Seamus protested.

"And Sharon wasn't?"

"The people there knew the Laytons. They didn't know Sharon near as well," Seamus said.

"What about yer precious motive, then?" Jimmy asked.

"We kind of talked about that last night—the land," Maura said impatiently. "Look, I didn't grow up around here, but from listening to a lot of you, I get the idea that land really matters to you, or to your families. I mean, you know who owned which field a century ago. Am I wrong?"

"Yer not, Maura," Seamus said. "I can't speak for the towns, but in the country it matters who owns what. People who build new homes here often as not build right next to or even over top of the old family cottage. So yeh may be on to somethin'."

"Thank you, Seamus." Maura turned back to the group to appeal to them. "We may not have all the facts, but isn't it possible that the Laytons bought back the field for their cattle business and got it cheap? It's simple enough to check property records, isn't it? That would be a motive, sort of." *Even if it was a long shot,* Maura added to herself.

"Mebbe, or not," Seamus said. "If yeh'd met the Laytons, yeh'd have a hard time seein' them as plotters and schemers, much less killin' anyone. And they were strapped for money, so how'd they manage to buy anything?"

"Seamus, I don't know. I'm just looking for possibilities. Do they still live there?"

"They do—or rather, the missus does. The mister died a few years back."

"So at least they managed to keep the business going back then. Which one of them could have done it?"

"Yeh mean the killing?" Bart said. "Denis or Ellen? The gardaí took a hard look at 'em at the time, since they were first on the scene, but it went no further. Hard to see either one doin' somethin' like that."

But they could see Diane doing it? "Do you know what a killer looks like, any of you? Bart? Seamus? Or look at it from the other side: can you imagine yourself killing anyone under just the right conditions?"

Some of the men exchanged glances. "In the heat of the moment, mebbe," Bart said. "Happens now and then. But planning it out ahead? Not likely. And of this lot, I'd know best how to do it. The rest of 'em would just muck it up."

"Fair enough. But somebody planned Sharon's murder. They knew she'd be alone. They knew she'd help if they appealed to her the right way. They brought the knife with them and then hid it so well, it's never been found. They made sure there was no evidence."

"And yer claimin' that Ellen or Denis Layton could've pulled this off?" Bart asked.

"Hey, you know I don't know either one of them. I don't know what kind of physical shape they were in or if either one of them could have stabbed Sharon more than once. Maybe it took the two of them working together. Maybe they planned to move Sharon's body but found they didn't have the strength to do it."

"Denis coulda dragged a heifer—he was a dairyman. Sharon woulda been easy fer him to shift," Joe said. "Mebbe Ellen too, back when I knew her."

"Okay. Maybe Ellen was the brains and Denis was the muscle. Or maybe it was always the plan to leave Sharon where she was found. Or they were making it up as they went. I can't say. But for now, are you willing to believe it's possible?"

"Say we do believe yeh—and I'm not saying we do—what is it you hope to do wit' this idea of yours?" Seamus asked.

It was a reasonable question, and suddenly Maura felt deflated. She hadn't thought that far, and she didn't know how police procedures worked in Ireland. Maybe in the back of her mind, she'd thought she'd just hand the solution to Sean and let him worry about the details. Or maybe she hadn't thought at all. "I . . . don't know. I'm not from here, remember? Does a murder case remain open forever until it's solved? Is there a special group that looks at cold cases? There's got to be a process for telling the gardaí, isn't there? Bart, can you tell me what has to happen?"

Bart gave her a long look. "Yer sayin' you think what you and this lot have worked out in the dead of night is strong enough to take to the gardaí and ask to reopen the case?"

"Are you telling us it's not?" Maura countered.

"You know who yeh can ask, Maura," Mick said neutrally.

"You mean Sean Murphy?" Bart said. "He was in nappies when all this happened. I'd have a better shot at makin' someone listen to me. If I thought yeh had a case."

"Sean's a garda now, and he's smart," Mick said. "And he's closer to the place than you are now, Bart. Convince him, Maura, and he'll take it to his boss. Maybe he's the best man fer it, since he has no horse in this race."

"What do you mean?"

"He wasn't involved in the past, no more than you were, so he can see it new, like."

Now Maura was torn between the two men. "Bart? You think we're way off base? I mean, I don't want to do an end run around you or push you to do something you don't want to. And I don't want to put Sean in an awkward position either. It's just that I know Sean. *And* his boss." She wasn't about to explain how and why to Bart.

"I'm not sayin' yer wrong, Maura," Bart told her. "Just that I'd look like a right fool if I took it back to my station and pretended we'd solved the whole thing overnight."

"But you were part of the investigation!"

Bart sighed. "I was, but I was at the bottom of the heap. I never saw anything that someone else didn't hand me to copy or file."

"Would Sean be risking his job if he poked this too hard and someone who did cover something up got mad? Either that or he'd look like he's sucking up, trying to make himself look good by solving this." Maura really wasn't sure which side of the argument she was on, and she knew she wasn't making much sense. Yes, she had a connection to Sean, but he was pretty junior at the Skibbereen station. Although Bart seemed to know who he was. Why? What would Sean do if she handed him their proposed solution to the case? Laugh at her or take it to the next level? She'd had some interactions with his boss,

Detective Inspector Patrick Hurley, and she thought he was a fair and honest man—and he'd believed her in the past when he had little reason to. Had he been involved in the original murder investigation? Did he have any kind of stake in solving this? Or covering it up?

She looked up to find most of the people in the room staring at her. How long had she been thinking? "Any ideas?" she asked.

"Give it a rest, and think on it some more," Mick said gently. "The gardaí will be busy enough sorting out the snow and all, makin' sure people are all right and safe. There'll be car crashes on the roads, no doubt. And the power's not even back yet. Give yerself a day or two. Nothing's gonna change."

Maura didn't want to give up, which surprised her. "Okay, this is where I think we are. The Laytons, husband and wife, are the best fit for our killer. You can tell me all you want that they're nice people and couldn't possibly have done this. But the logic is there." She scanned the ragtag group. "So here's the big question: do you think this is enough to take to Garda Sean Murphy? And if he says we're all crazy, it ends there. Bart thinks no. Diane, what do *you* want?"

Maura wanted to be sure that she wasn't coming off as a know-it-all, thinking she could walk in and solve a murder that had happened twenty years ago, in the course of one night. And on top of that, it wasn't her decision to make. She turned to face Diane. "Do you want me to take this to the gardaí, Diane? Or you can ask Bart to do it, if he's willing. There's nothing that says we have to, and it may stir up things for you that maybe you'd rather let alone. It can end here. Your choice."

Diane didn't answer immediately, taking a moment to study Maura's face. "Do you know, nobody ever took my side in this? Like I told you, my husband thought it was a grand joke, maybe because it kept people from looking too hard at him. I've made my peace with that—with him. I've gone on living my life, and I've no complaints. But I didn't kill Sharon, which means someone else did, and that person is still free. That's wrong. Is there anything to be gained by opening it all up again? Only justice. If you believe that matters."

"Is that a yes?" Maura asked.

"I suppose it is. If the gardaí don't want to touch it, you've done your part, Maura, and I'm grateful."

Maura turned back to the rest of the group, sitting or slouching around the room. "What about you guys? Do you think the story hangs together? Or were we just tired and bored and spinning tales last night? I'm not going to stick my neck out and then have all of you change your minds if someone comes to talk with you."

Glances were exchanged. Finally, Seamus spoke. "I think yeh've done a grand job of setting out the facts, Maura. And now that we look back at it, mebbe some angles were overlooked. Nobody's fault, just the way things were then. Mebbe it's worth takin' another look." He shifted his gaze to Bart. "You're the garda here, and you know the story from both ends. What's to be done?"

Bart was shaking his head before Seamus had stopped speaking. "It's not enough. Ye've given it yer best shot, all of yez, but most of what yeh've got is wild guesses and maybes. I'd be laughed out of the station."

Even though she'd expected that reaction, Maura felt a sharp stab of disappointment. She glanced at Diane, but Diane didn't look either surprised or upset. So this really was the end of the story?

Bart must have noticed her reaction, because he said kindly, "Take it to your friend Murphy, if you want, Maura, and see what he thinks. But he may tell you the same thing that I have, and that'll put an end to things once again."

Time to let it go, Maura. "Thank you. What you say is fair. Like I've said before, I'm the outsider, and I'd never heard of any of this before. I'm not going to pretend that I can see what a lot of gardaí and other people missed, but I've got fresh eyes and a different view of procedures, and that might be worth something. Plus, times have changed. So I might as well talk to Sean, off the record, kind of, and if it doesn't work out I'll let it go. Thank you all for at least giving it a shot. And thank you, Diane, for letting us pick your life apart—again."

"You mean well, Maura," Diane told her. "I hope you're right in your conclusions, but I've lost nothing if it ends here. I want to thank the rest of you as well."

Maura looked out the front windows and saw a car passing on the road, then another, and black pavement could be seen under the snow. A few people were standing in front of their homes or shops and shaking their heads. Life was resuming in Leap.

"If yeh've a shovel or a broom handy, we'll see to clearing in front of the place," Joe volunteered.

"If you'll clear the front so nobody breaks their neck getting in, I'd be grateful," Maura said.

Rose emerged from the kitchen, drying her hands on a tea towel. "I had flour and butter, so there're scones in the oven," she announced. "They'll be ready when you are."

And just like that, the men in the room were suddenly in action after their long night cooped up in the pub.

Twenty-Two

～

True to her word, Rose had a plate of scones steaming on the bar when the men tromped in, stamping what was left of the snow from their shoes or boots, jostling each other like boys. The fresh air and exercise had clearly done them good. Rose had also managed to make another pot of coffee and scramble some of the eggs from Billy's place.

As the men charged toward the bar, grabbing up plates, Maura slid behind it. "Rose, you are amazing. Yesterday, you weren't even sure that stove worked, and today you've produced a meal."

"We've the same type of stove at home. It's easy. I could show you how it works."

Maura laughed. "You know I don't cook. I'll leave it for you. But thank you for working things out."

After most of the men had helped themselves, Maura took a serving and went over to where Diane was sitting. She looked a lot more relaxed than she had the day before.

"You look better," Maura said as she sat down. "Or maybe more peaceful."

Diane smiled. "Actually, I don't know what I feel. You did a great job, Maura, but even so, the solution you've proposed seems kind of weak. I remember the Laytons, and I have trouble seeing them as killers. If some larger animal attacked their dog, maybe—they loved that animal. But to sit and plot a murder? It's hard to imagine."

"I understand, Diane, really. But Sharon died. That's a fact, like it or not."

"I know, I know. But over a piece of land? I can't really buy that."

"Look, I haven't been in Ireland long, but I have seen that people are really attached to their land, and so were most of their ancestors. I know that where I come from, there isn't the same kind of emotional connection—you buy a place to live, or to impress other people, or as an investment, but you're usually not heartbroken when you sell it. Not that I have any experience with all that—we always rented, and we moved several times."

"I guess I don't feel that either, Maura. I know the old place mattered to my grandparents, and they were very proud when they could leave it to me. But it hasn't been part of my life for a long time. I think it's time to let it go."

"What are you going to do now?" Maura asked, forking up eggs. She hadn't realized how hungry she was.

"I'll have to see what flights are available now."

"So you're leaving the country like you planned?"

Diane didn't meet Maura's eyes. "I appreciate what you've tried to do, Maura, but I don't see that it changes anything. Yes, I'm going home."

"Why'd you wait so long to sell your property?" Maura demanded.

"Sentiment? Selling it meant the real, final end of the whole thing, and I needed that. It's all right, Maura—I'm not disappointed, and I'm glad you tried. But once the phones and the power are back, I think I'll be going."

Maura battled mixed feelings. Maybe she was just thinking like an American, trying to fix things, but this wasn't her problem to fix. So why did she still want to?

No matter what Diane or the rest of them said, Maura was going to talk to Sean. Off the record. He might be young, but he was smart, and she trusted his judgment. If he said there was nothing to be done, she'd accept that.

Maura turned to the others in the room, who had been busy pretending they weren't listening to what Maura and Diane were saying. "Okay, gang, where are we?"

"Fair to middlin', I'd say," Jimmy volunteered. "A few dishes and glasses to be washed. And the stuff we trucked down fer sleepin' should go back to where it came from, upstairs. There's no more food, of course."

"Of course, but when did we turn into a restaurant? The rest of the shops should be open sometime today, and people can look out for themselves. So do we open as usual, with or without power?"

"We can do," Mick said. "As long as the taps keep workin' and we don't run out of drink. We're lucky we had a shipment last week, so we're good."

Maura checked the time. "It's, what—ten o'clock now? You can go home if you want, you know."

"There's no assurance that the lanes are clear, Maura, whatever the state of the main road," Mick reminded her. "Better we stay here fer a bit and see how it goes."

"Oh. Right. Tell me again that this kind of snow is rare around here?"

"Indeed it is," Jimmy said. "And there'll be plenty of talk about it later in the day. By the time the lads are done, there'll be a dozen feet of snow in the story, and the winds blowin' up a gale."

Maura noticed the young guys from the wedding party were now upright and scarfing down whatever food was left. They didn't look hungover—but they were guys, and they were young. Maura almost laughed—they were no more than a couple of years younger than she was, but next to them she felt old. "Joe?" she called out. "Will you get these guys home when the roads are open? Or wherever they're going?"

"No worries. And I've got help to get Bart's car out of the ditch."

With two more items settled, Maura made her way over to where Gillian sat and dropped into a chair. "How're you holding up?"

"A bit stiff after a night in your chair, but otherwise all right."

"Will you be going back to the manor house?"

Gillian looked uncertain. "I'm waiting to hear from Harry first, I suppose. No messages yet. And I don't know if anyone will have cleared the drive to the house. It's a long one, as you know, and there's only Tom O'Brien to see to it. But I guess it's more than that. As I said, Eveline has been happy about the baby, but the O'Briens think I'm an evil slut taking advantage of Harry. I don't feel like being cooped up with them in the house. May I just hang out here with you while I wait for Harry?"

"Of course you can," Maura said promptly. "But we're going to need to find more food at some point." She turned to Billy, dozing in the adjoining chair. "Billy, I'm sorry we cleared out your pantry. I'll make sure to replace whatever we ate." Maura didn't know the facts, but she guessed that Billy got by on a rather meager income, plus the free housing she gave him—not that she begrudged him that. He was definitely an asset to the pub, and he might be reluctant to take charity for playing the ongoing role of Wise Old Irish Codger.

He opened one eye and smiled at her. "I'm sure yeh'll make things right, my dear."

Maura looked up to Sean Murphy knocking at the front door, and she hurried to let him in. "Sean! How's the snow cleanup going? Would you like some coffee?"

"I can't stay, Maura—I'm only doin' the rounds to make sure everyone is all right and to see what will be needin' fixin'. How'd you pass the night?"

"We had a slumber party," Maura told him. When he looked blank, she said, "A sleepover? Anyway, the staff was all here and a bunch of other people who got stranded, so we just settled in for the night. We even put together some soup for people."

"Grand. So yeh've had no problems, then?"

Maura smiled. "For once, the fact that Old Mick never changed much helped us. He even left some kerosene lamps in the cellar, and we had plenty of fuel for the fire. We were fine."

"Then I'll be on my way to check on people who might not have fared so well."

"Let me walk you out," Maura said quickly, then followed him out the front door. "Listen, there's something I need to talk to you about. Not right now, obviously, because I know you're busy. But soon. Can you let me know when you've got some free time?"

"Is this police business, Maura?" he asked.

"In fact, it is. It'll keep, but it's important or I wouldn't be asking."

"Then I'll get back to yeh when I can, but I can't say when that might be. It's good that your lot came through the night so well, but there may be others who didn't."

"I understand. You go take care of your business. And thanks for checking on us, Sean."

She watched him trudge through what remained of the snow to his car and head back toward Skibbereen, skidding only slightly as he pulled away from the curb. Across the street, Anne Sheahan was sweeping off the front steps of the hotel. "Is everythin' all right?" Anne called out.

"We're fine here. You?"

"No worries. Yeh might have heard us singin' in the back, once we opened up the bar to all."

"Sorry I missed it. Listen, how're you fixed for food?"

"We're managin'. Yer out, I'm guessin'?"

"Pretty much. But we'll pay for whatever we eat."

"Come over when you've time, and you can see what's left. We'll settle up later. See you!" Anne took one last swipe at the snow and disappeared inside.

After she'd shut the door behind her, Maura told the group, "Anne says she'll feed us if we're desperate." Once again, she looked around the pub, trying to figure out how to keep herself busy since she couldn't go home and get some much-needed sleep and take a shower. She was interrupted by a knock on the door and turned to see Harry, looking haggard, and Maura guessed quickly that that was due to more than the weather. She opened it quickly. "Come in, please. Are the roads okay?"

"The main roads are fine, so long as you watch for ice. Let's hope the temperature doesn't drop." He looked past her. "Ah, Gillian, I thought I'd find you here. We need to talk."

Gillian looked at his pinched face and stood up, "Of course. May we use the kitchen, Maura? I'm guessing it's warmer than the back room."

"Sure, go ahead. Harry, is . . . ?" She didn't want to finish the question: *is Eveline gone?* Maura had met her a time or two and had been impressed by the old woman, who was more open-minded than her staff, apparently.

Harry nodded. "She is. It was an easy passing. Now I've a hundred things to do, but I need to talk to Gillian first, if you don't mind."

"Go, both of you."

They disappeared into the kitchen. "That's sad, even if we were expecting it," Maura said to no one in particular.

"She was a good woman," Billy said softly. "We won't see her like again."

"It'll mean some changes to the village, yeh know," Mick said.

Maura felt a flash of annoyance. "No, I don't know, because I haven't thought about it. I know the place itself will be turned over to the National Trust. Is that what you're talking about?"

"Mostly. Depending on what's done with it, it could bring in more tourists. They pass through here anyway, and if a historic manor house tempts them, they might stay on a bit, maybe stop in here at Sullivan's."

"Mick, Eveline's only just gone. I thought things moved slowly in Ireland. Are we going to see the National Trust sniffing around here this week?"

Mick's mouth quirked in a half smile. "I'd say that's not likely, but it depends on what documents were drawn up, whenever that happened. Within the year, mebbe?"

"Then we'll deal with that when it happens," Maura told him firmly. "And no, I'm not going to turn this into a Quainte Countrie Pub anytime soon, not just for tourists who may not show up."

"Nor would I expect yeh to. Just keep yer ears open, will yeh?"

"Don't I always?"

Gillian and Harry emerged from the back room. Harry gave Gillian a quick kiss, nodded at the rest, and hurried out the front door, leaving Gillian behind. Maura went over to her and said in a low voice, "Everything okay?"

"Yes. And no. I don't know. Harry's gone off to see Eveline's solicitor and then arrange for her burial, so we might know more later. He thought it made more sense for me to stay here with you than to go with him or to go back to the house. But he surprised me with something I hadn't expected."

"Are you going to tell us, or is it a big secret?" Maura asked.

"I don't think it's a secret, just not settled quite yet." Gillian raised her voice. "If you want to know what's going on, you might as well gather 'round." She waited while the others approached, although Diane stayed in the far corner. "As some of you may know, Eveline Townsend had use of the manor house for her lifetime, but now it reverts to the National Trust. Which means that Harry and I are out of a place to live, although the Trust won't be taking over tomorrow—we don't know exactly when, which is one reason Harry's gone on to Skibbereen just now. But Eveline made Harry her heir in return for his looking out for her these past few years and helping to pay the bills. She didn't own the house any more, but when that agreement was made, she specified certain items that were hers, and Harry will inherit those. So there'll be some money coming to him. I knew that before. But it's what he wants to do with it that I didn't know."

"And that is?" Maura said impatiently.

"He's gone and made an offer on the old creamery by Ballinlough—there'll be enough coming from Eveline to do that, or will when the estate is settled. He wants to fix it up so we can live there—there's a nice house tucked behind the big building where I had my studio."

"That sounds like a great solution, Gillian," Maura said. "You get to keep your painting space, and you'll have a home for all of you."

The men made some happy noises and turned back to their conversations. Maura said to Gillian, in a lower voice, "It *will* be the three of you, won't it?"

Gillian nodded. "Yes, Harry'd live there too. And the baby, of course. But there's a problem—Harry's work's in Dublin, so he'd be away much of the time or on the road."

"Don't you like to spend time alone? To work, when you're painting?"

"I would have said yes, but with a baby . . . I don't know what I think."

"Look, I'm no expert," Maura began, "but Harry's an accountant, right?"

"Yes. But most of his clients are in Dublin."

"But can't he do a lot of whatever he does on the computer? From here?"

Gillian's expression brightened just a bit. "You're right. He'd have to go to Dublin only when he needed to meet face-to-face with clients. And maybe he could find clients in Cork city or somewhere closer—like Skibbereen. And there are all those rich people around Schull, right? Thank you—I'm just so rattled that I'm not thinking clearly. And it is a lovely spot."

"It'll work out. And I'm guessing that Harry has actually put some thought into this—and wants to make you happy. That's good, isn't it?"

Gillian gave Maura a watery smile. "Thank you, Maura. Maybe he's finally decided to grow up."

Twenty-Three

❧

As opening time approached, a small cluster of men gathered outside the door, stamping their feet in what was left of the slush. *Might as well let them in now*, Maura reasoned. Sean wouldn't be coming back any time soon to check if she was sticking to the legal schedule. She unlocked the door again and smiled. "Come on in, guys. You look cold."

Rosy-faced men trooped in and spread out around the room, which quickly filled with the scent of damp wool with a whiff of manure—cows needed to be milked no matter what the weather. They seemed less interested in a drink than in sharing battle—er, snow stories with each other. As the conversations went on, as she had guessed, the reported depth of the drifts out in the country grew deeper, until Maura wondered if even the house chimneys had been visible—and if that was true, how had all these men managed to arrive at the pub so fast?

At some point, she realized that Diane had disappeared. Maura tracked her down in the kitchen, where she was using her mobile phone, and Diane said quickly, "I've been trying to find a flight out. I'm guessing there are a lot of stranded travelers, but I've found a seat at eight tonight."

So Diane was moving on with her life. Maura felt both disappointed and relieved. "I, uh, told Sean Murphy I wanted to talk to him when he had the time."

"That's the young garda who stopped in?"

"That's him."

"Maura, you've done enough. You don't need to bother him with this." Diane changed the subject quickly. "You know, you've got quite a place here."

"What do you mean? The pub?" Maura asked.

"Yes. From the outside, it looks like an ordinary village pub."

"That's what it is," Maura told her, confused.

"Ah, but you've got an interesting mix of people here—almost like a stage play, don't you know. Billy, there—he's the wise old man or maybe the judge watching and handing out opinions. Rose is the young innocent, but I haven't quite pegged her father Jimmy yet. Maybe he's the official naysayer, the gadfly who makes comments only so that others will contradict him—he likes to stir things up. Gillian is the fallen woman, and people aren't sure what they think about that in this modern day. Mick—now he's the enigma, and if this were a play, he might come up with some interesting surprise in the third act. You know, he'd turn out to be a Russian spy or the missing king of Ruritania. And the rest of the crowd is the Greek chorus, the audience to our little drama."

Maura shook her head. "And what about me? Where do I fit?"

"I'd say you represent justice. Or maybe truth—you can see clearly what others don't. By the way, that young garda—Sean, is it?—he's sweet on you, you know."

Maura sighed. Poor Sean—he wasn't very good at hiding what he felt. "That's what people keep telling me. I tell them I'm not ready to get involved with anybody right now—I'm still learning how to run the pub. I don't have the time or energy to start anything with him right now."

"You must have an interesting story of your own, Maura—how you ended up here, and you so young. Too bad we don't have time to talk more about it, but I know you have a business to run."

"I don't think my story is half as interesting as yours, and yes, I'd better get back to doing my job. Just tell me when you're leaving?"

"I promise," Diane said. "Maybe I'll go explore the town—I'm tired of being shut up in here. If I can borrow a pair of boots?"

Walking out of the kitchen, Maura said, "No problem. Mick, you mind if Diane borrows your boots for a short while?" When Mick nodded in assent, Maura stepped behind the bar and retrieved the waterproof boots, then handed them across to Diane. "Just watch your step—it's probably slippery in spots."

"I'll be careful, Maura. See you later!"

More and more men kept straggling in, and each new arrival resulted in the repetition of the same stories. There was snow everywhere, no surprise. There was a tree blown down on a lane Maura didn't recognize. Someone had heard on the radio that a ship had sunk outside the harbor. The power was coming back, but slowly and unevenly. At least nobody said any other storms were expected.

Before noon, Maura sent Rose across to the hotel to beg for food, and she returned with a couple of bags of bread and cheese and some more apples. "Anne says all her rooms are filled, but we've most likely got more mouths to feed here. Just be sure to tell them where the food's coming from."

"Can you do something with this stuff?"

"I'll go fire up the stove in back. Toasted cheese sandwiches coming up! And maybe an apple crumble—Anne gave me some sugar, and there's still flour as well."

The next time Maura looked up from pulling pints, she saw a middle-aged woman charge in the front door. It was hard to see what she really looked like since she was bundled up from head to toe in a knitted cap, quilted puffy coat, and fur-lined boots. She made a beeline for Jimmy, who was talking to a couple of men in the far corner. "Ah, Jimmy my love, there you are! I was worried sick that something had happened to you. Where's Rosie?"

"Hullo, Judith," Jimmy greeted her with lukewarm enthusiasm. "Rose's in the back makin' some food fer us all. Yeh didn't have to worry."

"You might've called, at least."

"Me phone died," Jimmy said. Which Maura suspected was not true but provided a handy excuse.

"Well, no mind, if all's well." The woman looked around the room. "Seems like yer doin' good business today." She spotted Maura watching the exchange. "Aren't yeh goin' ta introduce me, Jimmy? This young woman would be yer boss, then?"

Jimmy did not look happy, but he brought the woman over to the bar. "Maura Donovan, meet Judith."

The woman peeled off her gloves and extended a hand for Maura to shake. "It's grand to meet yeh, Maura. I'm Judith McCarthy. Looks like you've made a go of this place. Is Jimmy here behavin' himself?" Out of the corner of her eye, Maura saw Jimmy wince.

"Nice to meet you, Judith. I haven't seen you in here before, have I?"

"Nah, Jimmy keeps me under wraps. I'm livin' nearer to Drinagh, but I'm not one fer the pubs meself, and if I'm lookin' fer a pint, I'll go to the Gaelic Bar up there. I'm a workin' woman, like you. Only I've got cows to manage, rather than this lot." She waved at the small group of men in the room, and a few returned the greeting.

"Well, I'm glad you came by." Even if Jimmy wasn't. "How're the roads?"

"The Drinagh road's clear, but not the side roads so much. Yer up at Knockskagh, Maura?"

"I am. But I haven't seen snow around here before, so I don't know what the driving is like."

"The bog road will be fine, I'd wager, but yer hill—now that's another matter."

"That's kind of what I guessed. Can I get you anything?"

"A coffee would be grand. Then mebbe I should see if Rosie needs some help in the back. Jimmy never mentioned a kitchen."

"Probably because nobody's used it in years. But it came in handy last night, and Rose was the one who got it working." Maura poured a mug of coffee and slid it across to Judith.

"She's a sharp girl, she is. I keep tellin' her she should go to uni, do somethin' with herself."

"I agree with you."

Rose emerged from the back with a platter of sandwiches, golden brown on the outside and oozing cheese. "Take yer time, lads—there's more where these came from." Rose set the platter on the end of the bar. "Hi, Judith." Rose looked happier to see the woman than Jimmy had.

The men in the room were surprisingly polite as they lined up to help themselves, and the sandwiches disappeared quickly.

"Can I help yeh with those, Rose?" Judith asked.

"Sure, come on back. There's another batch cookin'."

Maura waited until Judith and Rose had gone back to the kitchen before turning to Jimmy. "So, Jimmy, anything you want to share?" she asked, smiling.

Jimmy muttered something under his breath. "That's Judith. She's decided we're a couple, and she's enlisted me own daughter to convince me."

"Looks like Rose is okay with that. And Judith seems like an impressive woman with a farm of her own. Congratulations, Jimmy." Maybe he wouldn't need to steal any more oil now.

"I'm told she's got a nice piece of land and a strong herd," somebody called out. Jimmy managed to look both pleased and pained at the same time.

Maura ducked out from behind the bar before Jimmy commented, and she waded through the crowd over to where Gillian sat. She dropped into a chair. "You okay? Want a sandwich?"

Gillian nodded. "Just thinking. And I'm famished. Billy could use one too."

"I'll snag a couple from the next batch. This is kind of a busy place to think," Maura commented.

"It's fine. Better than too quiet, with all these thoughts banging around my head. Like you said, if we bought the creamery and cleaned it up, I'd have a studio, and I could give classes there."

So Gillian was taking Harry's idea seriously. "That could work," Maura agreed cautiously.

"And I could keep the baby close by, maybe with a childminder some of the time."

"You could."

"It's a lovely site."

"It is."

Gillian laughed. "Ah, Maura, you're no help at all."

"What, you want me to tell you it's a bad idea? I don't think it is. You know the place—you'd have a place to work with good space and light, and it's easy to get to for students. I'll give extra points to Harry for coming up with the idea. Of course, there's probably a lot of work to be done to the place before you can live in it, and you wouldn't be able to help much for a while, and I don't know how handy Harry is, him being an accountant and not a carpenter . . ."

"That's more like it—poking holes in the idea," Gillian said. "You've been practicing your bartending."

"You mean supporting whatever opinion seems to be popular? Did I have a choice if I wanted to make this place work?"

"Now that you've given me both sides, what do you *really* think?"

Maura faced her squarely. "First, I'll tell you that I'd be happy if you stayed around—for selfish reasons. I don't have a lot of women friends, as you might have seen, and I don't want you to go away. Second, if Harry's really on board with the whole idea, and he follows through, that tells you something about how he feels about you. So I guess I'm saying you should go for it. If you need guys to help with the construction part, you could probably get out the word here at Sullivan's and find plenty."

Gillian smiled. "Thank you. If it weren't so hard to stand up from this chair in my condition, I'd hug you. Of course, I still have to talk to Harry, but I guess I'd say I'm leaning toward agreeing with you."

"Good." Maura looked around to see who could overhear, but no one was paying attention to them. "What do you think of Judith?"

"Based on the two minutes I've seen of her from over here? I think she'd do Jimmy a world of good, and it would free up Rose, wouldn't it?"

"My thoughts exactly. Any other problems you want to fix, while we're at it? Global warming? World peace?"

"Let's stop while we're ahead, shall we?"

Twenty-Four

❧

Judith emerged from the kitchen bearing another plate loaded with hot sandwiches. Rose followed behind her. Maura nodded at Gillian, then went up to Rose and said quietly, "Make sure Gillian and Billy get some, will you?"

"Of course. What's Gillian thinkin' about the old creamery and all?"

"I think she likes the idea. And I'm glad Harry came up with the plan. Judith's really something, isn't she?"

"She is that. I call her a force of nature. Da doesn't stand a chance."

Judith returned to the bar. "We make a good team, do we not, Rosie?"

"We do. I'll go wash up."

Judith leaned against the bar, scanning the room. She spotted Joe Minahane seated in the dark corner next to the fireplace. "Well, if it isn't my neighbor, Joe! What're yeh doin' here, and who's lookin' after the herd?"

Joe stood up—a touch reluctantly, to Maura's eye—and came over to the bar. "I was doing me bit as a good Samaritan, rescuing a stranded traveler—that'd be him over there. Bart Hayes from near Limerick, he tells me. Went off the road near the farm with a bunch of drunken lads after a weddin' in Rosscarbery, who were all but useless, and I couldn't see gettin' him out of the ditch in the snow with or without their help. The snow was comin' so fast, I didn't think I'd make it to Skib, so I came here."

"And the cows?"

"Called me wife before my phone went out so she'd know what's what. She can handle the milkin'."

"No doubt she can—she's too good for the likes of you," Judith said with a smile. She looked up in time to see Diane come back in, shucking off her borrowed boots inside the door. "Sure and that's not—"

"Diane Caldwell," Maura said quickly. "She's been here since last night—got stranded when her flight to London was canceled because of the snow." Maura watched Judith's expression carefully, but she seemed more intrigued than hostile.

"And do you know about—"

"What happened twenty years ago? I do now, and so does most of this crowd. Leave her be, will you?"

"I don't stick my nose in where it isn't wanted, Maura," Judith said a bit stiffly. She turned to Joe. "Didn't yer wife have some connection to what happened back then?"

"I've no idea what yer sayin', Judith," he said, although from his panicky expression, Maura was pretty sure he did.

Judith ignored his denial. "Yer Nora, she was a Dempsey before she married you, was she not? Sister to Ellen, who married the Layton man. Poor grazing land they had at his place. It was a good thing they got that other field back."

Rose had said that Judith kept cattle, so she'd know about that. Out of the corner of her eye, Maura noticed Bart straighten up. Funny that Joe hadn't mentioned anything about his wife's connection to Sharon's neighbors. Maybe it meant nothing, but the fact that he'd concealed it didn't look good.

Diane must have heard as well, and now she approached the bar. "Judith, is it? You already know I'm Diane. We had an interesting time last night, going over the old case. Some of us here thought the Laytons deserved a harder look. Bart here"—she gestured to Bart, who hadn't moved but was watching intently—"now, he's a garda, and he was on the case when it happened all those years back. He thought we were just blowing smoke here last night, but the Laytons came up in conversation. Joe, why'd you not mention that your wife was sister to Ellen Layton?"

"She had nothing to do with any of it," Joe said, his tone surly. "The gardaí talked to us back then. Nora was home with me and the kids and the cows."

"I'm glad to hear that," Diane said.

"So why didn't you bring it up, Joe?" Bart asked in a voice that sounded surprisingly official to Maura. "Everybody else seemed to have an opinion about what happened. Did yer wife never say anything?"

"I didn't want any trouble," Joe said, looking at his boots, "and we never talked about it. Nothin' to tell."

"Your wife was cleared when it happened," Bart pressed on. "So where's the trouble?"

"It might be she talked to her sister after it happened," Joe said reluctantly. "A *long* time after it happened."

Bart's expression was colder than before. "And might it be that Ellen said something to your Nora, then, that made you think a bit different?"

Joe avoided Bart's glance. "Mebbe."

"And would you be wanting to share that with us now? Seein' as how we've talked about almost everything else under the sun, includin' everyone's love life?"

Joe looked around the room: anyone who'd been at the pub the night before was watching him now. The newcomers shrugged and ignored them.

"Tell 'em, Joe," Judith prompted him, "or I'll tell what Nora told me. And I might get it wrong, you know."

Joe held up both hands. "All right, all right. Yeah, me wife is sister to Ellen Layton, but they didn't see much of each other after Ellen married and they went to live on her husband's father's place. Like everyone's said, it was poor land, and it took a lot of work. Yeh've heard that Denis and Ellen sold the land that the Morgans built on—they needed the money, but Denis came to regret it, for he found he needed the grazin' more. But the idea yez were kicking around last night—that he cooked up some grand scheme to kill Sharon Morgan and somehow take back the land—is daft. Anyways, Ellen kept to herself when it was all over the news—didn't come cryin' on Nora's shoulder then. And like you've heard, nobody was ever arrested, and the whole thing went quiet, did it not?"

"So what did Ellen tell Nora later?" Maura demanded. There had to be something that was making Joe so nervous.

"When Denis passed on years later, Nora went to the wake. Nora and Ellen had a coupla brothers—you'd know that,

Bart—but they'd had their own problems with the gardaí, mostly petty stuff, so they kind of drifted around. Didn't even show their faces at the wake."

"One of them was living at the farm, helping the Laytons, when the murder happened—is that not right?" Bart asked.

"He did, now and then. Jacky, that was. The youngest. He'd been helpin' out fer years. When Denis died, he moved in permanent, like, and he's still there. Ellen couldn't handle the cows by herself—not that Jacky's much help—but what else is she to do?"

"Was this Jacky a suspect?" Maura demanded.

"Ellen and Denis told the gardaí he was home all night— after he'd come back from the pub in Schull, where plenty of people seen him. No one could prove otherwise. Besides, the gardaí had fixed on Diane here as the killer. So nothing ever came of it."

Maura was thinking about shaking the story out of Joe. A lot of the people she'd met at the pub liked to spin stories over a pint, but Joe was trying to avoid telling this one. "So what did Ellen finally say to Nora?"

Joe seemed to shrink into himself, and he wouldn't look at anyone. "She told Nora that she'd lied to protect her brother, and her husband did as well. She had no idea if Jacky was home or not, but she couldn't swear he wasn't—he could've been out with the herd. She felt she couldn't say nothin' because Denis needed his help on the farm, and Jacky needed the work and a place to live. But she said he always was a bully."

"That's pretty vague, Joe," Bart said. "Was there more?"

Joe nodded. "After the gardaí had come and gone back then, Ellen told Nora she found something that made her wonder, and she asked him about it. Jacky fed her some kind of story and told her to shut up. And she did."

Bart said, almost to himself, "The gardaí took Ellen's word and her husband's, and the brother gave them the same story, if I recall. If Ellen did find something that troubled her after we'd talked with her, she never said anything more to us."

"So the brother's still working the farm with Ellen?" Maura asked.

"If workin's the right word," Joe muttered. "But you did have a part of it right, Maura—Denis was able to buy the land back cheap, and that kept them going. There was no love lost between him and Jacky, but it might be that Ellen never shared her doubts with him."

Everyone was silent for a few moments, apart from the patrons who hadn't heard the story the night before, and finally Bart spoke. "It seems to me it might be a good idea fer the gardaí to talk to this brother and to Ellen again. Don't get yer hopes up, Diane—it could mean nothing, and if Ellen and Jacky stick to their stories, that's the end of it."

"I understand, and I appreciate your taking it seriously," Diane told him. "If nothing comes of it, so be it."

Bart nodded. "I've a mind to pay a call on the Skibbereen garda station. And if I'm going to do that, I'd best sort out this lot from the weddin'." He crossed the room and corralled the four young men, who seemed to be on their way to drowning their hangovers with more drink. Then Liam and Donal joined the discussion and apparently volunteered to take their new friends to wherever they were supposed to be staying.

Bart returned to their small group. "Me car's still in the ditch, Joe. Think we can get it out now?"

"I've a truck back at the farm that should do the trick. You want to leave now?"

"I think we should. Diane, will you be here the rest of the day?"

"I can be. I'll be flying home tonight."

"I'll let you know what they say," Bart told her.

"Talk to Inspector Hurley there—he's a good man, and he'll listen to you," Maura said.

"Thank you fer yer hospitality, Maura. I can't recall a more interestin' evening in years. Joe, let's go." Bart seemed to have taken control, and Joe followed him meekly.

Diane and Maura watched them go. "Well," Diane said, "do you think this will change anything?"

"Diane, I can't say," Maura told her, "But I've seen stranger things happen around here."

* * *

The crowd ebbed and flowed throughout the day. Judith hung around for a while, helping Rose with the food, then the washing up. After a couple of hours, she gave Jimmy a quick kiss—much to his embarrassment—and left with a cheerful wave. Otherwise, the crowd was made up mainly of men, which left Maura wondering whether they'd left their wives at home to deal with restless children and any snow cleanup. She couldn't really complain because at least they were paying for their drinks now.

Liam and Donal returned mid-afternoon after delivering the wedding boys to wherever they were going. Maura wondered what they'd made of the night—or if they'd even noticed anything unusual was happening.

Shortly after two, the lights came back on, greeted by much cheering. Maura was briefly startled to realize how many other noises came with it, like the humming of the refrigerator behind the bar. She'd have to retire the antiquated but still useful lamps to the basement. Or maybe keep them in a handier place in case the power went out again—there was still plenty of winter to come. From what she could see through the crush of bodies, the snow outside was melting fast, as if the last twenty-four hours were being erased in front of her eyes.

Finally, around three, the men began to trickle out reluctantly to go home to chores and children. Maura guessed that some might be back later, or there might be a whole new crop in the evening. The snowstorm would go down in local history as a memorable event to be hashed over for years to come. Unless it was followed by worse, but Maura couldn't bring herself to worry about that yet.

She turned to her staff, who were looking a bit ragged. "We made it. You think there'll be another crowd tonight?"

"If what's left of the snow doesn't turn to ice," Mick said.

"Do any of you want to go home, clean up? Mick, are you going to try to go up and see Bridget?"

"I thought I might if yeh can spare me."

"For an hour or two, sure. I'd like to know she's safe. And I have a selfish reason too—I want to know if I can get home tonight."

"I'll let yeh know. I'm guessin' the hill'd be the worst of it."

"That's what Judith said. Jimmy, I think you've got a winner there." Jimmy mumbled something that Maura probably didn't want to hear.

Maura lowered her voice. "You know, you've been in a lousy mood for a while now, Jimmy. You don't want to be with Judith? Or married?"

"That's me own business," he told her, his tone surly.

Maura wasn't about to back down. "Well, if you're working here, it's my business. You've been almost rude to some of our patrons. Including Diane."

Jimmy gave her a long look, then his shoulders slumped. "Rosie and me, we've been on our own fer a while now. It works for us."

"Jimmy," Maura said impatiently, "in case you haven't noticed, Rose is pretty much grown up. She might have plans of her own, beyond cooking supper for you. Things are going to change whether you like it or not. And Judith seems like a good woman."

"She is that. Yer still angry about that oil business?"

"I'll forget about it as long as it doesn't happen again. Fair enough?" Jimmy nodded, and Maura added, "You want to take an hour or two off?"

"Nah, 'cause Judith'd probably ambush me in me own home."

"What about Rose? She's been working hard, and she deserves a break."

"I'm grand, Maura," Rose said cheerfully. "I had a fine time in the kitchen, feeding all the people."

"And you did an amazing job, Rose. Thank you, from all of us."

Mick said, "I'd best be on my way before it gets dark."

"Let me know if you can't make it back." Bridget had no doubt weathered the storm just fine in her small, sturdy house, but she was far from young and might need some help with fuel or even getting the door open. "And give my love to Bridget."

"I'll do that." Mick too found his coat and left.

Diane had retreated back into herself, working her mobile phone, probably looking for a way home. Would her husband meet her at the airport? Were they all waiting to see if anything came of Bart's visit to the gardaí in Skibbereen? Assuming Joe had gotten his car out of the ditch. And what could they hope for after twenty years?

Maura doled out a few pints, collected empty glasses and crumpled napkins, and wiped off tables, until she looked up to see Sean Murphy at the door. She hurried to greet him. "Hey, Sean. Don't take this the wrong way, but you look lousy."

"Then my face matches what's inside. Could you do me a coffee?"

"Of course. Sit down before you fall over."

Sean followed her to the bar, where he sat and shrugged off his coat. Maura started a fresh cup of coffee—now that the power was back, she could use the fancy machine again. While she waited, she asked, "Was everybody all right?"

"About what yeh'd expect. A tree down here and there. A fence broken, and the cows strayed. No fires, thank God."

"And the roads?" Maura slid a mug of coffee across the bar to him.

"All but dry, now that the weather's turned."

"Almost like it never happened," Maura said. Poor Sean—he looked exhausted. "Can you at least go home now and take a nap? Or are you still on duty?"

"I'm on my way there now, but I wanted to tell yeh that yer Bart Hayes stopped by the station."

"Did you talk to him?"

"He asked for the inspector. They were still talking when I came out."

"Is that good or bad, do you think?"

"I can't say." Sean drained his coffee. "I've only half a brain workin' right now, Maura, seein' as how I've been up all night. But I thought you'd be wanting to know: if you and yer lot came up with something last night, and Bart thought enough of it to bring it to the inspector, then the gardaí are taking it seriously." Sean stood up. "I'll be goin' home now, but if I learn anything new, I'll let yeh know."

"Thank you, Sean—we appreciate it." She escorted him out the door, noting that the snow really was almost gone now, except in shady corners.

When she shut the door and turned back to the room, Gillian piped up. "Things are happening?"

"So it seems. Bart Hayes was still at the station when Sean left to come here. We'll just have to wait and see. Have you heard from Harry?"

"No. I'm guessing he's still at the solicitors' office, assuming he and they all made it to Skibbereen. Or maybe at the estate agent's—I'm sure they'd be eager for the commission on the old creamery. But first, Harry had to learn how much ready money he'd have and when it would be available before he could buy the creamery. And I've got a deadline of my own."

"The baby, you mean," Maura said. "Of course. And you won't want to be nine months' pregnant or taking care of an infant with guys running around, tearing things down, and hammering new things up."

"Exactly. Which gives us three months. Of course, maybe we can stay at the manor that long, but we'd have to let the O'Briens go. I'm sure Harry'd rather not face telling them, although I think he's planning to give them something for their years of service."

"It's not like Eveline's passing is a surprise."

"True, but they've been with her for years, and I'm not sure what lies in store for them. But that's not my problem." Gillian studied Maura's face. "Do you know, Diane's lucky to have found you."

"Why?"

"First, because you listened to her. Second, you believed her. Third, you managed to convince a bunch of half-drunk strangers to believe her—or at least question the official story. Fourth, you seem to have made the gardaí believe you. Maybe the stars are aligned in Diane's favor."

"Well, it may all lead exactly nowhere. I don't want to get anybody's hopes up."

Gillian looked past Maura, and her expression brightened. "Ah, there's the man himself," she said. "How'd it go, Harry?"

Harry made his way over to Gillian's seat and leaned over to kiss her. "Couldn't be better, love. I think we're set."

Gillian looked over his shoulder at Maura and winked. "See? The stars are aligned."

Twenty-Five

❧

Another wave of people started turning up at Sullivan's shortly before four. Mick returned just before it began. "Yeh'll have no trouble with the lane, Maura," he told her. "And Bridget's fine. She was after tellin' me about all the big snows of the past, else I would have been here sooner."

"I'm glad to hear that, Mick." It was a relief to know that she could get home without problems: after another busy day, she desperately craved some time alone and a shower. But that was for later, and she couldn't exactly leave while business was so good. Worse, right now she was on edge. If Sean was right, the gardaí had taken their story seriously enough to look harder at it, but that might not lead anywhere. She was prepared for that, but she wanted to know. And she assumed Diane did too.

She noticed Gillian and Harry heading for the door and was so busy that she could do no more than wave. At least Gillian looked happy. Harry really had stepped up, and maybe things would actually work out for them, at least for a while. Maura knew as well as anyone that plans didn't always work out as expected, but people had to try. Just look at Jimmy! He had seemed content with things just the way they were, and then Judith had somehow wormed her way into his life and started rearranging it for him. Was that good or bad? *Good for Rose*, Maura had already decided—Rose might actually get a chance at a life of her own now. Judith looked like a woman who knew her own mind, although what she saw in Jimmy still mystified Maura. But maybe Judith was exactly what Jimmy needed.

As for herself, Maura realized she was coming up on a year in Leap. Well, nine months. The first few months had been kind of a blur, what with grieving for Gran and then trying to take in what Gran had done for her, fixing it with Old Mick so she would inherit the pub and his house. And then she'd had to learn how to manage a pub and employees and how to live in a country she'd never seen before. Things had worked out pretty well— with the help of other people, freely offered and given. Maybe that was what she was doing with Diane: paying it back. Trying to help, although Diane hadn't asked for it.

When there was a lull, Maura went over to where Diane sat and dropped into a chair. "How're you holding up?"

"After this long, I guess I think 'what will be, will be.' If anything changes, the gardaí know where to find me. I saw Gillian and Harry leaving. Everything all right there?"

"Harry came by to collect her, and they're off making plans. All good, I promise."

"I'm glad for them."

Maura stood up and crossed to room to where Billy sat. She perched on the chair next to his by the fire. "How're you doing, Billy?"

"I think I'll be heading to me own place soon. These old bones need a good rest."

Maura paused a moment, struggling to put her question into words. "Billy, what do you think is going to happen now?"

"Ah, Maura . . . I'm thinkin' the gardaí got it wrong back in the day. That's not to blame them—it was a big crime, and there was more than one station called in to help. Which was both good and bad."

"Why do you say that?"

"Because it's the local station that knows the local people. Someone should have looked harder at the Dempsey man. He'd been in trouble before, in Schull. But whoever it was talked to Ellen believed what she told them, and she never changed her story. At least after . . . whatever happened, Jacky Dempsey stayed out of trouble, so far as we know."

"Billy, I have to ask this, but don't laugh. How does it happen that Bart, who's a garda and part of the original investigation, goes off the road in front of Joe's home, and Joe just happens to be married to Nora, who's Ellen Layton's sister, and Nora got the story from Ellen years ago? And then Joe and Diane end up here at the same time and turn the whole story on its head?"

Billy smiled. "Ah, Maura, that's how things work in West Cork. And it's about the family—and loyalty. I'm guessin' that Ellen felt she couldn't betray her brother, at least not to the gardaí, but came the time when she had to share with Nora. And Nora kept quiet as well because family came first."

"And Diane was an outsider. I guess I see that. After all, here I am—if it wasn't for my grandmother, I'd be an outsider too, and I wouldn't be here."

"Family's important, Maura. The one you come from—and the one you choose. That's why we all stick close." Billy fumbled for his cane next to his chair. "I'd best be on my way before I can't move at all."

"Take it slow, Billy, and watch out for icy patches."

After she had watched to make sure that Billy had made it safely to his own front door, Maura was surprised to hear the pub's phone ringing—that was a rare event. She didn't even know if they needed a landline, but it had come with the place, and she hadn't changed it, since the cost was so low. She located it under the bar and answered tentatively. "Sullivan's."

"Maura? It's Patrick Hurley."

That was the last person she had expected to hear: the head of the local gardaí. "Uh, hello. Can I help you with something?" She tried to appear casual as she pulled the phone as far away from the bar as she could and turned her back on the small crowd. She wasn't sure whether she wanted everyone to hear what she was saying—or to know she was talking to the gardaí.

"It's more a case of helping you, I'm guessing. Bart Hayes has been here since he got his car back on the road, but then, you knew he was on his way. What we didn't expect was to see Nora Minahane and her sister Ellen Layton here not long after."

Maura managed not to drop the phone. "They came in by themselves? You didn't, uh, invite them?"

"Turns out Joe Minahane told Nora that Diane was at your place and that the lot of you had been talking about the old murder, and she decided that Ellen should tell us everything for her own safety."

"Jacky Dempsey still living with her?"

"He is, and if word gets back to him about what's been going on, Ellen might pay the price—Jacky's got a temper, and there've been incidents with him before. She's made the right choice."

"Where is he now?"

"We've men out looking for him, and we've alerted the Schull gardaí."

"And Ellen's told you what happened?"

"She has." The detective cleared his throat. "Maura, this goes against a lot of rules, but I hear Diane Caldwell is planning to leave soon, and Ellen wants to meet with her before she goes. Could the two of you come to the station?"

"Now?" Maura turned to look at the crowd: Mick and Jimmy could handle it, at least for a while. "Uh, yeah, sure. We'll be there as soon as we can."

As she returned the phone to its regular place, Maura realized that most of the people in the pub, including her staff, were staring at her expectantly. "What?" Her tone was sharper than she had expected, and she felt she should apologize somehow. "Sorry. That was the gardaí in Skibbereen. They want to talk to Diane, and I'm going to take her over there now."

"Have they arrested anyone?" someone asked.

"I didn't ask. I'll be back later, and I'll fill you in then. Mick, Jimmy—can you cover?"

"Sure. You'd best go now," Mick said.

As Maura approached Diane, she couldn't read her expression. It was an odd mix of hope and fear. "What's happened?" Diane asked.

"Outside," Maura said tersely. "Grab your coat."

Diane complied, and they walked out the front door. On the way to the car, Maura said, "Joe's wife and her sister Ellen showed up at the garda station while Bart was there. Ellen wants to talk to you."

"What has she said?"

"I don't know, but I'm going to make a wild guess that we got it right, because otherwise I doubt Detective Hurley would ask to see us now. We'll find out soon enough."

Diane said little as they drove the short distance to Skibbereen. Maura wasn't sure what to say—or think. It seemed like they'd been right. All that casual talk in the pub the night before had somehow produced enough pieces that the answer had come out. Not that she wanted to take all the credit, and she didn't want to make the gardaí look bad, but they'd found at least some part of the truth. She should be happy, shouldn't she? Still, Jacky Dempsey was out there somewhere, and he still might be a threat. He'd gotten away with murder, and just because he'd behaved himself for the last twenty years didn't cancel that out. And he'd kept his sister Ellen quiet for all that time. How had Nora managed to escape the family?

When Maura had parked near the garda station, Diane spoke for the first time. "Will Ellen be in any trouble? I mean, for concealing evidence of a crime or whatever you call it here?"

"I can't tell you. If Joe was telling the truth about what his wife told him long after the murder, then Ellen Layton really didn't know what happened, although she might have suspected. You could probably argue that she should have told the gardaí her suspicions, but it sounds like Jacky wasn't admitting anything, and she was scared of him. Plus, she needed his labor to keep the farm going. People like Billy keep telling me that family comes first. But this doesn't seem like a good example. You ready?"

"I think so. You know this detective?"

"I do. He's good at what he does, and he's fair."

They walked into the small vestibule, gave their names to the person at the front desk, and were escorted to a conference room that Maura knew better than she wanted to. They sat together at one end of the long conference table there and waited silently until Detective Hurley opened the door and escorted two middle-aged women in before following them and shutting the door behind him. "Please sit," he told the women, who had to be the Dempsey sisters. "Before we start, I want to make something clear. This meeting is not happening. I am divulging information that I should not make public, but I think Maura and Diane have earned the right to hear it, and I trust that they won't spread it any farther until it becomes public information, which should happen shortly. Do you all understand that?"

The four women nodded silently.

"Then let's begin. There is no recording being made of what we say today, if you're concerned. I assume you all know who the others are?"

"Hello, Ellen," Diane said. "It's been a long time. And you must be her sister, Nora," Diane turned toward the second woman, whose resemblance to Ellen was clear. "Thank you for coming forward, both of you."

Ellen Dempsey Layton looked small and sad—her hair badly in need of cutting, her clothing worn and faded but very clean. *Was that what keeping an awful secret for decades did to you? Sucked the life out of you?* Maura wondered. *Or was it the hard work of keeping a failing dairy farm going? Not to mention living with a brother who she was probably pretty sure was a murderer.*

"Can we get on with it?" Ellen said suddenly. "I asked to meet with yez because it's time the truth came out. And to apologize, if I can, fer doin' this to yeh, Diane. You'd done nothin' to deserve it. But once the circus began, there was no stoppin' it."

"I used to see you walking your dog," Diane said. "With your husband. Are you still raising the dogs?" Maura wondered if she was trying to calm Ellen.

Ellen nodded. "I am—Denis is gone now, as you may know. The dogs, they bring in a bit of money now and then."

"There was a dog there that night, wasn't there?" Diane prompted.

Ellen nodded. "There was. Me brother Jacky took her out fer a walk—seemed odd to me then, for he rarely offered, but I wouldn't say no. It were late, and it was rainin', so I let him. He was gone fer a while. I thought I could hear Pansy barkin' out somewhere over the fields, but I figgered she'd scared up a rabbit or somethin'. When Jacky came back, poor Pansy was all wet and muddy. He were pretty muddy himself."

No blood? Maura wondered. But best not to interrupt Ellen now.

"So it were the next mornin'," Ellen went on after a pause, "and me husband and me were walking Pansy again, and that's when we found . . . her. The woman, Sharon. The gardaí know the story after that." She glanced again at the detective. "They asked me often enough."

Ellen swallowed before continuing. "She were just lyin' there, all bloody, Sharon was. Made me sick, it did."

"You can skip that part, Ellen," Diane said. "When did you begin to think your brother might have had something to do with it?"

"It were January, right? And Jacky weren't wearin' his coat, the one he wore to go out and see to the cows. They were in the big shed, but they needed feedin' and milkin' and all. A couple days later, I found the coat out in the barn behind some hay and thought mebbe he'd forgot it there. So I brought it in to clean it up, and that's when I saw the blood on it. I tried to ask him about it, and he said a cow had got cut on a bit of metal and got blood on it, and I should stop botherin' him about it. So I stopped."

Ellen paused again, gathering her courage. Her sister remained silent but laid a hand over Ellen's, and Ellen resumed her story. "He were an angry man, then and now. Denis's da's farm failed, and Denis took it over. Me da's farm was long gone, but he'd left Jacky out of it because he'd already had his troubles with the gardaí, and he had no love fer farmin'. But Jacky had no place to go, and Denis and me, we needed an extra hand with the cows, so we took him in. He did what he had to do at the farm and no more, and he acted like he owned the place even before me husband passed away. He was one for the drink, but he didn't much like pubs, so he'd stay home with his bottle. The drink made him angrier."

"He never married?" Diane asked.

Ellen smiled grimly. "What woman would have him? He had no land, no work of his own. And he would have to have treated a woman right. I don't know if he knew how."

"What did he want with Sharon, then?"

"Story was, Sharon Morgan was . . . well, it was said that she liked the men. She'd been carryin' on with Diane's husband, hadn't she? Maybe Jacky thought she'd be an easy mark. But he never admitted to anything, so I'm no more than guessin'."

"You knew?" Diane asked, dismayed.

"We seen yer man sneaking over, now and then," Ellen said.

Diane shook her head. "How did Jacky get Sharon out of the house that night?" Diane prompted her.

Ellen turned to her. "That's why he took the dog, I'd say. He must've tied her to a fence, which Pansy did not like, and that's what set her to barkin'. And then he could've gone knockin' on Sharon's door to ask her to help findin' Pansy, who'd slipped away from him in the dark. She knew the dog, yeh see, and Jacky must have said he was my brother, so she didn't think twice about helpin' him."

"Was he drunk?" Diane said.

Ellen looked away then. "He was, but I didn't think he could come to any harm just walkin' the dog. I never thought . . ."

Ellen swallowed again, then sat up straighter. "I don't know what Jacky had planned. Maybe he thought she'd ask him in and give him a cup of tea or something stronger. But that didn't happen."

Nora finally spoke. "Yeh've been too soft on that boy all yer life, Ellen. I'd have straightened him out if I'd been around." Nora turned to the rest of the table. "He had no luck with women, but he never figgered it was his fault. It was worse when he was drinkin'. He must have made his move on Sharon once she'd opened the door to him, but she was all in a hurry to get into her boots and find poor Pansy. When he finally made his grab fer her and she figgered out what he wanted, she wasn't havin' any of it and told him as much, and he went blind with rage, or so I'm guessin'. Weren't the first time he'd lost control like that. His brothers still have the scars to this day."

"He had a knife?" Diane asked.

"He carried one by habit," Ellen said, relieved to talk about something less distasteful to her. "The cows are always after gettin' into tangles, and it's handy to have. He probably never thought about usin' it, until the end . . ."

Diane spoke again after a long silence. "You know he stabbed her many, many times. And then he left her there on the ground, not even knowing whether Sharon was dead or alive. He remembered to retrieve the dog and walked back to your house, and he hid the bloody coat on the way. Ellen, did you know? Or suspect? Then or only later?"

"May God forgive me, I didn't want to know. If we wanted to keep the farm, Denis and me, we needed him. We couldn't pay anyone else. So I didn't ask, and I don't think Denis ever suspected a thing. But there was the coat, and Jacky jumped all over me when I asked about that. Over the years, he let slip a word or two, especially after he'd been drinkin'. When the murder came up in the news now and again, he'd get this funny look on his face, almost like he was smilin'. He might've hit a woman a time or two when he went to a pub—the gardaí in Schull might know of that. I'm sorry—I know I should've said something, but we would've lost the farm without his help, and then where would we have gone? We'd nothin' else. And he was my brother."

Diane turned to Detective Hurley. "Is this enough to arrest Jacky Dempsey?"

Detective Hurley looked at her, his face neutral. "I'm fairly sure the case against him is strong. We'll bring him in as soon as we find him, and we'll have the warrant shortly."

"And that will be the end of it," Diane said, almost to herself.

"No, wait!" Maura interrupted, unwilling to let this go with so many loose ends. "What happened to the Morgan land, Ellen?"

Ellen looked at her blankly for a long moment. "Me husband bought the place mebbe a year later. The husband—Paul, was it?—he didn't want nothin' to do with it anymore and was glad be rid of it. We needed it fer the cows, see, and he made us a good deal."

So she had been on the right track the night before, in a way, Maura thought, *but she hadn't known about Jacky.* But he was the gardaí's problem now.

Diane finally spoke, looking at Ellen again. "Ellen, thank you for coming forward now. It's been hard on me, living with this, so I can't imagine how much worse it must have been for you all these years, wondering if your brother was a killer and sharing a home with him."

"Thank you, Diane," Ellen answered. The two women exchanged a long, wordless look.

Then Diane turned to the detective, "Thank you as well for listening to Bart and for moving this forward."

Detective Hurley smiled wryly. "It was Maura who convinced Bart Hayes, which is no easy thing to do. I've come to trust her instincts. What's more, this unfinished case has been a thorn in the side for the gardaí here for years, and we'll be glad to see the back of it with a successful conclusion."

"I'm glad yer all so happy, but what are we to do now?" Nora demanded belligerently. "We can't go home and wait for Jacky to kill us in our beds, fer sure he'll know who blabbed."

"Mrs. Minahane, unless someone has told him about what went on at Sullivan's last night, he has no idea we're searching for him, and most likely he'll be at the farm. I'm sure we'll find him quickly."

Nora looked only partially mollified. "Might be we'll stick around Skib until that happens, fer he won't think to look fer us here. I'll let Joe know to keep his eye peeled fer him."

"Detective, once you do find Jacky, can we talk about it at the pub?" Maura asked. "You know how fast word spreads, and we've got a lot of curious people there—or will have soon enough."

"I'll be sure to let you know when he's found." He smiled at Maura. "And thank you for your help. Diane, what are your plans?"

"I've booked a flight for tonight."

"Then most likely I won't be seeing you again. Let me apologize for all the trouble we've caused you."

"Thank you," Diane said gravely. "I can't exactly say I forgive you, but I do understand. And I appreciate that you let Ellen talk to us."

"It seemed the least I could do. I'll see you out."

Twenty-Six

~

It was time to get back to Sullivan's: it was already close to five, and Maura expected a busy night. They made their way out to Maura's car without speaking, and once they were seated, Maura turned it on and cranked up the heat. "What do you want to do now?"

Diane looked blindly out the front window. "I . . . don't know . . . It's been twenty years. Mark and I, we were happy at the cottage, and then Sharon was killed, and somehow I became the favorite suspect, and things just dragged on and on . . . And here we are, all these years later, and it might actually be over."

"Did you ever meet Jacky Dempsey?"

"Not that I can recall. It sounds awful of me, but mostly we stuck to our own kind. Mark and I wouldn't have had much to do with an uneducated cattleman, even if he did live nearby. And we wouldn't have expected Sharon to do that, any more than we would. This Jacky sounds a bit unstable. Poor Ellen."

"Why do you say that? Her keeping silent really screwed up your life."

"But I can understand her reasons, in a way. Certainly, she was wrong, but she was weak and frightened and didn't see any other choices."

Maura felt little pity for weak women like Ellen, but she wasn't going to argue with Diane. "What time's your flight?"

"Eight. And I still have to turn in the rental."

"You sure you won't stay around until they catch the guy?"

Diane's mouth twitched. "I've had his sister's apology. I doubt he's going to tell me he's sorry—he probably blames Sharon for leading him on."

"Do you want to wait at Sullivan's? You don't have to leave for the airport for an hour or two."

"Why not? I've nothing left to do."

Maura navigated her way back to Leap and parked. Inside Sullivan's, more people gathered. Maura could hear Liam and Donal tuning up in the back room—acoustic, even though the power was back. Getting ready for their gig tonight—she kept forgetting about that. The music sounded a bit wistful, she thought, muffled by the thick walls and the doors.

She slipped behind the bar, then tapped a spoon on a glass. When she finally had everyone's attention, she said, "We've just come from the Skibbereen garda station. It looks like Diane Caldwell has been cleared of the murder of Sharon Morgan. The gardaí are now looking for Jacky Dempsey, based on new information from his sister. We'll let you know when he's found."

Diane resumed what now seemed to be her permanent seat in the corner, and Maura joined her there. "That inspector of yours—he's an intelligent man, that one," Diane said.

"You were expecting a local dummy?"

"No, but I suppose I didn't believe he would have an open mind. As you might guess, I have few happy memories from my interactions with the gardaí."

"Detective Hurley does care about doing the job right. And he listened to some wacky theories from me when he had no reason to. He's not your typical by-the-rules kind of guy."

"I suppose I've lived in cities for too long—I forget that there are decent people in jobs like his."

"And the ones before weren't? Decent, I mean?"

"I don't mean to say that. I think they were simply over-whelmed and uncertain. You won't know this, since you've only just arrived, but this part of Ireland was still quite isolated then. That's one of the reasons people like me came here—for the peace and quiet. And the beauty of the land. The gardaí simply weren't prepared to deal with a gruesome high-profile murder."

Maura looked at her critically. "You know, I thought you'd be angrier now that you'd been dragged through this for so long."

Diane smiled ruefully at Maura. "What good would that do me? They got it wrong, but not out of malice or laziness. And now they've finally gotten it right. I might wish it had taken less time, but they got there in the end."

"Have you talked to your husband since all this started?"

"I texted him when I found I'd be delayed, but I didn't want to share the details until I knew the outcome."

Not exactly a warm and supportive relationship there, Maura said to herself. *Was it ever?* But who was she to judge? "What will he think?"

"As I've said more than once, he thought the whole accusation was a joke at the start, and then he was surprised that the case dragged on so long. And then he more or less forgot about it all, since the English papers didn't follow the case, and I didn't bring it up. He was more interested in how much I'd realize from the sale of my grandparents' property. I know you're probably too polite to ask, but it's less than he expected."

"Do you still plan to sell the property?" Maura asked.

"I've signed a contract. I suppose I could still withdraw, but I don't know if I want to."

"Do you need the money?"

"No. If we had, I'd've sold the place years ago. I hated to part with it. It was the last piece of my childhood, in a way. Would I be welcome here now, when the news gets round?"

Maura remembered Diane's hands caressing the shabby old salt shaker—was it only yesterday? She must still feel some attachment to the old place to have brought it with her. "I can't answer that," Maura said. "If anyone had asked me would I be welcome here, I would have laughed in their face. But I was wrong. It might not be as hard as you think."

"They remembered your gran, Maura, and they honored her memory, I assume. She kept in touch with people here?"

"Yes, not that she ever told me."

"Ah, there's the difference. Any memories of me in West Cork are bad ones, and I didn't contact anyone after I left. People here *wanted* to like you, but they were happy to hate me."

"That's just sad," Maura said. *But probably true*, she added to herself.

Maura gazed around the room. Everything seemed to be running smoothly, and there was a steady stream of people wandering in and out of the back room, where Liam and Donal had started playing in a kind of haphazard way. Irish musicians didn't pay much attention to schedules, she'd found.

What an odd couple of days this had been! If there was such a thing as a book called *Pub Management for Dummies*, battling blizzards and solving old crimes—at the same time!—were probably not categories. When would Ireland stop surprising her?

She wandered back to the kitchen, which was as clean as such an old place could be. It had the basics, even though the stove was no doubt older than she was, although not quite as old as Billy—a thought that made her smile. It worked, kind of, but if she decided to expand and start offering food, she'd have to get a more modern one, and that would probably be expensive. And there would also be various fees and licenses for serving food that she'd never even heard of. And inspections. And approvals. Maybe she wouldn't rush into it. Or she could ask Rose to do the legal homework if she really did want to cook. So much to learn and so little time to look into it all.

Mick appeared in the doorway. "Sounds like yer meetin' went well. Any more wrongs to right?"

"Not likely. I don't go looking for these things, you know."

"Maybe you attract them like a magnet, since yer country is so violent."

Maura bristled. "More than around here, maybe, but most of the US is pretty peaceful. There are only a few states where people walk around in public wearing guns." Sad but true: if it was *no* states, she would be happier. She'd known more than one person in her high school class who had been shot on a dark Boston street. "I never got lunch, and we owe Billy some food. If you'll cover here, I'll go and ask him what he needs and then go to the Costcutter and see if they've got anything in."

"You go on then. We're fine here."

Maura grabbed her coat and hurried the twenty feet or so to Billy's door at the end of the building. She knocked and after a few moments heard slow shuffling approaching. "Billy? It's Maura," she called out, waiting. After another thirty seconds, he reached the door and opened it, smiling.

"Ah, Maura, please come into where it's warm."

"Thanks. I'm glad to hear your heat is working. I was going to get something to eat and then I remembered that we ate a lot of what was in your pantry. If you'll tell me what you need, I'll pick it all up together."

"Ah, don't trouble yerself," Billy said, dropping into his chair and waving Maura toward one opposite.

"Billy, it's no trouble, and we owe you. What did the boys borrow? Milk? Bread? Eggs?"

"All those and a bit o' cheese as well. Thank you, Maura. What's the news?"

Maura leaned against the door. "Diane and I just got back from the garda station. Detective Hurley invited us to talk with Ellen Layton, and she told us as much as she knew of the story. Add what Bart Hayes told them, and they expect to arrest Jacky Dempsey for the murder."

"Ah," Billy said and stopped.

"You don't sound surprised, Billy," Maura said.

"I can't say that I am. The Dempseys tried to make a go of the farm, but even with Denis Layton runnin' the place, it didn't do well. Ellen's brothers weren't interested, so they went lookin' fer easier ways to make a livin'. Dairy farmin's hard work, yeh know. Jacky was always the bad seed."

"And you know this why?"

"When yeh've been around as long as I have on this earth, you hear things, and you know people."

Maura couldn't argue with that. "Judith seems to be making dairy farming work for her. Do you think Jimmy is up to it?"

Billy waved a dismissive hand. "Ah, he'll find a way to weasel out of the work, I've no doubt. Probably say he's important to the runnin' of Sullivan's. But Judith's a strong woman, and she'll handle him."

Maura wasn't convinced, but she wished Judith luck. Maybe marrying Judith would sweeten Jimmy's mood, although she wasn't going to count on it. "So I'll get you eggs, bread, milk, and cheese and drop them off here. Will you be coming by the pub later?"

"I may do, after a bit."

"Then I'll see you later." Maura gave him a last smile and let herself out to make the trek to the Costcutter.

Twenty-Seven

The walk up the street to the store gave Maura some time to think—time alone had been in short supply recently. When the murder had happened, people—including the gardaí—had been happy to assume that the killer had been an outsider rather than one of their own. Maura respected the loyalty that people felt for each other, especially when they'd known each other all their lives, as had their families known each other for decades. But that didn't justify ignoring the truth. The only result of that bias had been years of suspicion and a general feeling of dissatisfaction that nothing had ever been proved. The unsolved case still troubled people.

Well, now it was solved, which should satisfy people. Jacky Dempsey didn't sound like a man who had a lot of friends who'd care.

When she reached the store, Maura found the shelves pretty much picked over, which didn't surprise her after what Rose had told her. "You got new stuff coming soon?" she called out to the older woman behind the register, who she recognized but whose name she didn't know.

"Here's hopin'! Like a pack of wolves, it's been—you'd think people were planning fer a siege or the like. But I didn't like to put a limit on what they could take. There's a truck due in the mornin', I'm told. What do yeh need?"

"Probably the same thing as everyone else. Most of what I need is for Billy Sheahan—we kind of borrowed most of his food for breakfast."

"Ah, well then—wouldn't want the man to starve. I've got some bread and stuff put away in the back, and I'll let you have it—fer Billy." The woman disappeared toward the back of the store, and Maura found herself staring at the day-old newspapers in a rack near the register. She wondered what the headlines would look like in the next edition.

"I'll put yer stuff in a sack, shall I?"

"Please." Maura waited while the woman disappeared through a door at the rear and emerged with a carry bag a minute later. "What do I owe you?"

"Ah, I'll put it on yer tab, shall I?"

She had a tab? She must have inherited Old Mick's. Rose would know. "Thanks."

"Give my best to Billy," Hannah called out as Maura went out the door.

One task accomplished, Maura thought as she set off back toward the pub. She rapped on Billy's door when she reached it and handed him the bag when he opened the door.

"I'll be down to yer place directly," he said. "Once I've had me supper, that is." Billy lifted the bag and smiled at her and then closed his door.

Back at Sullivan's, Maura opened up a can of some pasta prod-
uct, dumped it in a bowl, and heated it briefly in the microwave.
That was lunch—or was it supper? She was startled when the
door flew open, slamming against the wall, and Sean Murphy
strode in, looking flushed with excitement. Maura did a double
take, taking a harder look at him. "Sean, have you been fighting?"

"I have indeed," he said, looking very pleased with himself.
"And I've news fer yeh. We've got yer man Dempsey."

"That was fast! Wait, weren't you off duty today?"

"The inspector wanted everyone on hand to look for the man,
so I was called in."

The small crowd had fallen silent, and then everyone started talking at once, surging toward the bar. Maura raised one hand. "Hold
it!" She turned to Sean. "Can you talk about it? Publicly, I mean?"

Sean grinned. "It'll be on the telly soon enough."

Maura eyed the crowd. "Okay, then. But first, Sean, looks like
that shiner could do with some ice. If we have any, that is."

"Ta, Maura. I hardly noticed."

The Irish gardaí—and Sean in particular—rarely resorted
to violence, so for Sean to come in sporting battle injuries was
startling. She couldn't wait to hear the story, but she thought
some first aid might be needed first. Before she could do anything about it, Rose handed her a plastic bag filled with ice and
wrapped in a towel. She passed it over the bar to Sean.

"Something to drink?" she asked.

"Coffee, if yeh don't mind. I've got to get back to the station,
but I thought Diane deserved to hear the news from one of us
rather than on the news."

Diane passed through the small crowd, and she stopped next to Sean at the bar and faced him. "He's in custody?"

"He is. The warrant's on its way," Sean told her triumphantly.

Diane's face gave nothing away. She studied him, as if to reassure herself that he wasn't kidding. "Where'd you find him?"

"At the Layton farm, where he's been all these years. He thought he was safe there—he never believed his sister would tell us anything. We're still talkin' to the gardaí in Schull about him, fer it's hard to believe he'd've stayed out of trouble fer long, and I'm guessin' he's been a guest of theirs before."

"Does he know yet that it was his sisters who finally turned him in?"

"That I can't tell you, but he didn't declare that he was innocent. We have the right man, and with his sister's story and a few comments he might have made when we came to talk with him, not to mention assaulting a garda or two, I don't think there'll be any problem holdin' him. It's just paperwork now."

"Oh." Diane was finally beginning to process the reality. "Thank you for telling me. Us."

"The whole country'll know soon enough." Sean nodded at the television over the bar, which somebody had turned on without the sound. The news broadcast was on, and the crawl at the bottom of the screen read "Arrest of man in Sharon Morgan case."

Maura was pretty sure it would be a busy night at the pub.

Sean finished his coffee. "I'll be gettin' back to the station now, but I wanted to be the one to tell yeh." The small crowd of men parted once again to let him pass to the door, but not without a few of them slapping him on the back as he passed.

When he was gone, they closed ranks once again, clustering around the bar, looking expectant. *Like a herd of cows at feeding time*, Maura thought irreverently. "I'm thinking this calls for drinks all around," Maura told them. "Mick, can you handle that?" When he nodded, she turned to look for Diane, but she'd retreated to her corner and was gathering up her things.

When Maura approached her, Diane said, "You did it. You found out what really happened. You convinced the gardaí. And they've caught him. I never thought I'd see this day. And I don't know how to thank you."

"For a start, you don't have to thank me," Maura told her. "I just got things started. The rest was luck."

"More than that, Maura. You've got a sharp mind, and you pointed out some things that others missed. And you've got a good place here. Friends. A home."

"Well, when I showed up here last March, I thought I'd be gone in a week, but I guess Ireland kind of gets to you. But you're still going back to England?"

"You had people here, didn't you?" Diane said, ducking the question.

"Same as you—grandparents. I never knew about any relatives around here. But it seems they all knew about me."

"And how is that working for you?"

"Not too bad, actually," Maura said with a reluctant smile. "At least I admitted I didn't know what I was doing, and people were willing to help."

"So now you're paying it forward. You've helped me, like others helped you."

"I guess," Maura admitted. "But when we started yesterday, I just thought maybe you didn't get treated fairly. And I know some of the gardaí around here, and I respect them. We gave them a chance, and they got it right."

"And it was your doing, Maura." Diane smiled, then glanced at her watch. "Make my farewells for me, will you?"

"What, you don't want to stay and enjoy the celebration? It's for you, you know."

"No, but thank you. You enjoy the credit. And I'll be forever grateful."

Maura was startled to feel the prick of tears. "Will you be coming back, do you think?"

Diane smiled. "Maybe. We'll see. Do you have a back way out?"

Maura led her to the back door past the bathrooms, then watched as she got into her car and drove off toward Cork and the airport and London and her husband. Diane's life had been changed here in Cork two decades earlier, and it felt right that it should be changed again here. As for her part, Maura had only done what she thought was right.

But now she had a business to run and a pub filling rapidly with people who wanted the "real" story behind solving an old and very cold case. That was her business.

Mick came up behind Maura and said quietly, "She's gone?"

Maura nodded. "She is. She didn't feel like celebrating."

"Yeh know, yeh've a knack fer this."

"For what?" she asked without turning around, her eyes still on the crowd.

"Bringin' people together and, I dunno, making them look at things in a new way?"

"That's partly because I'm American. And I've been lucky," she said.

"Some people are born with luck. Diane, say, has had a long spell of bad luck until she bumped into you. Gillian? Still hangin' in the balance, but she and Harry are together now, and it might stick, and yeh might've had a hand in that. Jimmy's onto a good thing with Judith, even if he doesn't see it, and that'll free up Rosie to do what she wants, and I know yeh'd like to help her."

Now Maura turned to face him. "Are you saying I get credit for all those things?"

"Not likely. But you might've given them a push in the right direction."

"Mick, if I've got this kind of power, I'm going to be scared to open my mouth."

"I wouldn't worry yerself—it's all good. Enjoy it, will yeh?"

"Right," Maura muttered. And then she stopped herself. After most of a year, she was beginning to understand how people in West Cork thought. What's more, she had come to appreciate the support they had given her from the day she had arrived. She had made friends, and she had a place in the community. Maybe Diane had been right: she was beginning to pay it forward. That felt good.

She turned to the gathering crowd. "So tell us what happened, Maura Donovan!" someone called out.

"Order another round, and I'll tell you what you want to know," Maura said, smiling.

Acknowledgments

Ireland is a lovely, peaceful place where crime is fairly low—and where the gardaí (the Irish police) usually know who committed the crime before they even look for the culprit. It's that small a country.

Murder is taken seriously there because it's so rare: while the number of police officers per capita in Ireland is about the same as in the United States, the homicide rate is far lower. As you might guess, that can be a problem for mystery writers, who usually look for a murder to open their stories.

So I was happy when I came upon an unsolved murder that took place in 1996 in West Cork—one that was fairly high profile, involving film people from England and France, outsiders who did not mix well with the local population. The case still makes headlines today, twenty years later, as legal battles ebb and flow, and it remains an open case.

Of course, I started thinking, "What if...?" What if newer technologies could add any new information? What if the makeup and mind-set of the Irish gardaí had changed? And what if my young American Maura Donovan, raised in big-city Boston, could take a fresh look at what had happened? So I threw together Maura, her staff, her friends, her bar patrons, and the prime candidate for the murderer (never arrested, always suspected) in Sullivan's Pub on a snowy evening and waited to see what would come out.

There's still no solution, officially, but I may have come up with an idea or two. But keep in mind that this is not a true crime story. There are no interviews with the people involved or analysis of the records. This is a fictionalized account of how the murder *might* have happened.

The community of writers provides a wonderful support network, and none of my books would have happened without Sisters in Crime and the Guppies and Mystery Writers of America. The resources that are now available to writers—from forensics to police procedures to the psychology of criminals—are amazing, and we have no excuse for getting facts wrong. Special thanks go to Sergeant Tony McCarthy of the Skibbereen gardaí, who's been helpful not only for explaining how things are done in Ireland but also for being willing to talk to me about crime in Ireland in general. Thanks also to the people in Leap and Skibbereen who I have come to count as friends—people who are willing to answer my dumb questions. Particular thanks go to Matt Martz and the crew at Crooked Lane Books for grabbing this book up and taking it to the next level and to my agent, Jessica Faust of BookEnds, for making it happen.